NANCY DREW®

girl detective

PAPERCUTZ

NANCY DREW GRAPHIC NOVELS AVAILABLE FROM PAPERCUTZ

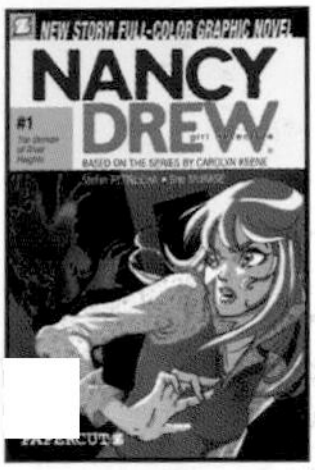
NEW STORY! FULL-COLOR GRAPHIC NOVEL
NANCY
DREW
PAPERCUTZ

#1 "The Demon of River Heights"

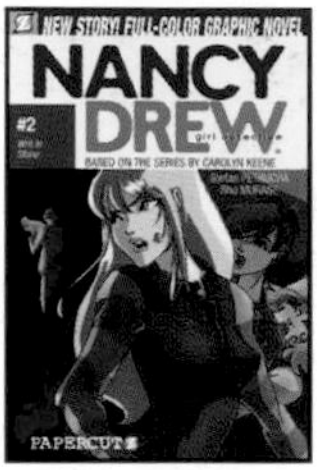
NEW STORY! FULL-COLOR GRAPHIC NOVEL
NANCY
DREW
PAPERCUTZ

#2 "Writ In Stone"

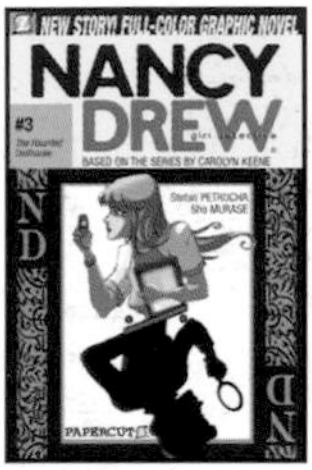
NEW STORY! FULL-COLOR GRAPHIC NOVEL
NANCY
DREW
PAPERCUTZ

#3 "The Haunted Dollhouse"

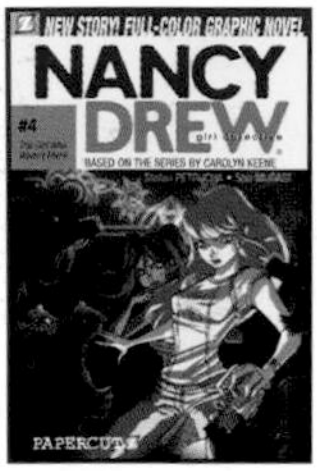
NEW STORY! FULL-COLOR GRAPHIC NOVEL
NANCY
DREW
PAPERCUTZ

#4 "The Girl Who Wasn't There"

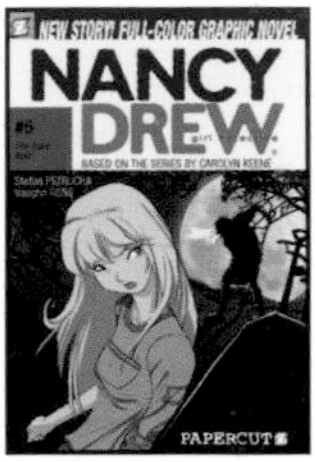
NEW STORY! FULL-COLOR GRAPHIC NOVEL
NANCY
DREW
PAPERCUTZ

#5 "The Fake Heir"

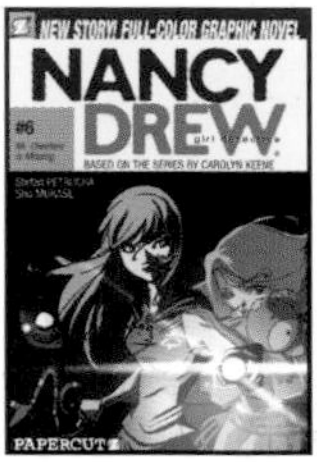
NEW STORY! FULL-COLOR GRAPHIC NOVEL
NANCY
DREW
PAPERCUTZ

#6 "Mr. Cheeters Is Missing"

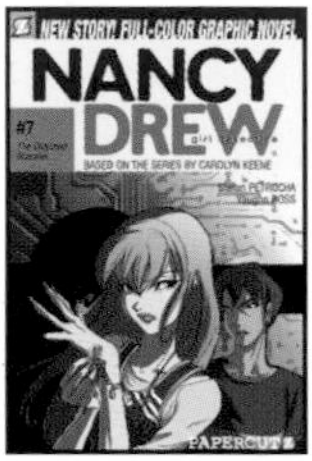
NEW STORY! FULL-COLOR GRAPHIC NOVEL
NANCY
DREW
PAPERCUTZ

#7 "The Charmed Bracelet"

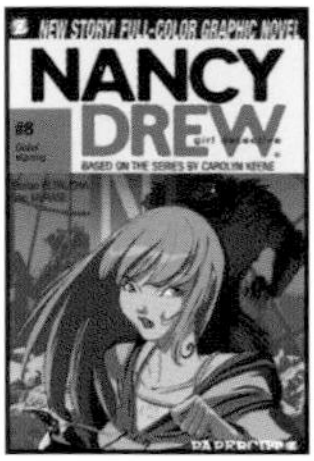
NEW STORY! FULL-COLOR GRAPHIC NOVEL
NANCY
DREW

#8 "Global Warning"

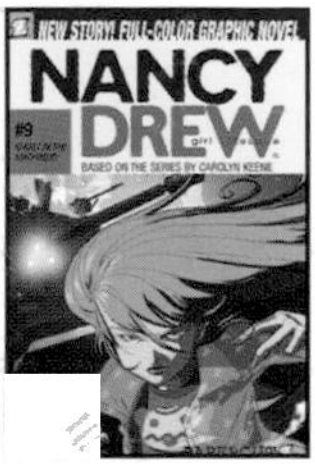
NEW STORY! FULL-COLOR GRAPHIC NOVEL
NANCY
DREW

#9 "Ghost In The Machinery"

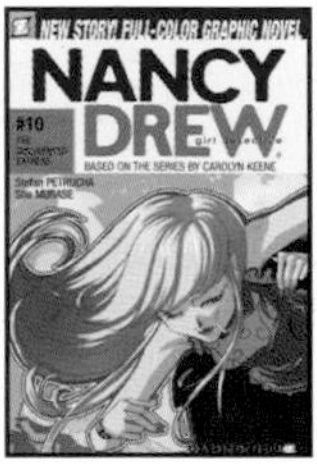
NEW STORY! FULL-COLOR GRAPHIC NOVEL
NANCY
DREW

#10 "The Disoriented Express"

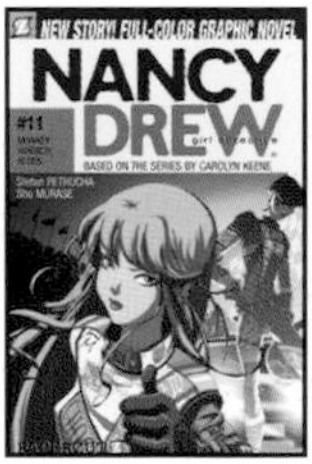
NEW STORY! FULL-COLOR GRAPHIC NOVEL
NANCY
DREW

#11 "Monkey Wrench Blues"

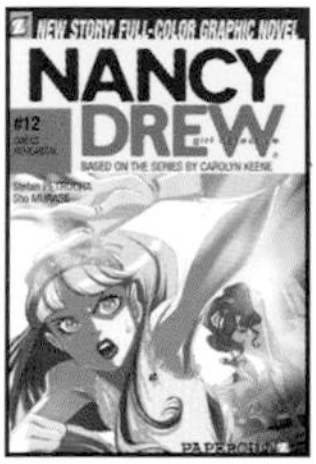
NEW STORY! FULL-COLOR GRAPHIC NOVEL
NANCY
DREW

#12 "Dress Reversal"

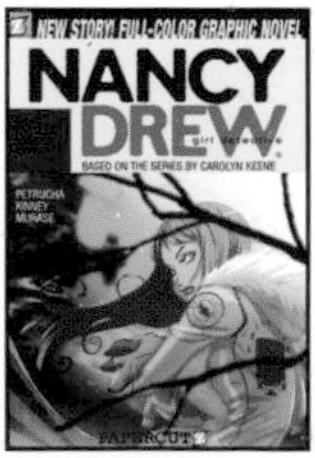
NEW STORY! FULL-COLOR GRAPHIC NOVEL
NANCY
DREW
PAPERCUTZ

#13 "Doggone Town"

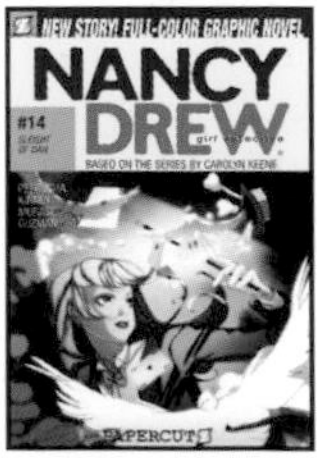
NEW STORY! FULL-COLOR GRAPHIC NOVEL
NANCY
DREW
PAPERCUTZ

#14 "Sleight of Dan"

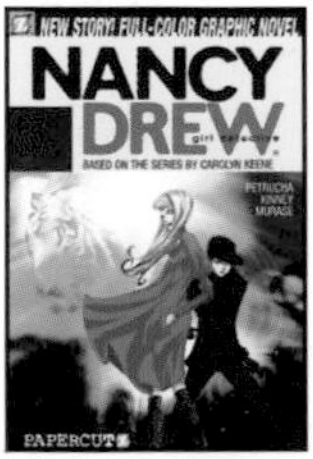
NEW STORY! FULL-COLOR GRAPHIC NOVEL
NANCY
DREW
PAPERCUTZ

Coming November '08
#15 "Tiger Counter"

$7.95 each in paperback, $12.95 each in hardcover.

Please add $4.00 for postage and handling for the first book, add $1.00 for each additional book.

Please make check payable to NBM Publishing. Send to:

Papercutz, 40 Exchange Place, Suite 1308 New York, NY 10005, 1-800-886-1223

www.papercutz.com

NANCY DREW

#14 DREW girl detective ®

Sleight of Dan

STEFAN PETRUCHA & SARAH KINNEY • Writers
SHO MURASE • Artist
with 3D CG elements and color by CARLOS JOSE GUZMAN
Based on the series by
CAROLYN KEENE

New York

Sleight of Dan
STEFAN PETRUCHA & SARAH KINNEY – Writers
SHO MURASE – Artist
with 3D CG elements and color by CARLOS JOSE GUZMAN
BRYAN SENKA – Letterer
MIKHAELA REID and MASHEKA WOOD – Production
JIM SALICRUP
Editor-in-Chief

ISBN 10: 1-59707-107-2 paperback edition
ISBN 13: 978-1-59707-107-9 paperback edition
ISBN 10: 1-59707-108-0 hardcover edition
ISBN 13: 978-1-59707-108-6 hardcover edition

Printed in China.
Distributed by Macmillan.

10 9 8 7 6 5 4 3 2 1

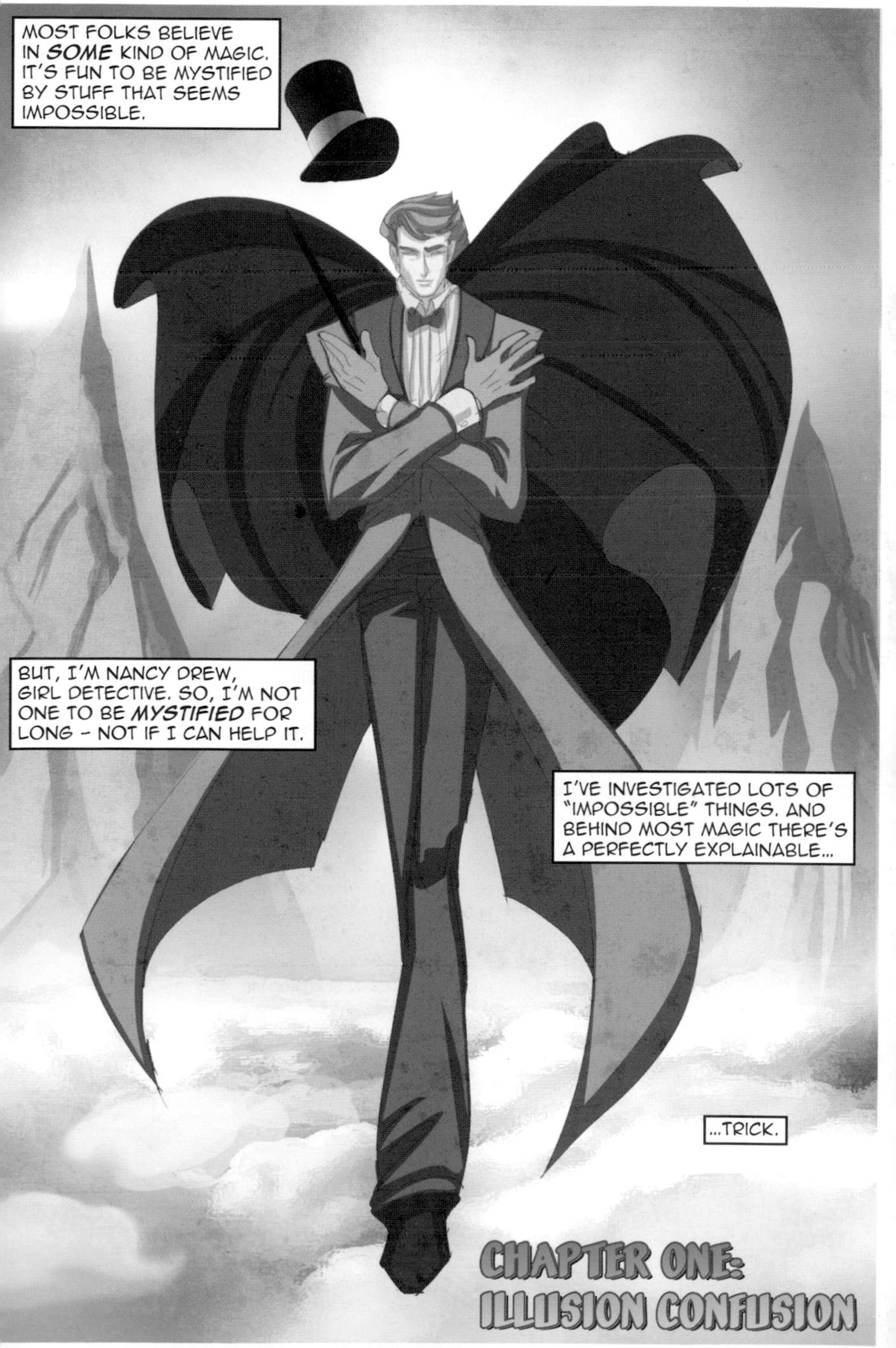
MOST FOLKS BELIEVE IN *SOME* KIND OF MAGIC. IT'S FUN TO BE MYSTIFIED BY STUFF THAT SEEMS IMPOSSIBLE.
BUT, I'M NANCY DREW, GIRL DETECTIVE. SO, I'M NOT ONE TO BE *MYSTIFIED* FOR LONG – NOT IF I CAN HELP IT.
I'VE INVESTIGATED LOTS OF "IMPOSSIBLE" THINGS. AND BEHIND MOST MAGIC THERE'S A PERFECTLY EXPLAINABLE...
...TRICK.
CHAPTER ONE: ILLUSION CONFUSION

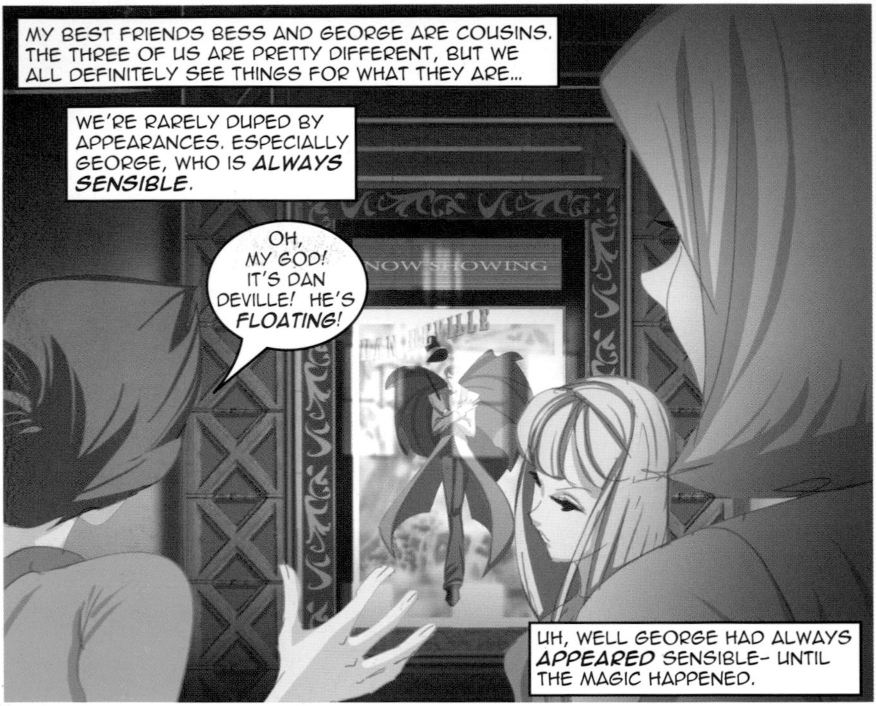
MY BEST FRIENDS BESS AND GEORGE ARE COUSINS. THE THREE OF US ARE PRETTY DIFFERENT, BUT WE ALL DEFINITELY SEE THINGS FOR WHAT THEY ARE...
WE'RE RARELY DUPED BY APPEARANCES. ESPECIALLY GEORGE, WHO IS ***ALWAYS SENSIBLE***.
OH, MY GOD! IT'S DAN DEVILLE! HE'S ***FLOATING***!
NOW SHOWING
UH, WELL GEORGE HAD ALWAYS ***APPEARED*** SENSIBLE- UNTIL THE MAGIC HAPPENED.

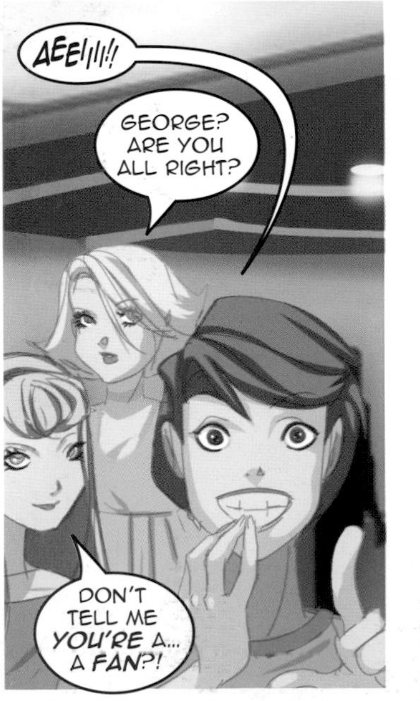
AEEIIII!!
GEORGE? ARE YOU ALL RIGHT?
DON'T TELL ME ***YOU'RE*** A... A ***FAN***?!

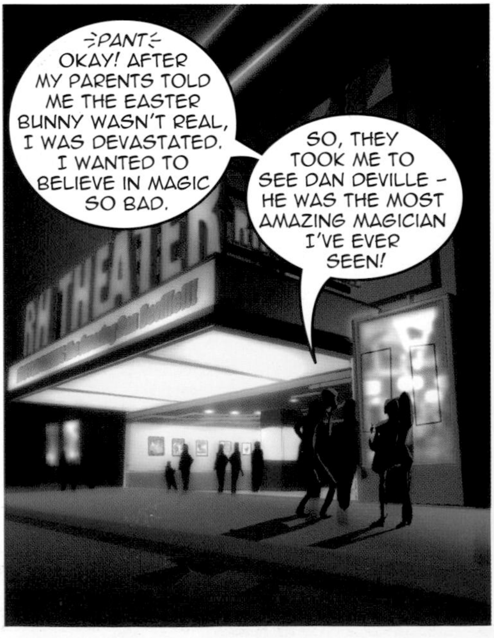
PANT
OKAY! AFTER MY PARENTS TOLD ME THE EASTER BUNNY WASN'T REAL, I WAS DEVASTATED. I WANTED TO BELIEVE IN MAGIC SO BAD.
SO, THEY TOOK ME TO SEE DAN DEVILLE - HE WAS THE MOST AMAZING MAGICIAN I'VE EVER SEEN!
RH THEATER

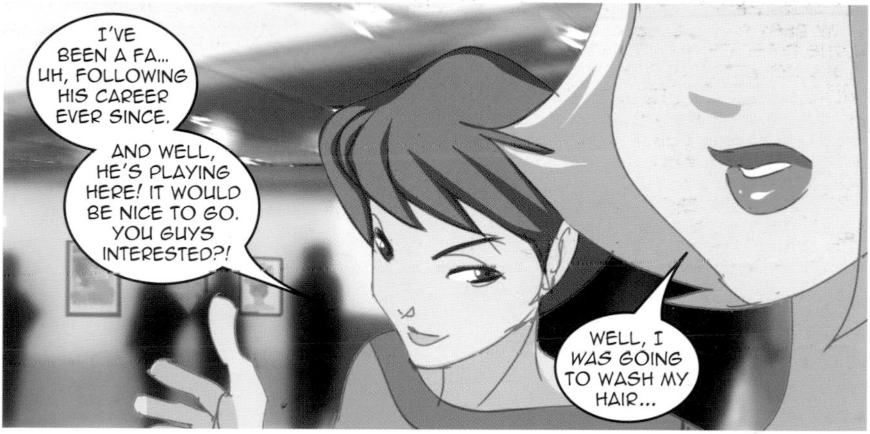
I'VE BEEN A FA... UH, FOLLOWING HIS CAREER EVER SINCE.
AND WELL, HE'S PLAYING HERE! IT WOULD BE NICE TO GO. YOU GUYS INTERESTED?!
WELL, I WAS GOING TO WASH MY HAIR...

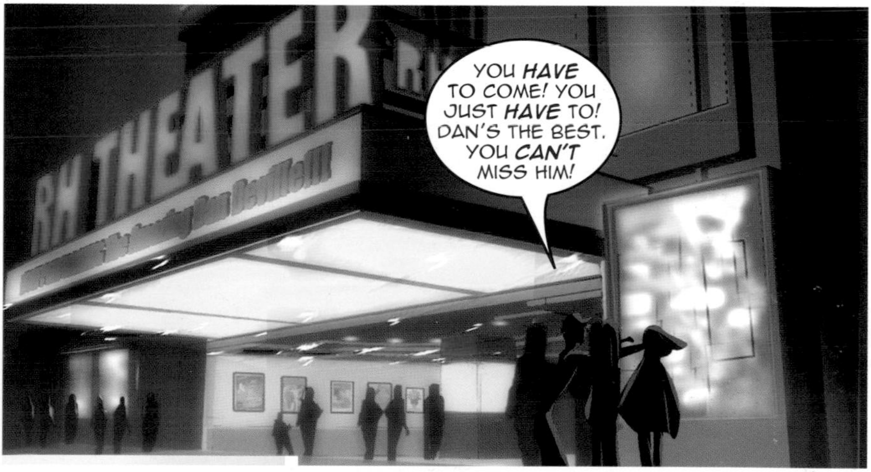
RX THEATER
YOU *HAVE* TO COME! YOU JUST *HAVE* TO! DAN'S THE BEST. YOU *CAN'T* MISS HIM!

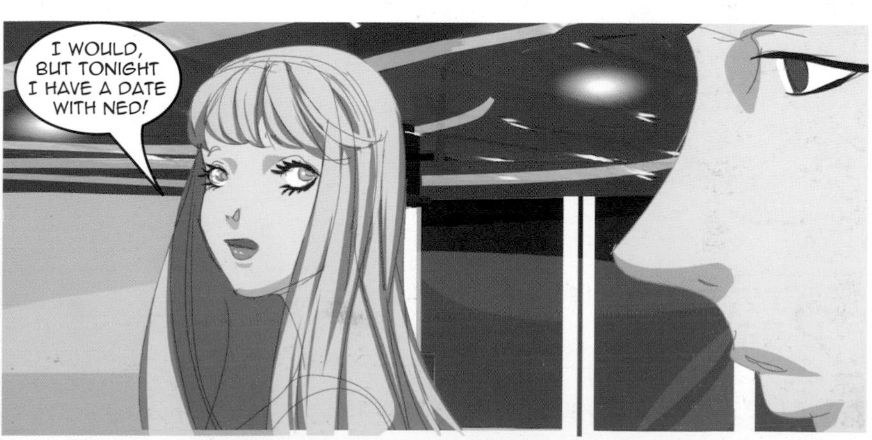
I WOULD, BUT TONIGHT I HAVE A DATE WITH NED!

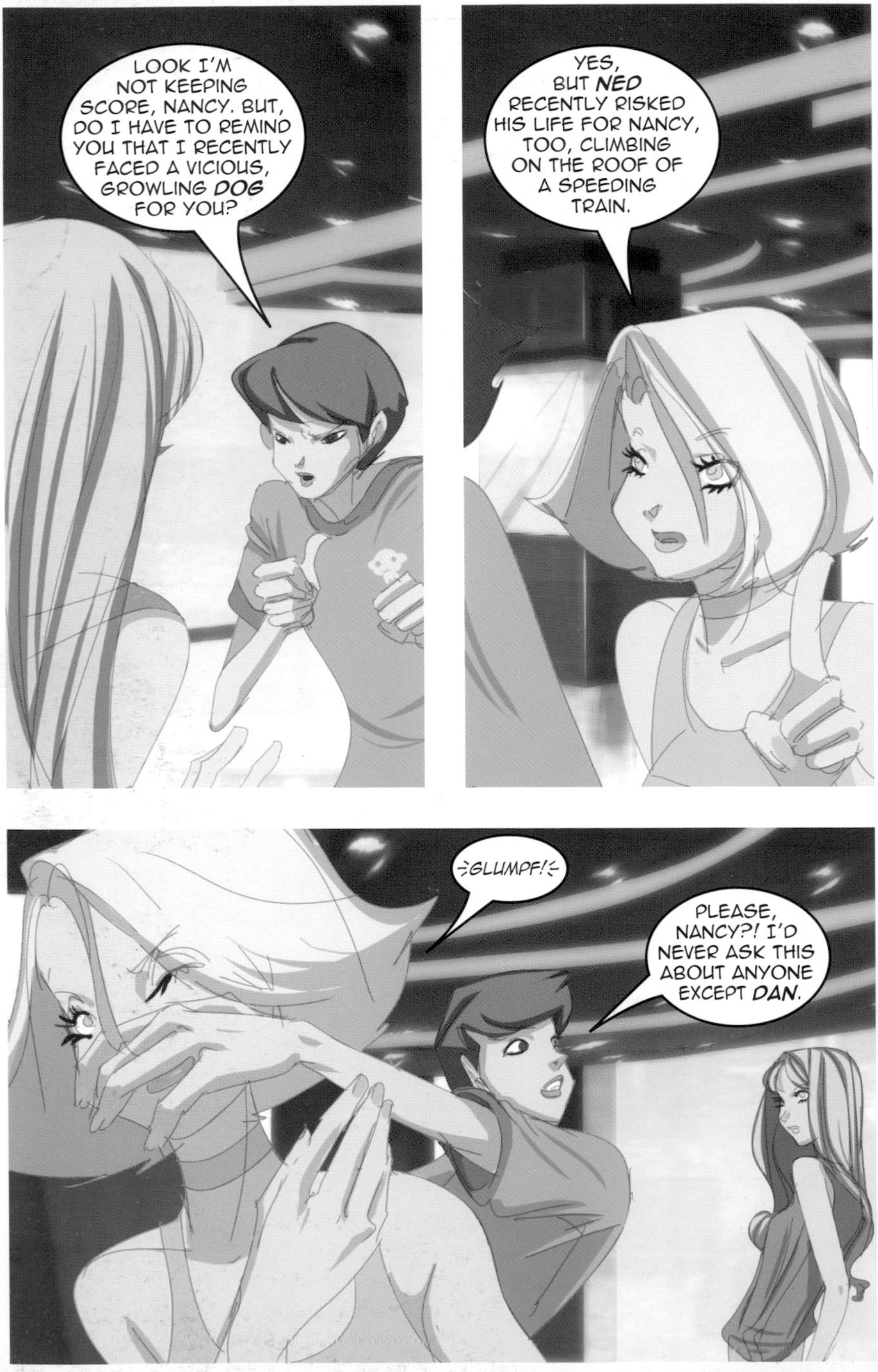
LOOK I'M NOT KEEPING SCORE, NANCY. BUT, DO I HAVE TO REMIND YOU THAT I RECENTLY FACED A VICIOUS, GROWLING DOG FOR YOU?
YES, BUT NED RECENTLY RISKED HIS LIFE FOR NANCY, TOO, CLIMBING ON THE ROOF OF A SPEEDING TRAIN.
GLUMPF!
PLEASE, NANCY?! I'D NEVER ASK THIS ABOUT ANYONE EXCEPT DAN.

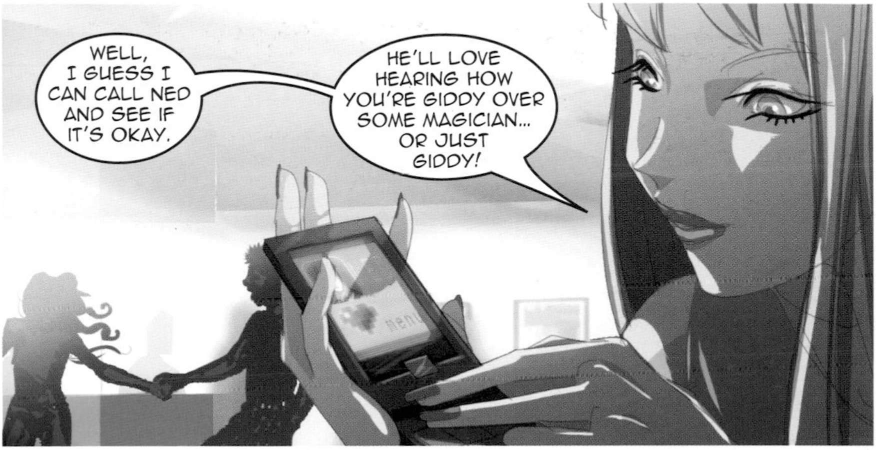
WELL, I GUESS I CAN CALL NED AND SEE IF IT'S OKAY.
HE'LL LOVE HEARING HOW YOU'RE GIDDY OVER SOME MAGICIAN... OR JUST GIDDY!

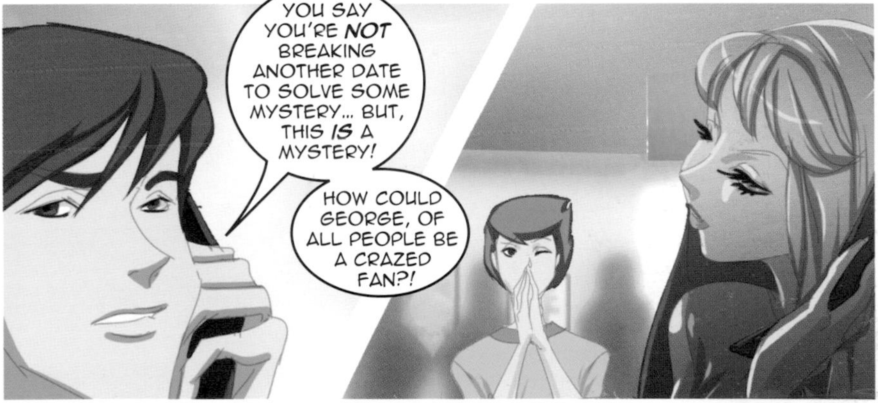
YOU SAY YOU'RE NOT BREAKING ANOTHER DATE TO SOLVE SOME MYSTERY... BUT, THIS IS A MYSTERY!
HOW COULD GEORGE, OF ALL PEOPLE BE A CRAZED FAN?!

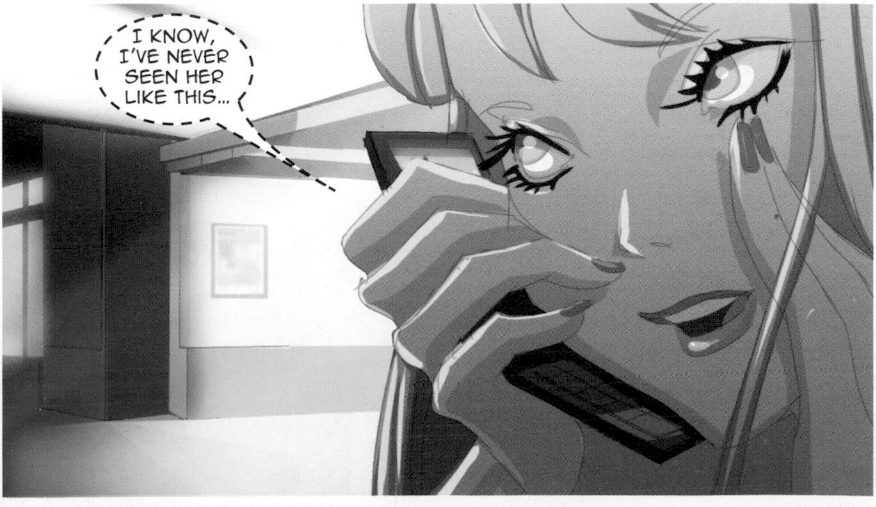
I KNOW, I'VE NEVER SEEN HER LIKE THIS...

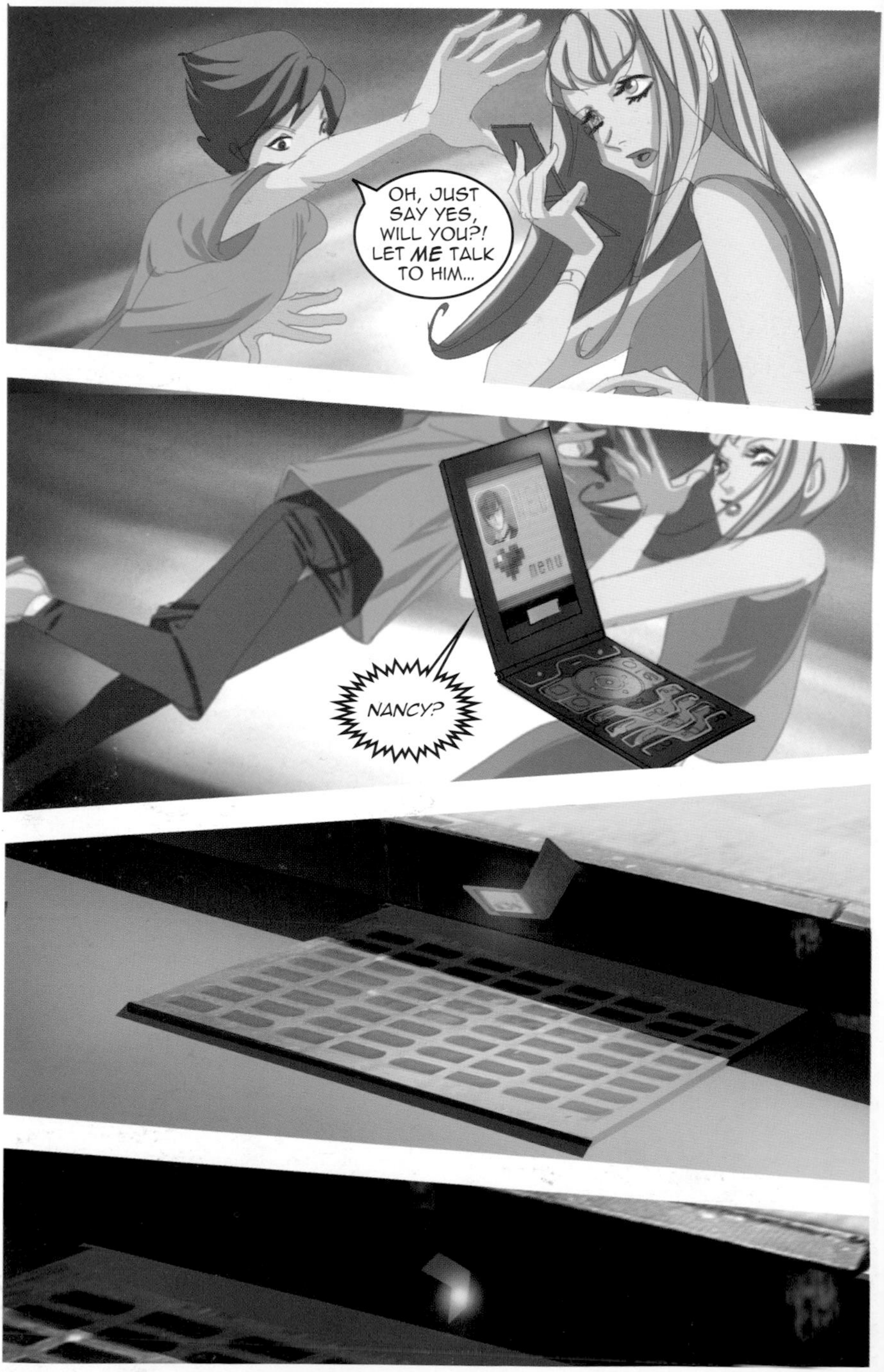
OH, JUST SAY YES, WILL YOU?! LET *ME* TALK TO HIM...
MENU
NANCY?

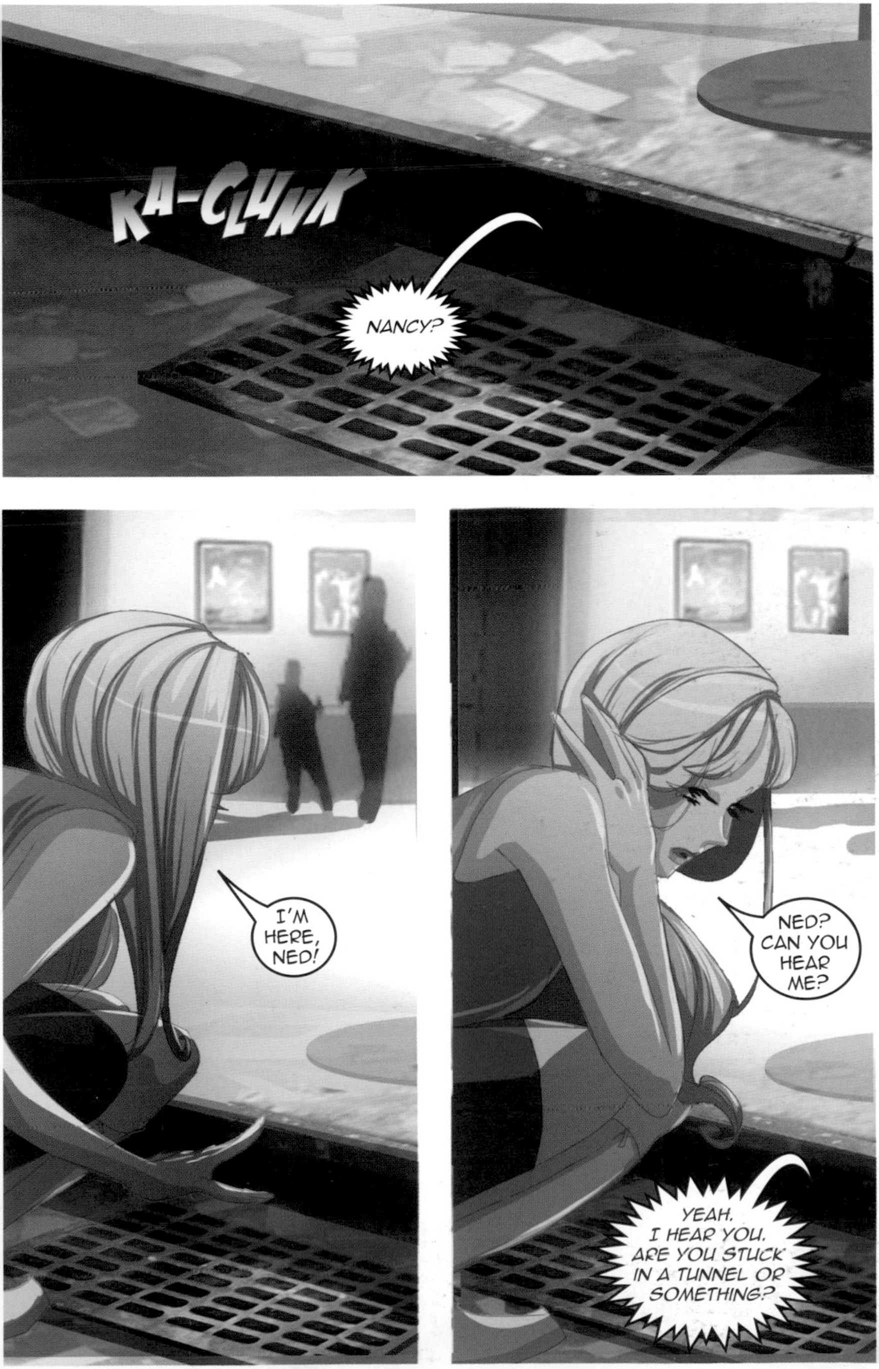
KA-CLUNK
NANCY?
I'M HERE, NED!
NED? CAN YOU HEAR ME?
YEAH. I HEAR YOU. ARE YOU STUCK IN A TUNNEL OR SOMETHING?

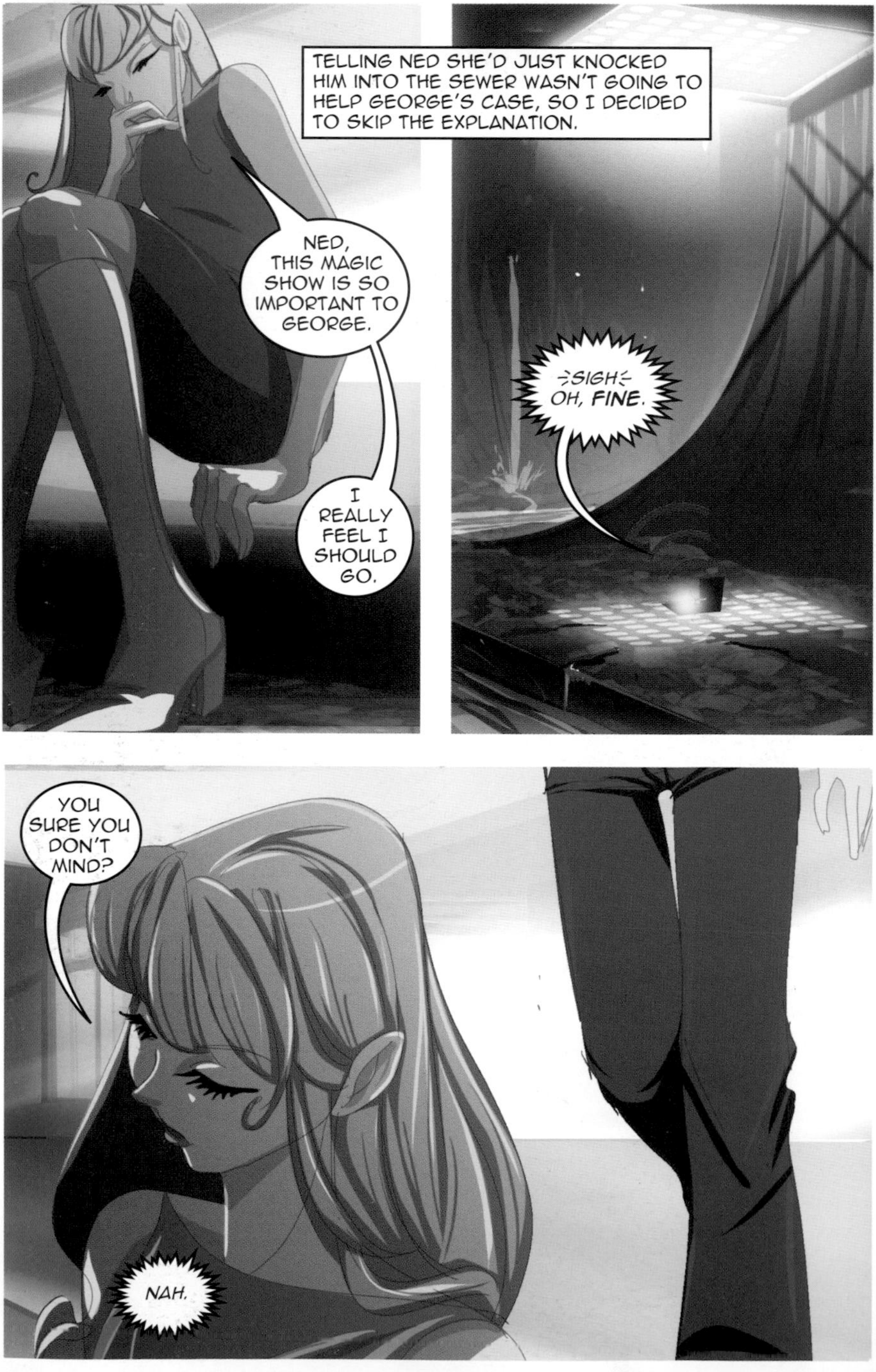
TELLING NED SHE'D JUST KNOCKED HIM INTO THE SEWER WASN'T GOING TO HELP GEORGE'S CASE, SO I DECIDED TO SKIP THE EXPLANATION.
NED, THIS MAGIC SHOW IS SO IMPORTANT TO GEORGE.
I REALLY FEEL I SHOULD GO.
=SIGH= OH, **FINE**.
YOU SURE YOU DON'T MIND?
NAH.

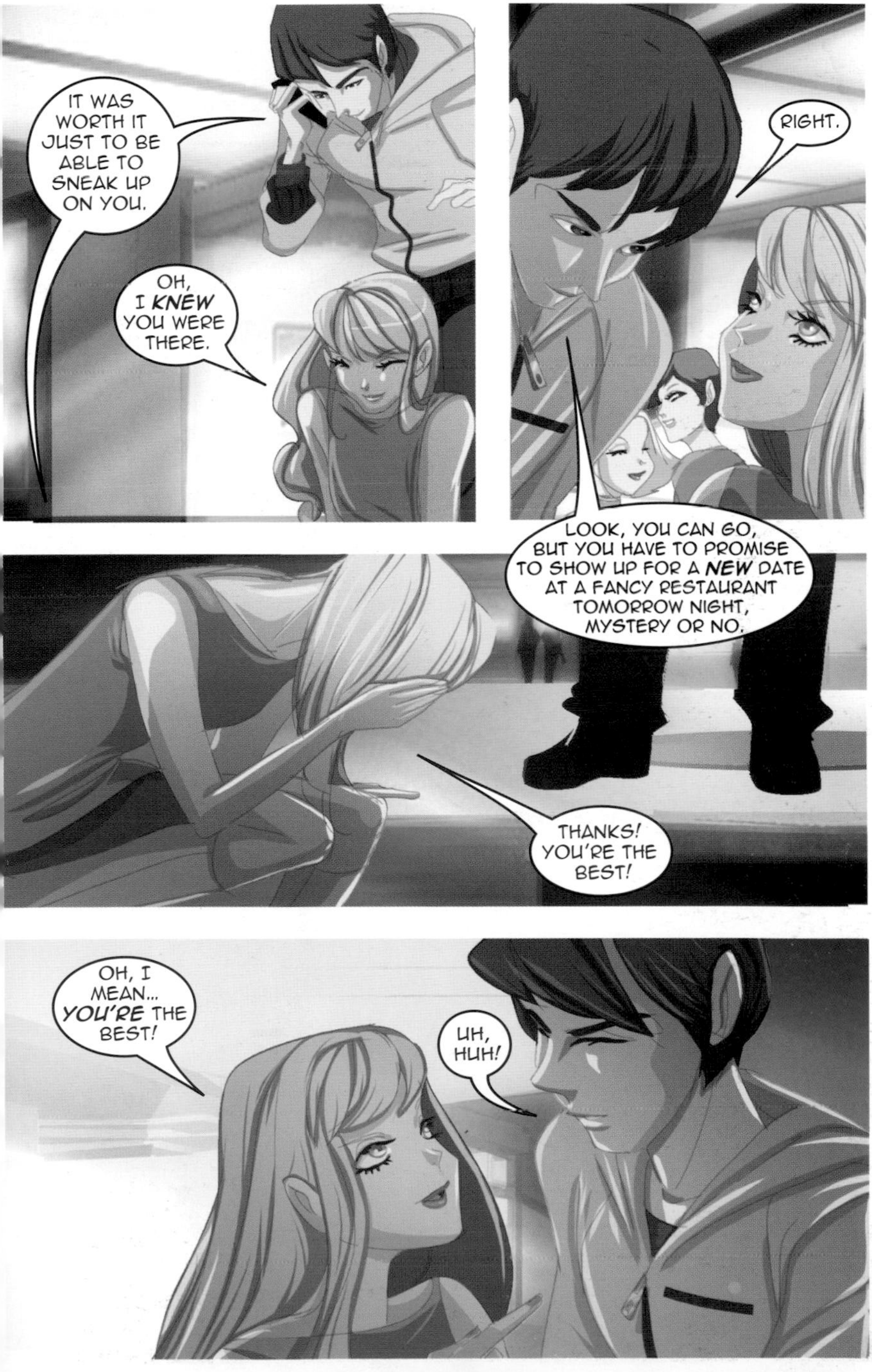
IT WAS WORTH IT JUST TO BE ABLE TO SNEAK UP ON YOU.
OH, I *KNEW* YOU WERE THERE.
RIGHT.
LOOK, YOU CAN GO, BUT YOU HAVE TO PROMISE TO SHOW UP FOR A *NEW* DATE AT A FANCY RESTAURANT TOMORROW NIGHT, MYSTERY OR NO.
THANKS! YOU'RE THE BEST!
OH, I MEAN... *YOU'RE* THE BEST!
UH, HUH!

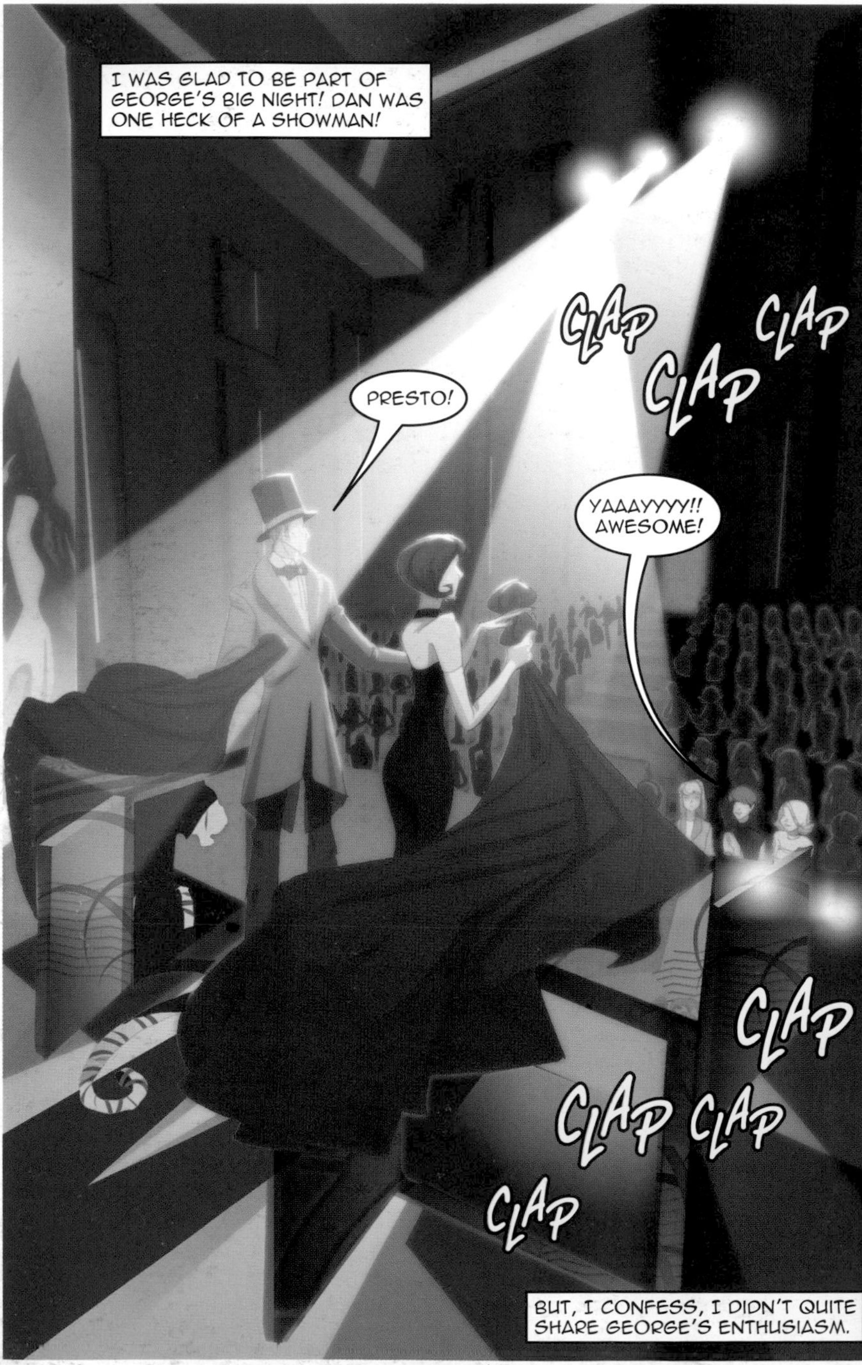
I WAS GLAD TO BE PART OF GEORGE'S BIG NIGHT! DAN WAS ONE HECK OF A SHOWMAN!
CLAP
CLAP
CLAP
PRESTO!
YAAAYYYY!! AWESOME!
CLAP
CLAP
CLAP
CLAP
BUT, I CONFESS, I DIDN'T QUITE SHARE GEORGE'S ENTHUSIASM.

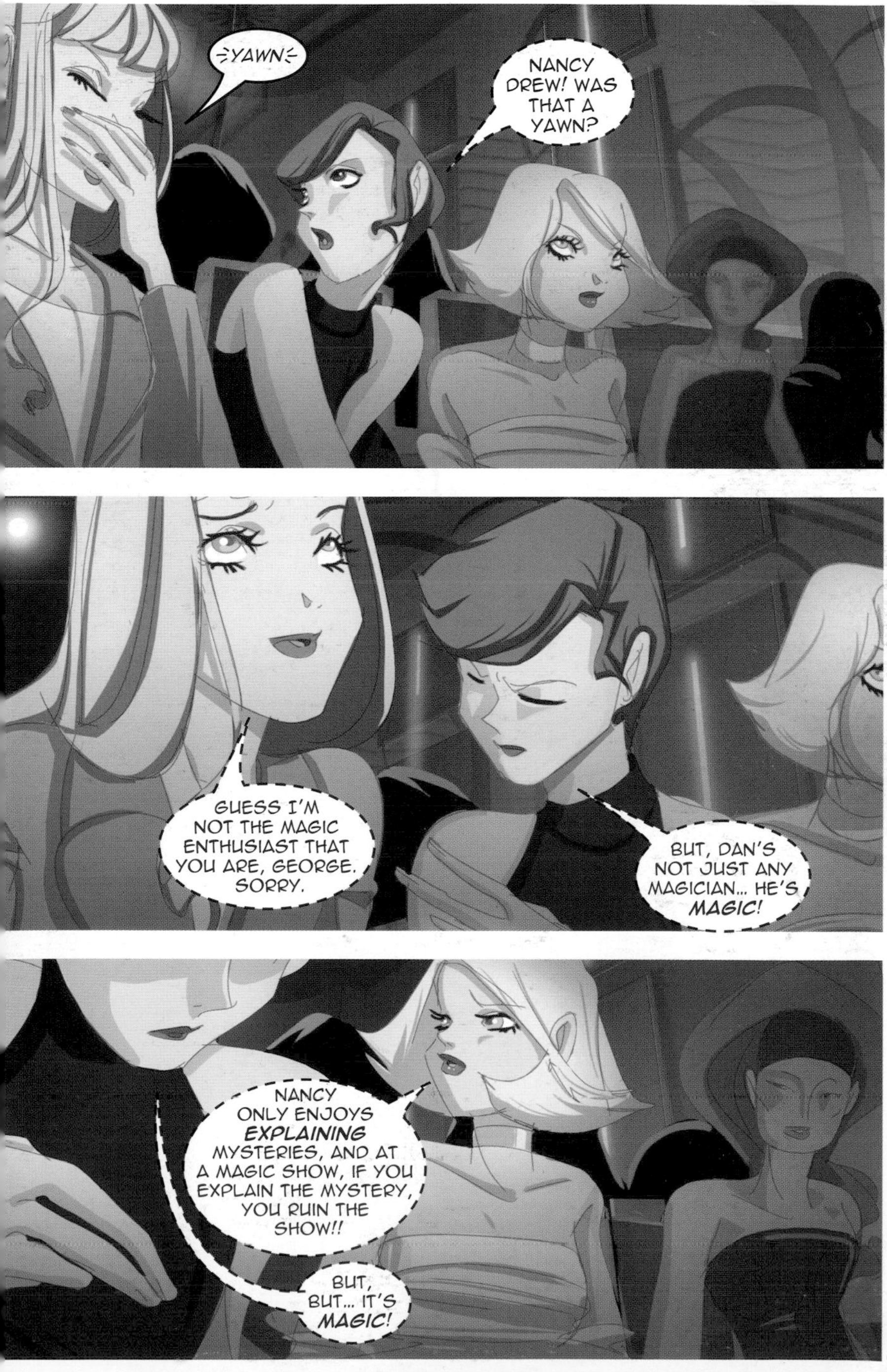

YAWN
NANCY DREW! WAS THAT A YAWN?
GUESS I'M NOT THE MAGIC ENTHUSIAST THAT YOU ARE, GEORGE. SORRY.
BUT, DAN'S NOT JUST ANY MAGICIAN... HE'S *MAGIC*!
NANCY ONLY ENJOYS ***EXPLAINING*** MYSTERIES, AND AT A MAGIC SHOW, IF YOU EXPLAIN THE MYSTERY, YOU RUIN THE SHOW!!
BUT, BUT... IT'S *MAGIC*!

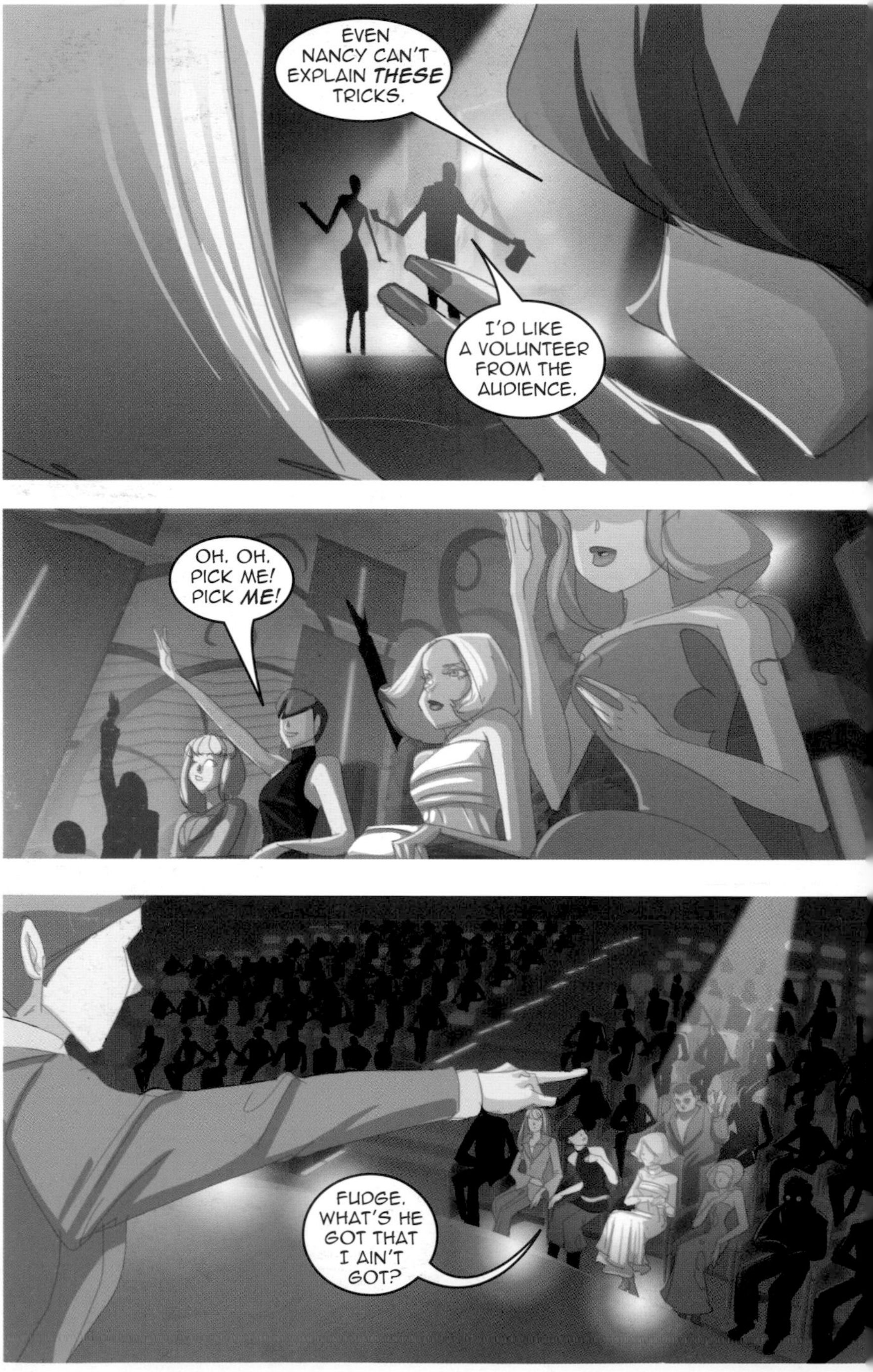
EVEN NANCY CAN'T EXPLAIN *THESE* TRICKS.
I'D LIKE A VOLUNTEER FROM THE AUDIENCE.
OH. OH. PICK ME! PICK *ME*!
FUDGE. WHAT'S HE GOT THAT I AIN'T GOT?

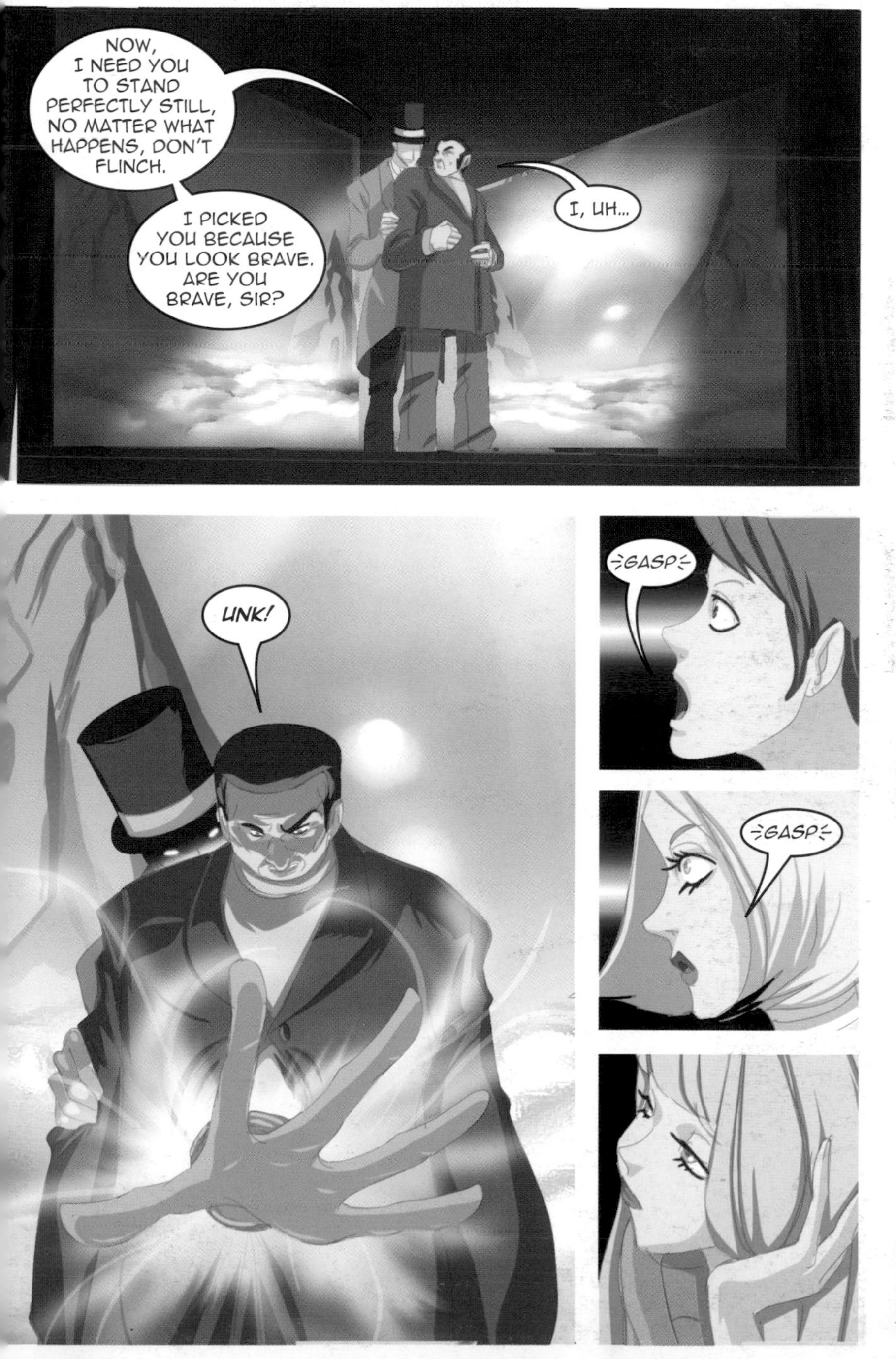
NOW, I NEED YOU TO STAND PERFECTLY STILL, NO MATTER WHAT HAPPENS, DON'T FLINCH.
I PICKED YOU BECAUSE YOU LOOK BRAVE. ARE YOU BRAVE, SIR?
I, UH...
UNK!
GASP
GASP

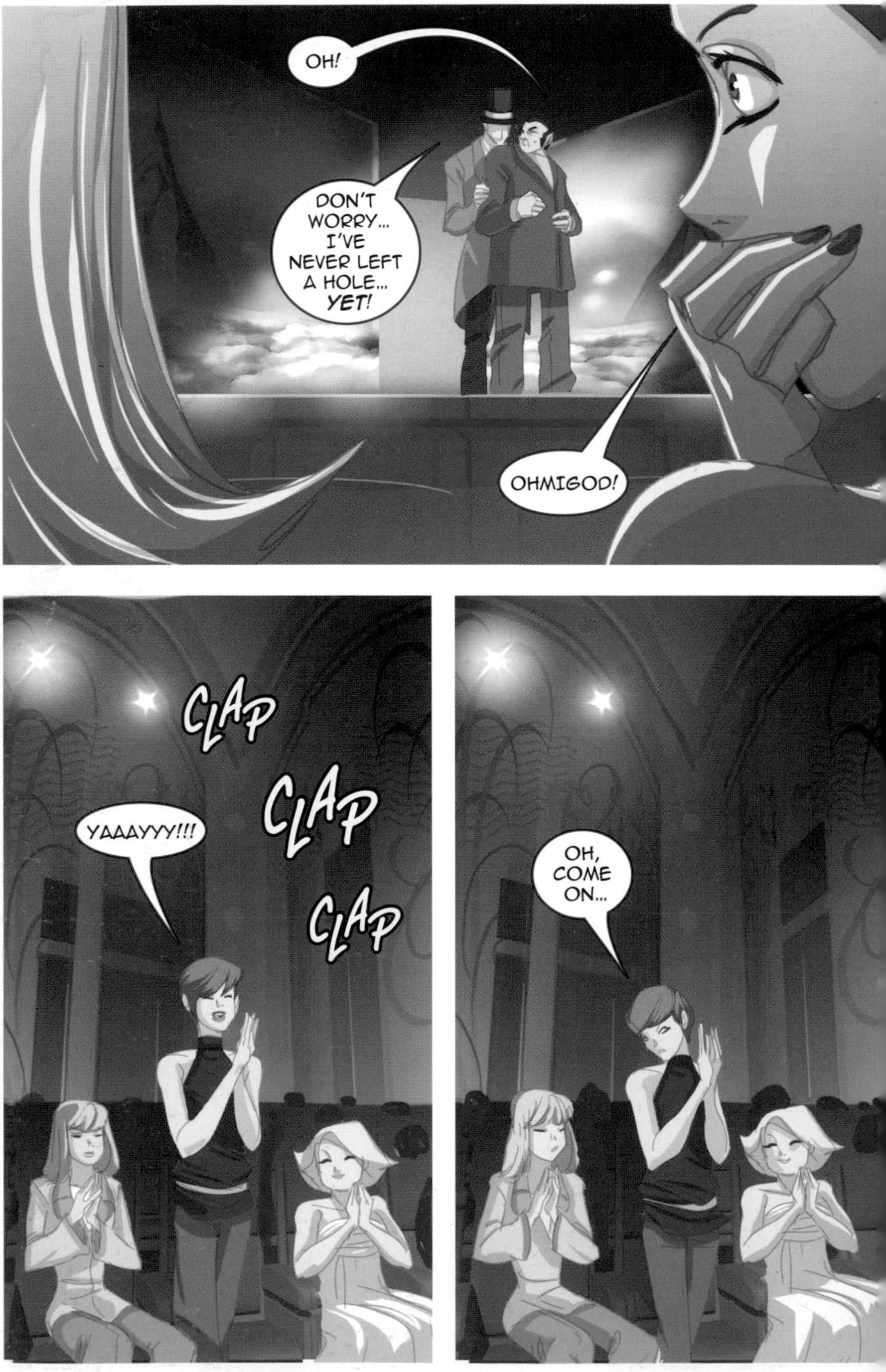
OH!
DON'T WORRY... I'VE NEVER LEFT A HOLE... YET!
OHMIGOD!
CLAP
CLAP
CLAP
YAAAYYY!!!
OH, COME ON...

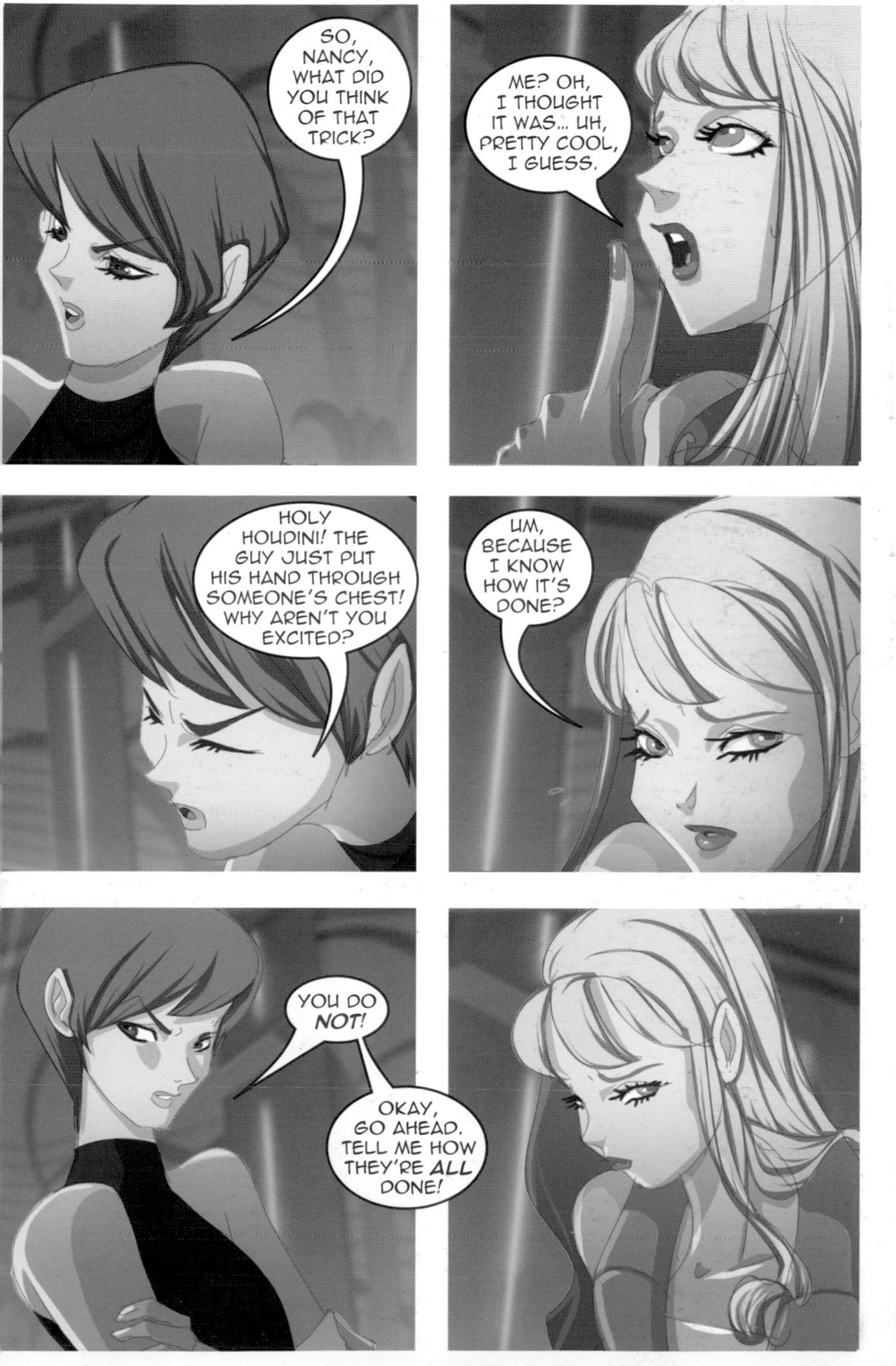
SO, NANCY, WHAT DID YOU THINK OF THAT TRICK?
ME? OH, I THOUGHT IT WAS... UH, PRETTY COOL, I GUESS.
HOLY HOUDINI! THE GUY JUST PUT HIS HAND THROUGH SOMEONE'S CHEST! WHY AREN'T YOU EXCITED?
UM, BECAUSE I KNOW HOW IT'S DONE?
YOU DO NOT!
OKAY, GO AHEAD. TELL ME HOW THEY'RE ALL DONE!

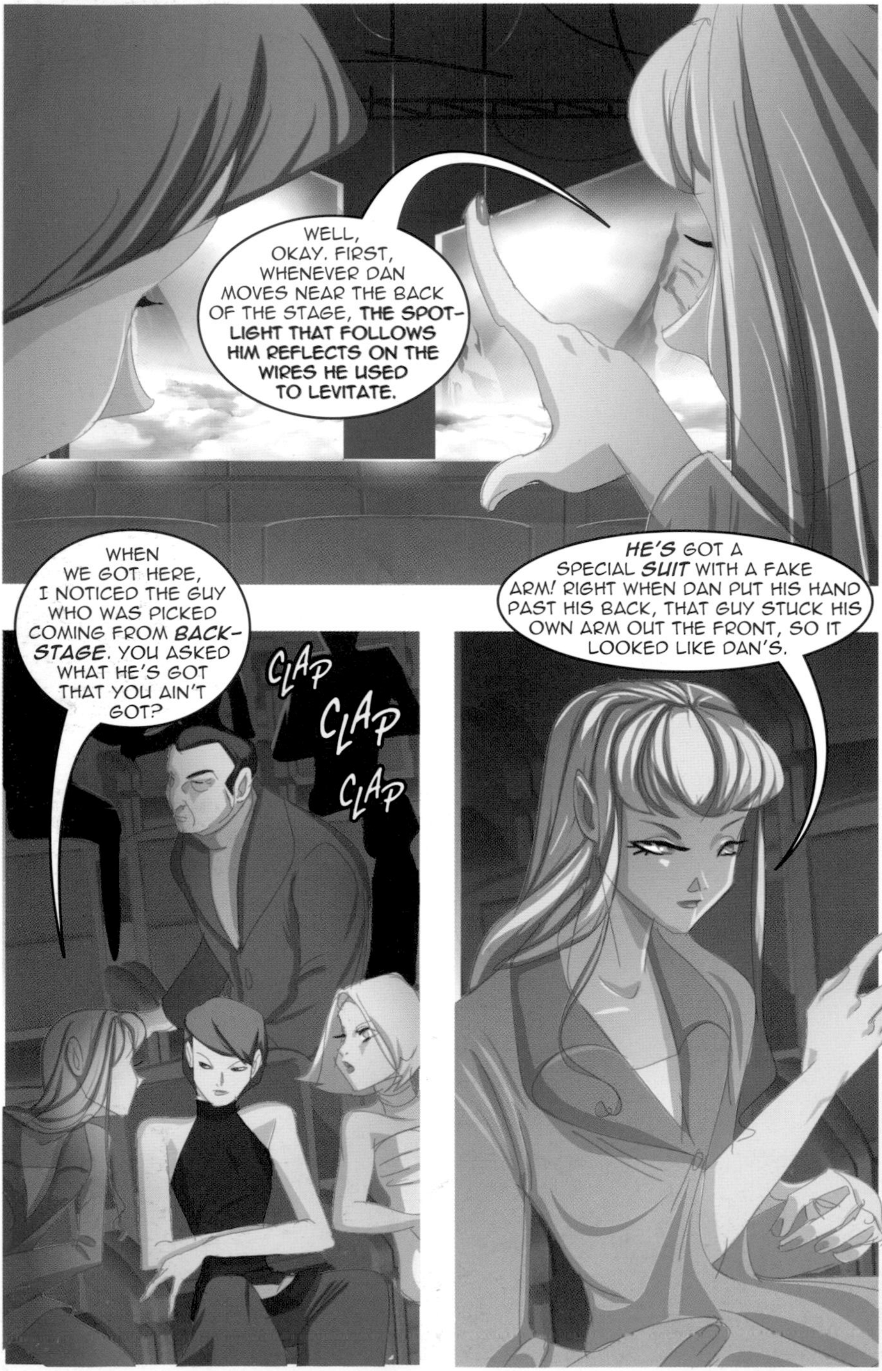
WELL, OKAY. FIRST, WHENEVER DAN MOVES NEAR THE BACK OF THE STAGE, THE SPOT-LIGHT THAT FOLLOWS HIM REFLECTS ON THE WIRES HE USED TO LEVITATE.
WHEN WE GOT HERE, I NOTICED THE GUY WHO WAS PICKED COMING FROM BACK-STAGE. YOU ASKED WHAT HE'S GOT THAT YOU AIN'T GOT?
CLAP
CLAP
CLAP
HE'S GOT A SPECIAL SUIT WITH A FAKE ARM! RIGHT WHEN DAN PUT HIS HAND PAST HIS BACK, THAT GUY STUCK HIS OWN ARM OUT THE FRONT, SO IT LOOKED LIKE DAN'S.

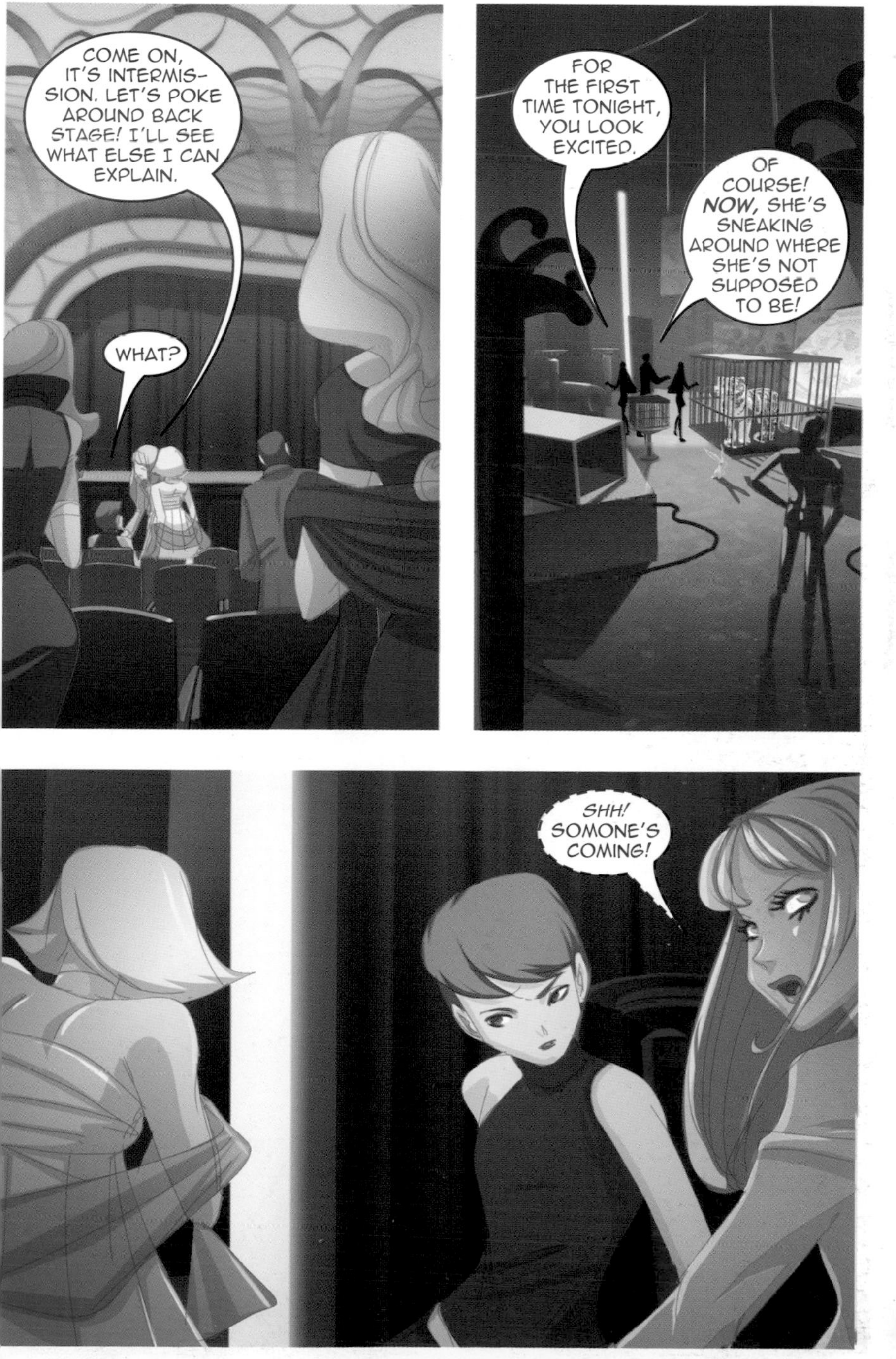
COME ON, IT'S INTERMIS-SION. LET'S POKE AROUND BACK STAGE! I'LL SEE WHAT ELSE I CAN EXPLAIN.
WHAT?
FOR THE FIRST TIME TONIGHT, YOU LOOK EXCITED.
OF COURSE! NOW, SHE'S SNEAKING AROUND WHERE SHE'S NOT SUPPOSED TO BE!
SHH! SOMONE'S COMING!

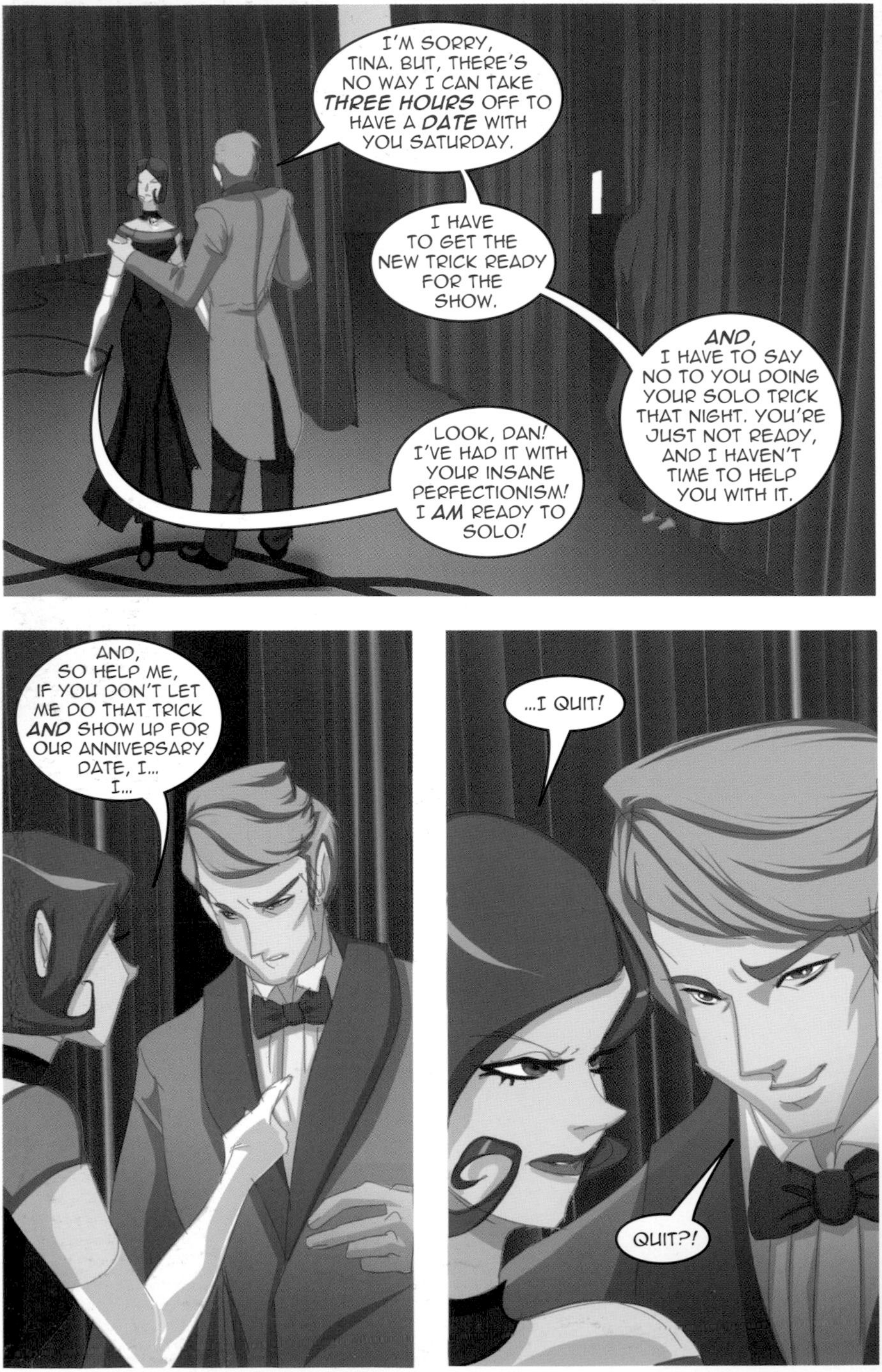
I'M SORRY, TINA. BUT, THERE'S NO WAY I CAN TAKE THREE HOURS OFF TO HAVE A DATE WITH YOU SATURDAY.
I HAVE TO GET THE NEW TRICK READY FOR THE SHOW.
AND, I HAVE TO SAY NO TO YOU DOING YOUR SOLO TRICK THAT NIGHT. YOU'RE JUST NOT READY, AND I HAVEN'T TIME TO HELP YOU WITH IT.
LOOK, DAN! I'VE HAD IT WITH YOUR INSANE PERFECTIONISM! I AM READY TO SOLO!
AND, SO HELP ME, IF YOU DON'T LET ME DO THAT TRICK AND SHOW UP FOR OUR ANNIVERSARY DATE, I... I...
...I QUIT!
QUIT?!

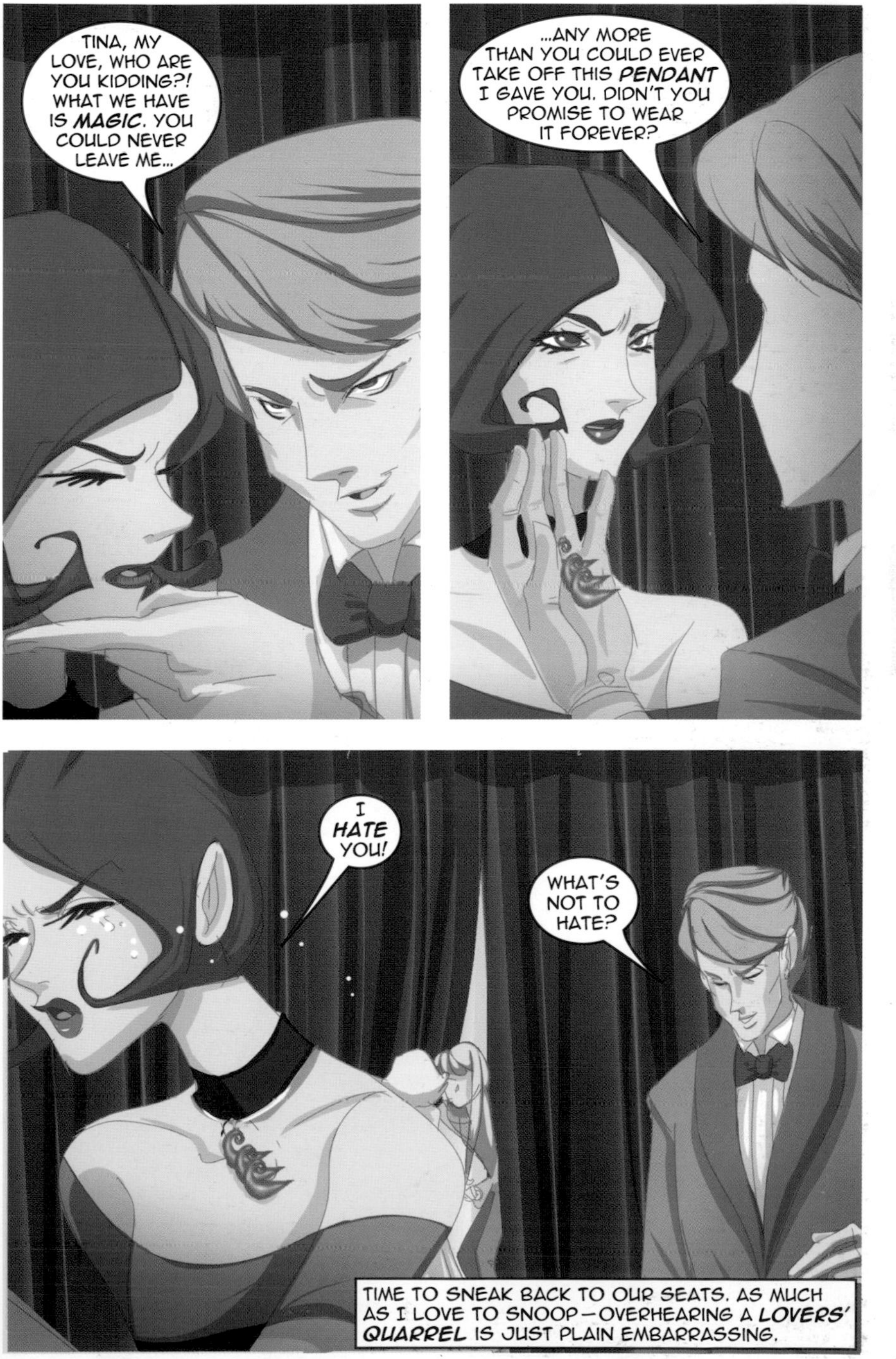
TINA, MY LOVE, WHO ARE YOU KIDDING?! WHAT WE HAVE IS MAGIC. YOU COULD NEVER LEAVE ME...
...ANY MORE THAN YOU COULD EVER TAKE OFF THIS PENDANT I GAVE YOU. DIDN'T YOU PROMISE TO WEAR IT FOREVER?
I HATE YOU!
WHAT'S NOT TO HATE?
TIME TO SNEAK BACK TO OUR SEATS. AS MUCH AS I LOVE TO SNOOP—OVERHEARING A LOVERS' QUARREL IS JUST PLAIN EMBARRASSING.

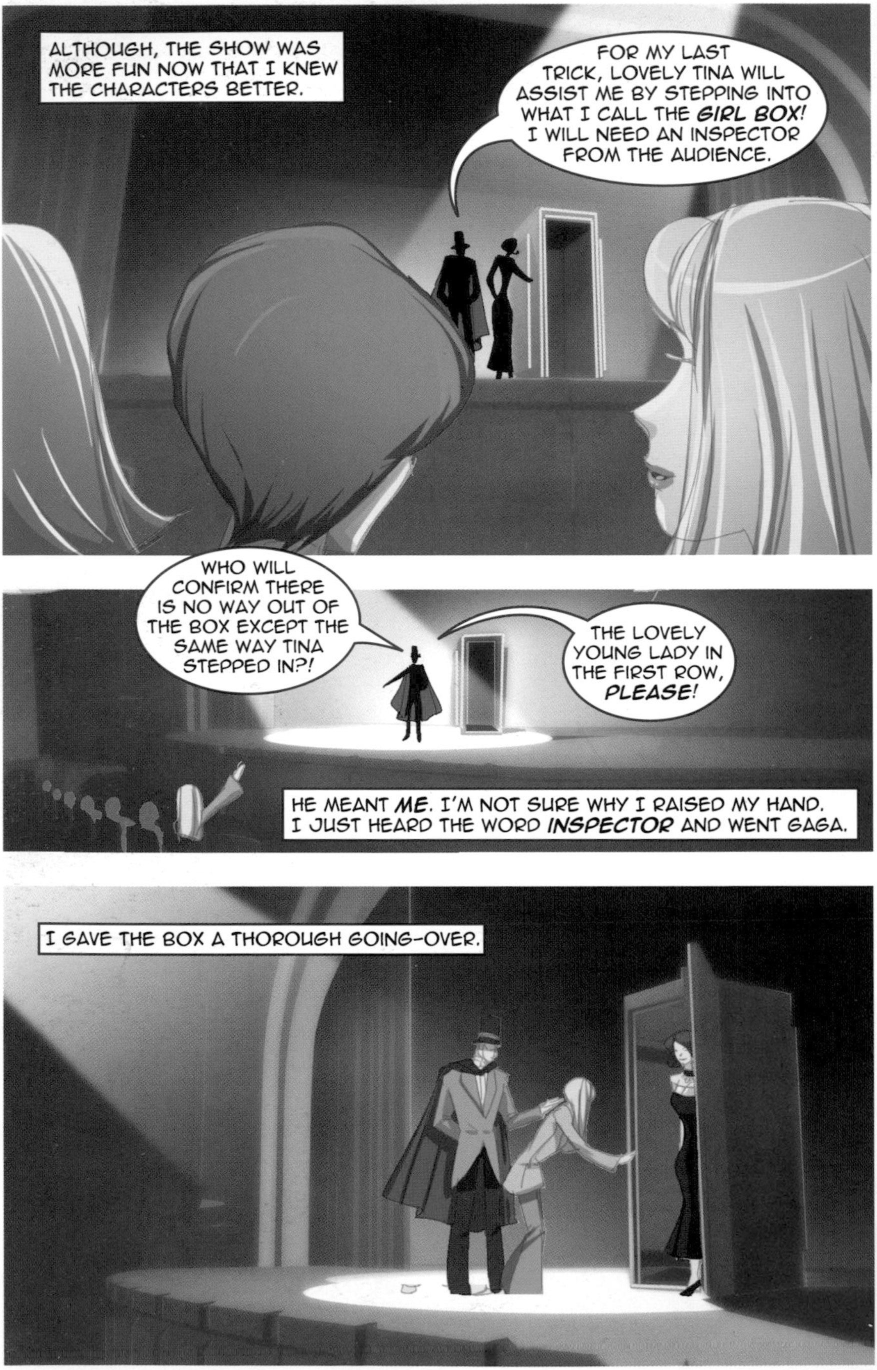
ALTHOUGH, THE SHOW WAS MORE FUN NOW THAT I KNEW THE CHARACTERS BETTER.
FOR MY LAST TRICK, LOVELY TINA WILL ASSIST ME BY STEPPING INTO WHAT I CALL THE ***GIRL BOX!*** I WILL NEED AN INSPECTOR FROM THE AUDIENCE.
WHO WILL CONFIRM THERE IS NO WAY OUT OF THE BOX EXCEPT THE SAME WAY TINA STEPPED IN?!
THE LOVELY YOUNG LADY IN THE FIRST ROW, ***PLEASE!***
HE MEANT ***ME***. I'M NOT SURE WHY I RAISED MY HAND. I JUST HEARD THE WORD ***INSPECTOR*** AND WENT GAGA.
I GAVE THE BOX A THOROUGH GOING-OVER.

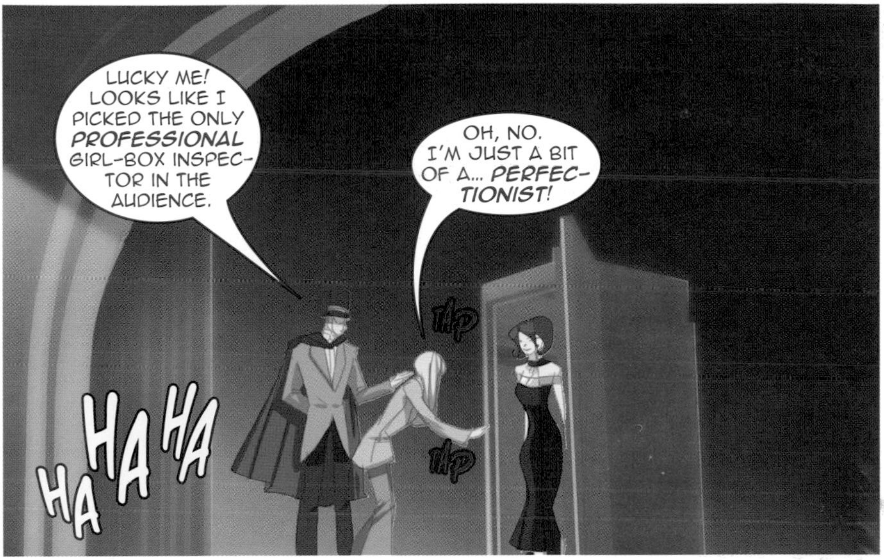
LUCKY ME! LOOKS LIKE I PICKED THE ONLY *PROFESSIONAL* GIRL-BOX INSPECTOR IN THE AUDIENCE.
OH, NO. I'M JUST A BIT OF A... *PERFECTIONIST!*
TAP
TAP
HA HA HA HA

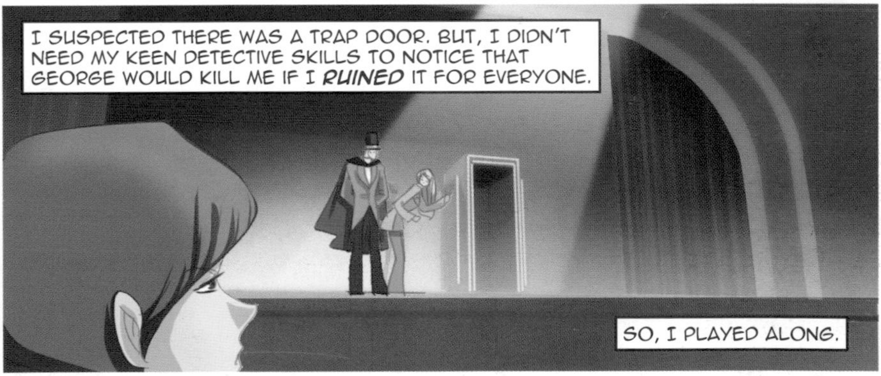
I SUSPECTED THERE WAS A TRAP DOOR. BUT, I DIDN'T NEED MY KEEN DETECTIVE SKILLS TO NOTICE THAT GEORGE WOULD KILL ME IF I *RUINED* IT FOR EVERYONE.
SO, I PLAYED ALONG.

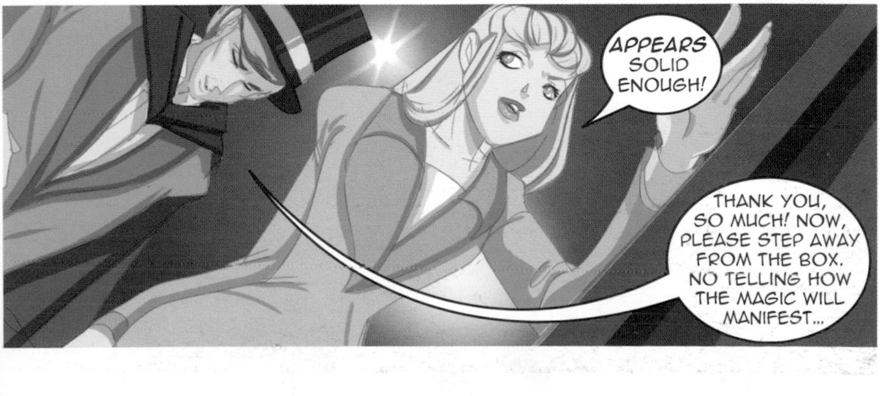
APPEARS SOLID ENOUGH!
THANK YOU, SO MUCH! NOW, PLEASE STEP AWAY FROM THE BOX. NO TELLING HOW THE MAGIC WILL MANIFEST...

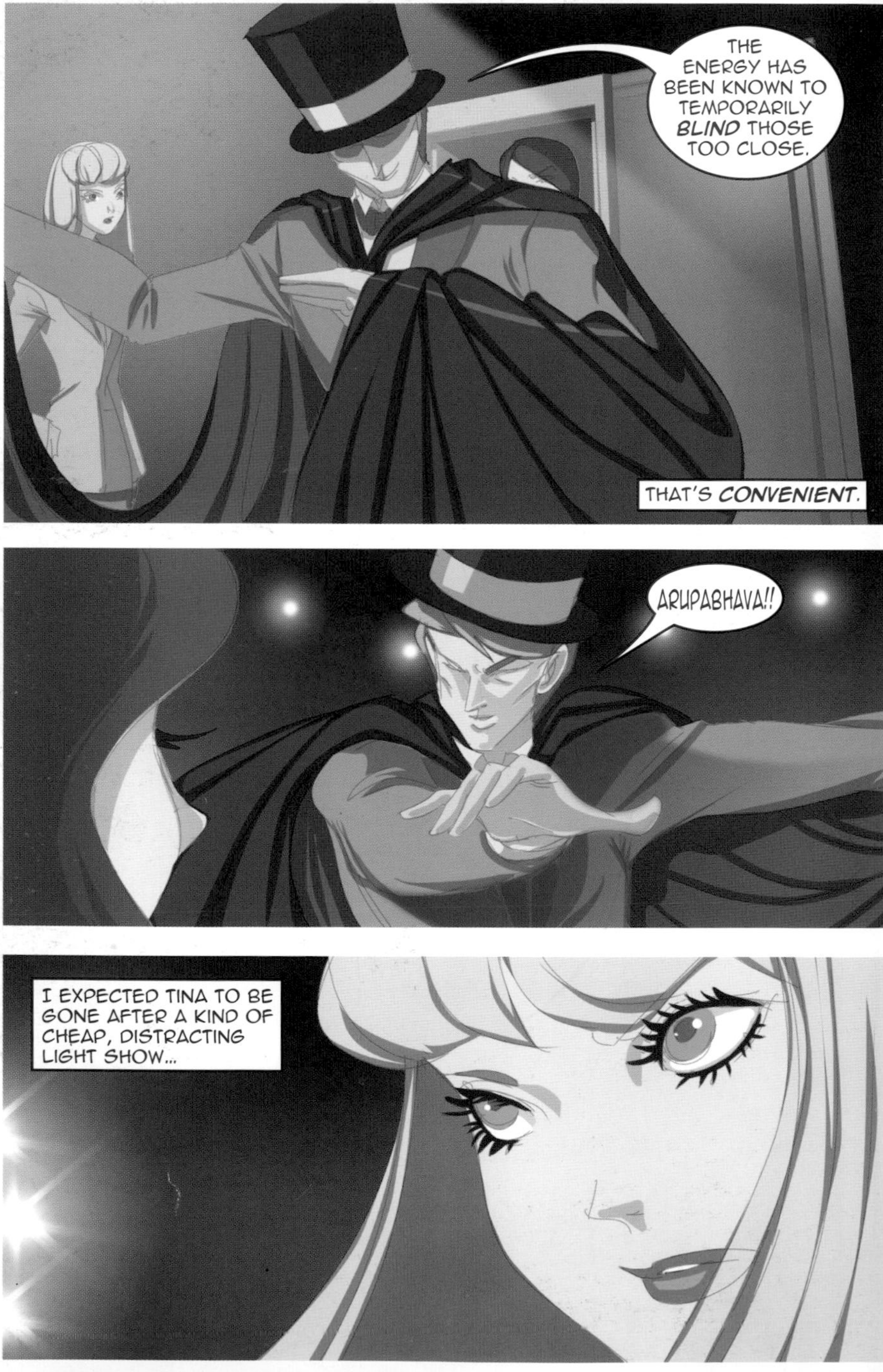
THE ENERGY HAS BEEN KNOWN TO TEMPORARILY BLIND THOSE TOO CLOSE.
THAT'S CONVENIENT.
ARUPABHAVA!!
I EXPECTED TINA TO BE GONE AFTER A KIND OF CHEAP, DISTRACTING LIGHT SHOW...

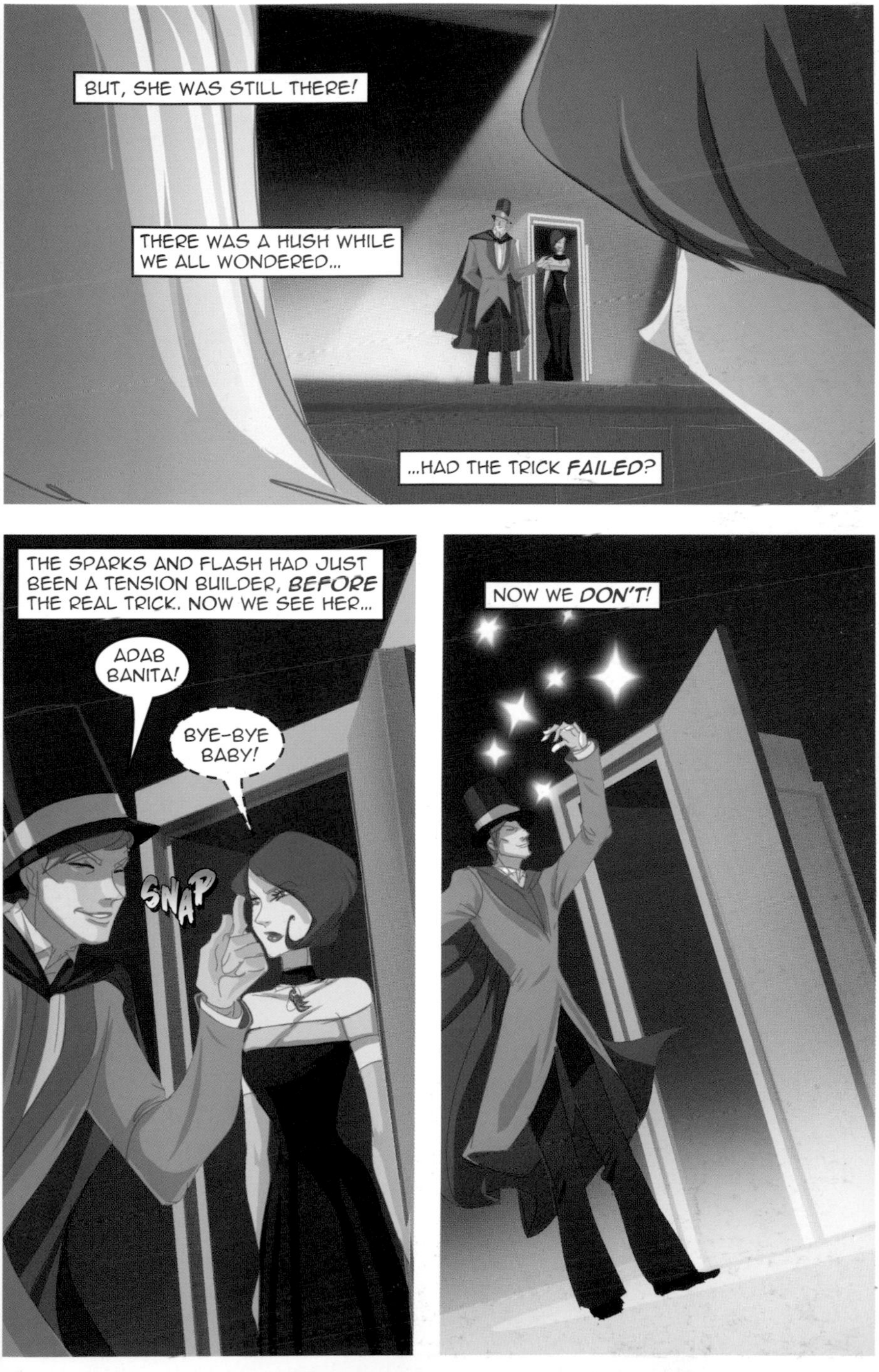
BUT, SHE WAS STILL THERE!
THERE WAS A HUSH WHILE WE ALL WONDERED...
...HAD THE TRICK *FAILED*?
THE SPARKS AND FLASH HAD JUST BEEN A TENSION BUILDER, *BEFORE* THE REAL TRICK. NOW WE SEE HER...
ADAB BANITA!
BYE-BYE BABY!
SNAP
NOW WE *DON'T*!

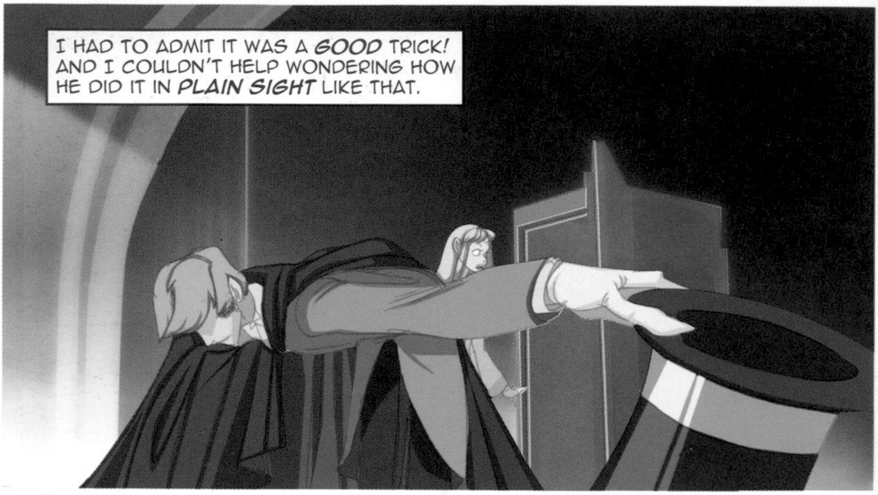
I HAD TO ADMIT IT WAS A GOOD TRICK! AND I COULDN'T HELP WONDERING HOW HE DID IT IN PLAIN SIGHT LIKE THAT.

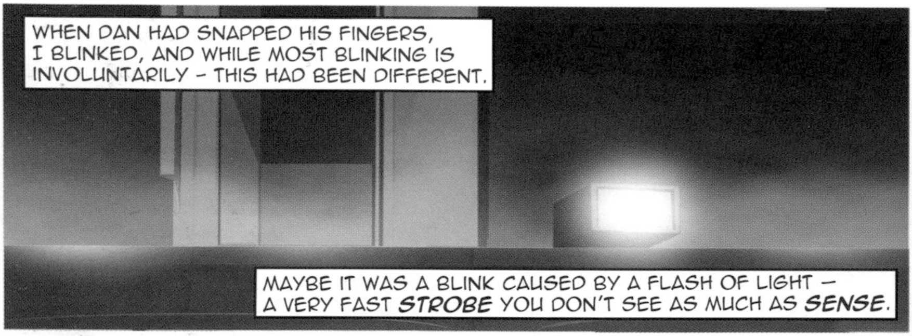
WHEN DAN HAD SNAPPED HIS FINGERS, I BLINKED, AND WHILE MOST BLINKING IS INVOLUNTARILY – THIS HAD BEEN DIFFERENT.
MAYBE IT WAS A BLINK CAUSED BY A FLASH OF LIGHT – A VERY FAST STROBE YOU DON'T SEE AS MUCH AS SENSE.

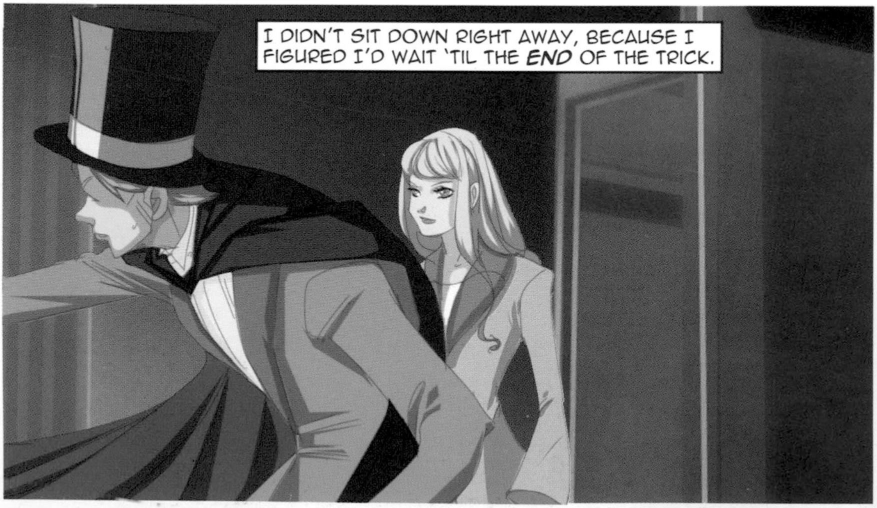
I DIDN'T SIT DOWN RIGHT AWAY, BECAUSE I FIGURED I'D WAIT 'TIL THE END OF THE TRICK.

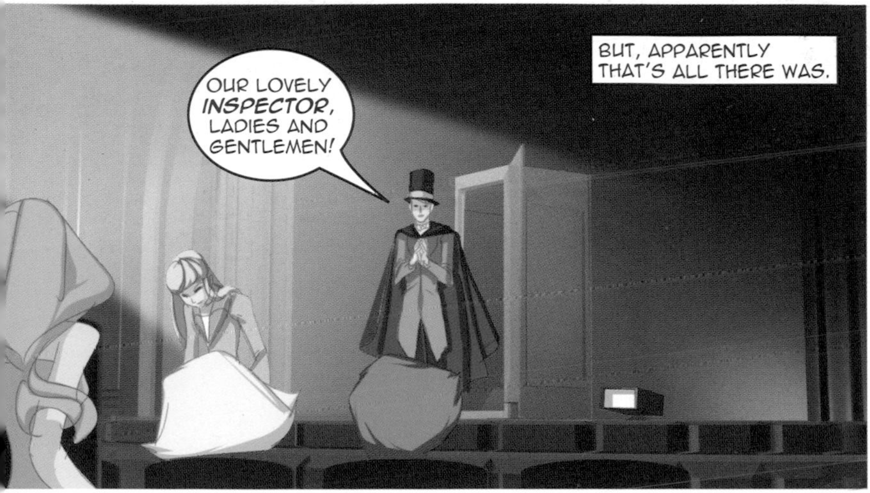
BUT, APPARENTLY THAT'S ALL THERE WAS.
OUR LOVELY INSPECTOR, LADIES AND GENTLEMEN!

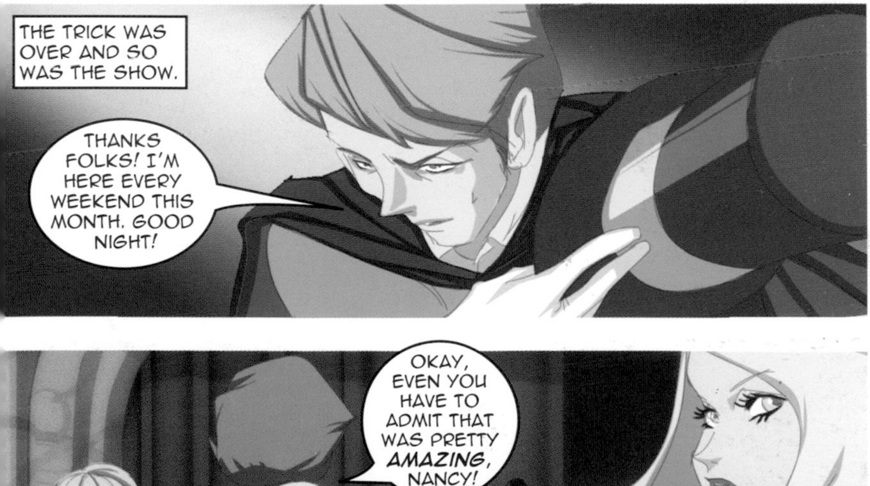
THE TRICK WAS OVER AND SO WAS THE SHOW.
THANKS FOLKS! I'M HERE EVERY WEEKEND THIS MONTH. GOOD NIGHT!

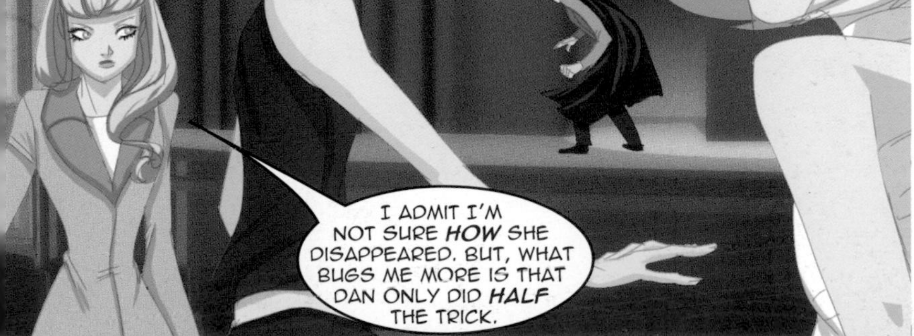
OKAY, EVEN YOU HAVE TO ADMIT THAT WAS PRETTY AMAZING, NANCY!
I ADMIT I'M NOT SURE HOW SHE DISAPPEARED. BUT, WHAT BUGS ME MORE IS THAT DAN ONLY DID HALF THE TRICK.

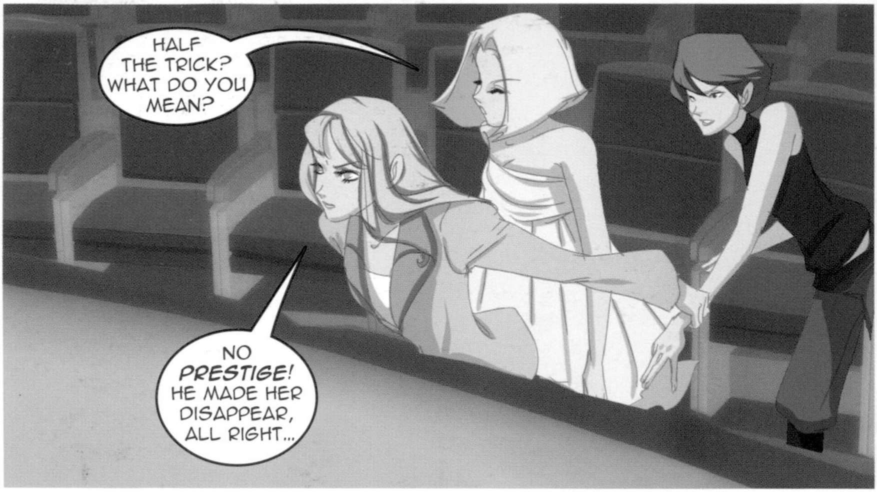
HALF THE TRICK? WHAT DO YOU MEAN?
NO *PRESTIGE!* HE MADE HER DISAPPEAR, ALL RIGHT...

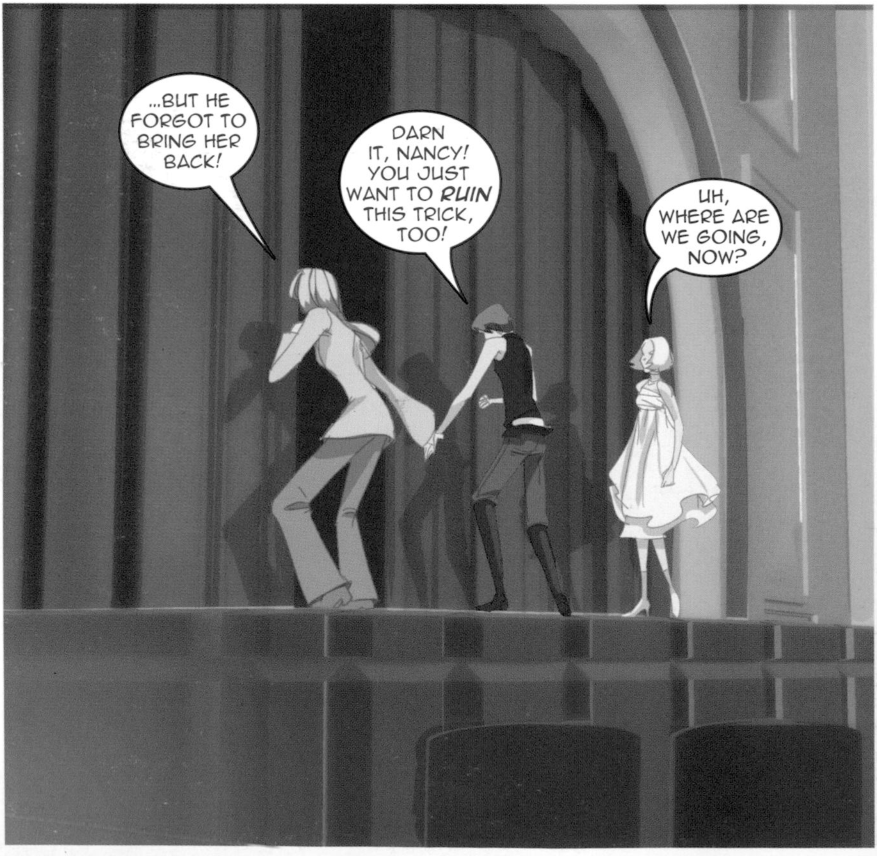
...BUT HE FORGOT TO BRING HER BACK!
DARN IT, NANCY! YOU JUST WANT TO *RUIN* THIS TRICK, TOO!
UH, WHERE ARE WE GOING, NOW?

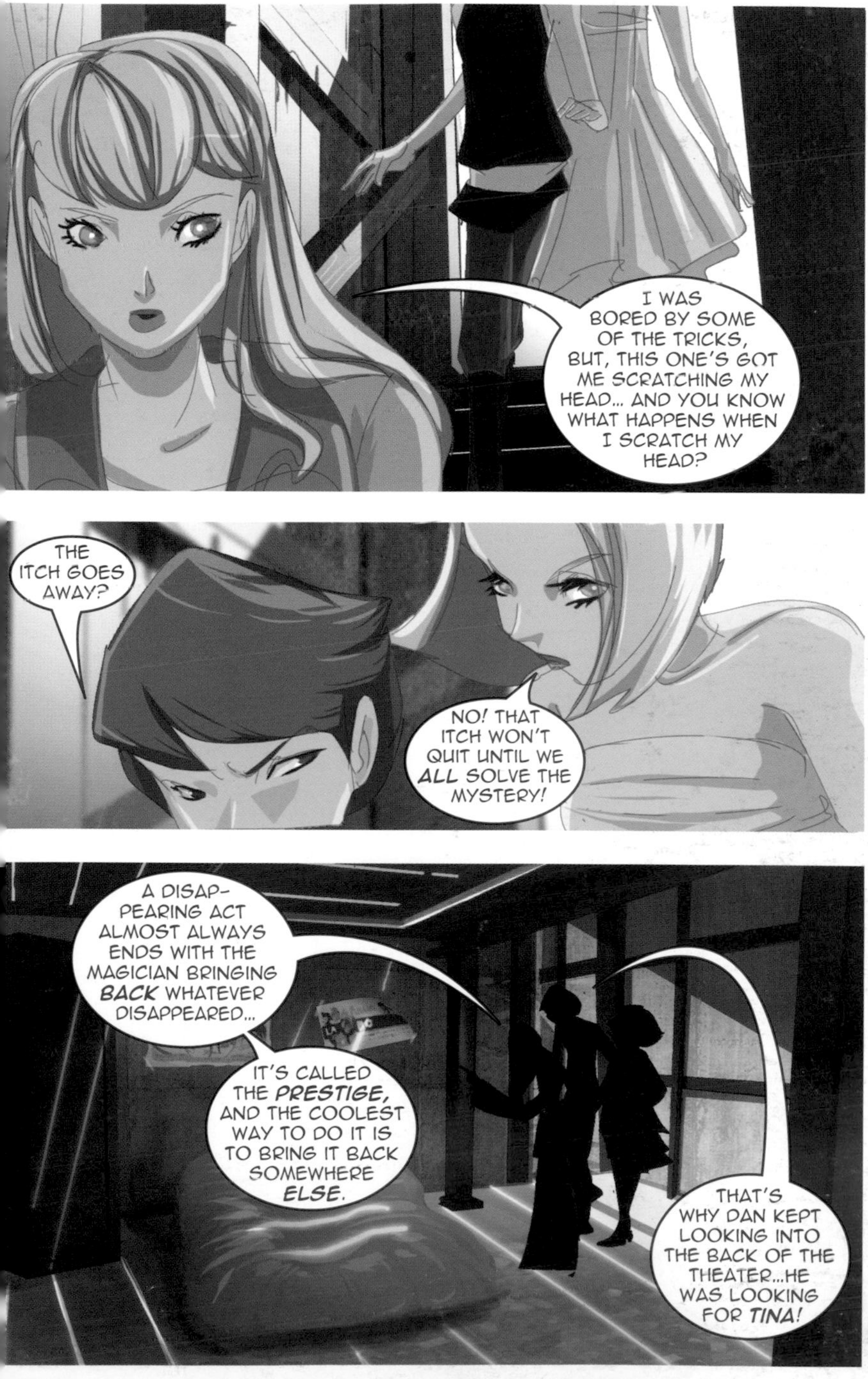
I WAS BORED BY SOME OF THE TRICKS, BUT, THIS ONE'S GOT ME SCRATCHING MY HEAD... AND YOU KNOW WHAT HAPPENS WHEN I SCRATCH MY HEAD?
THE ITCH GOES AWAY?
NO! THAT ITCH WON'T QUIT UNTIL WE ALL SOLVE THE MYSTERY!
A DISAP-PEARING ACT ALMOST ALWAYS ENDS WITH THE MAGICIAN BRINGING BACK WHATEVER DISAPPEARED...
IT'S CALLED THE PRESTIGE, AND THE COOLEST WAY TO DO IT IS TO BRING IT BACK SOMEWHERE ELSE.
THAT'S WHY DAN KEPT LOOKING INTO THE BACK OF THE THEATER...HE WAS LOOKING FOR TINA!

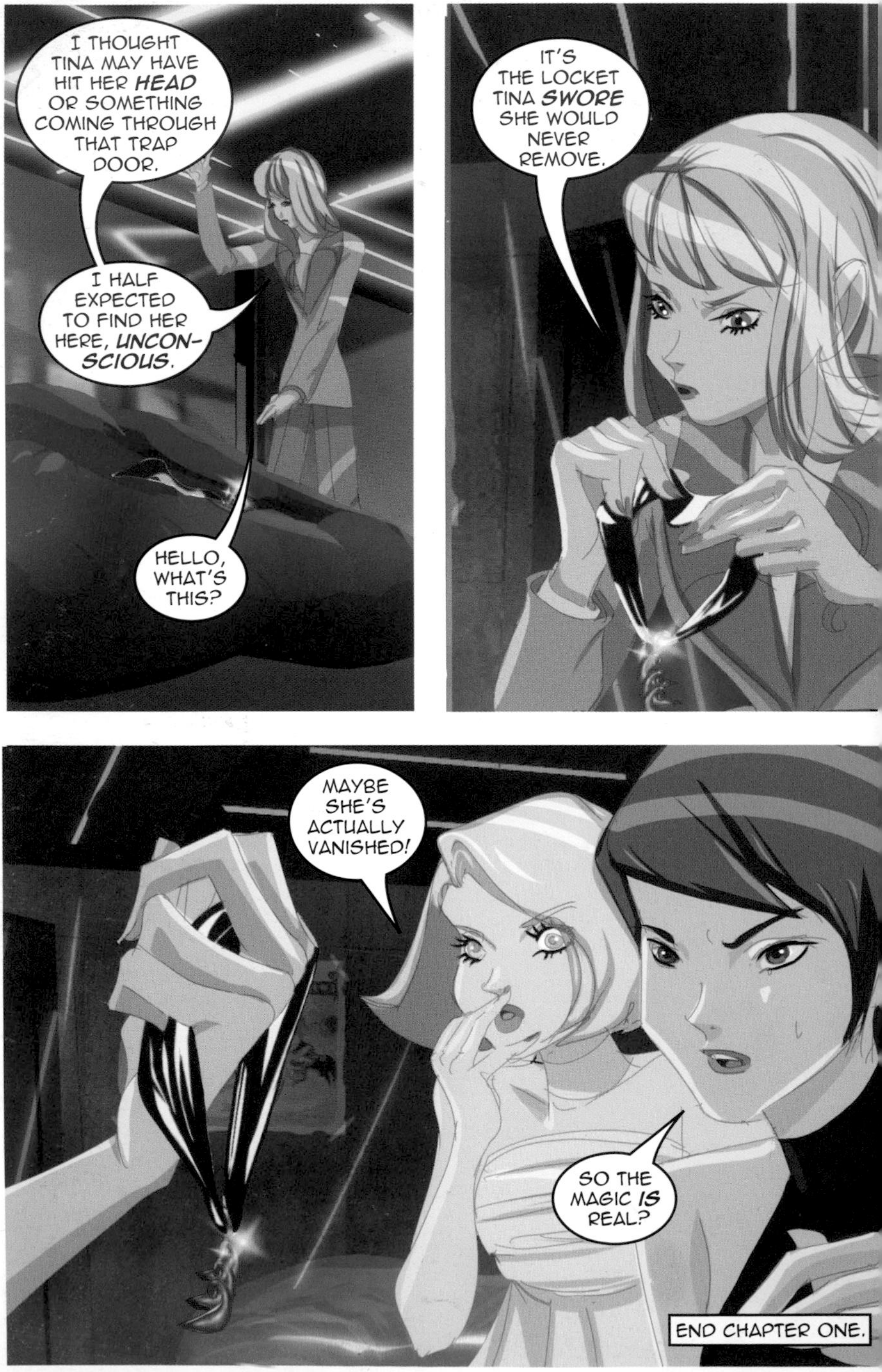
I THOUGHT TINA MAY HAVE HIT HER **HEAD** OR SOMETHING COMING THROUGH THAT TRAP DOOR.
I HALF EXPECTED TO FIND HER HERE, **UNCON-SCIOUS**.
HELLO, WHAT'S THIS?
IT'S THE LOCKET TINA **SWORE** SHE WOULD NEVER REMOVE.
MAYBE SHE'S ACTUALLY VANISHED!
SO THE MAGIC **IS** REAL?
END CHAPTER ONE.

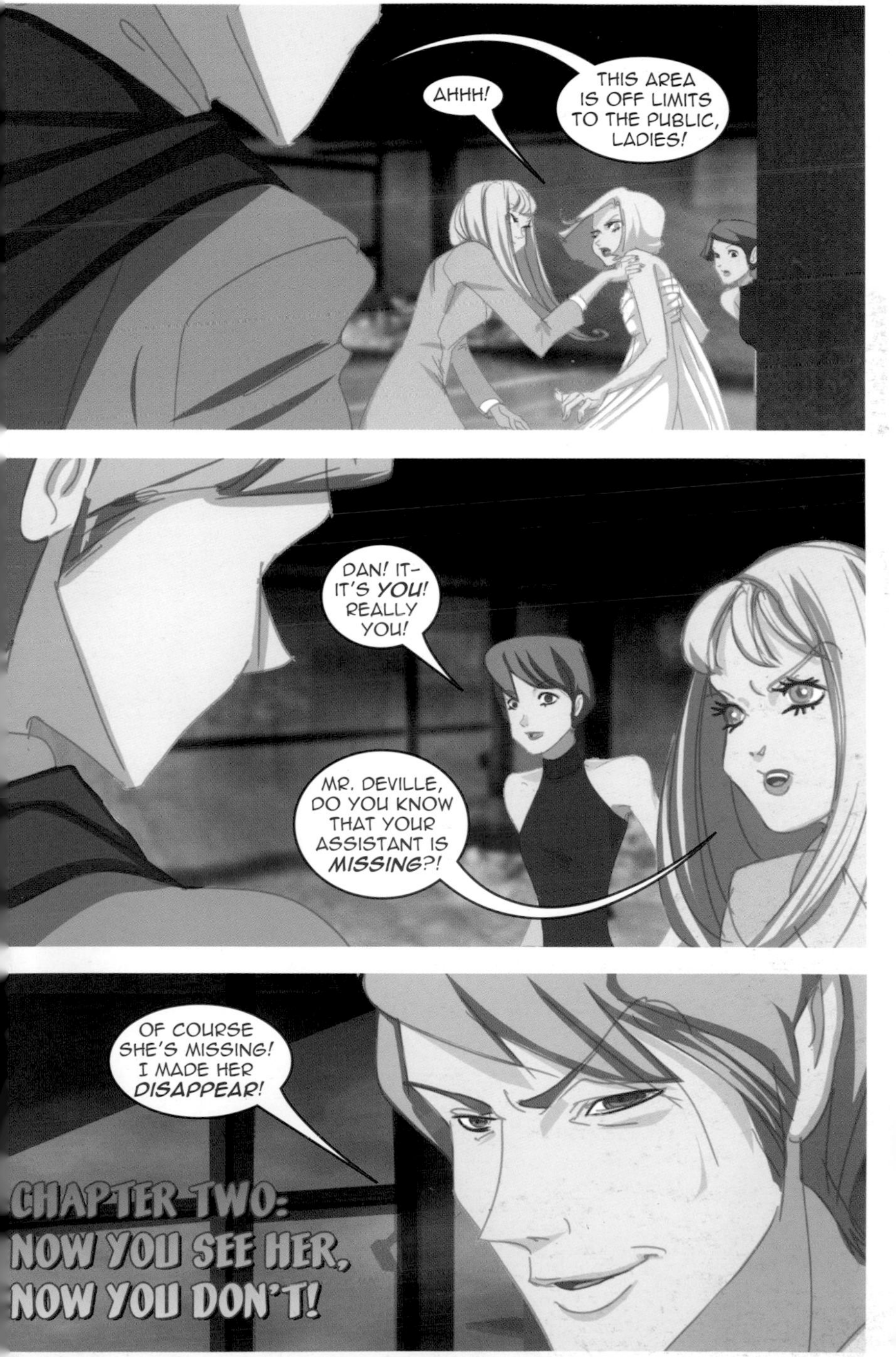
THIS AREA IS OFF LIMITS TO THE PUBLIC, LADIES!
AHHH!
DAN! IT- IT'S YOU! REALLY YOU!
MR. DEVILLE, DO YOU KNOW THAT YOUR ASSISTANT IS MISSING?!
OF COURSE SHE'S MISSING! I MADE HER DISAPPEAR!
CHAPTER TWO: NOW YOU SEE HER, NOW YOU DON'T!

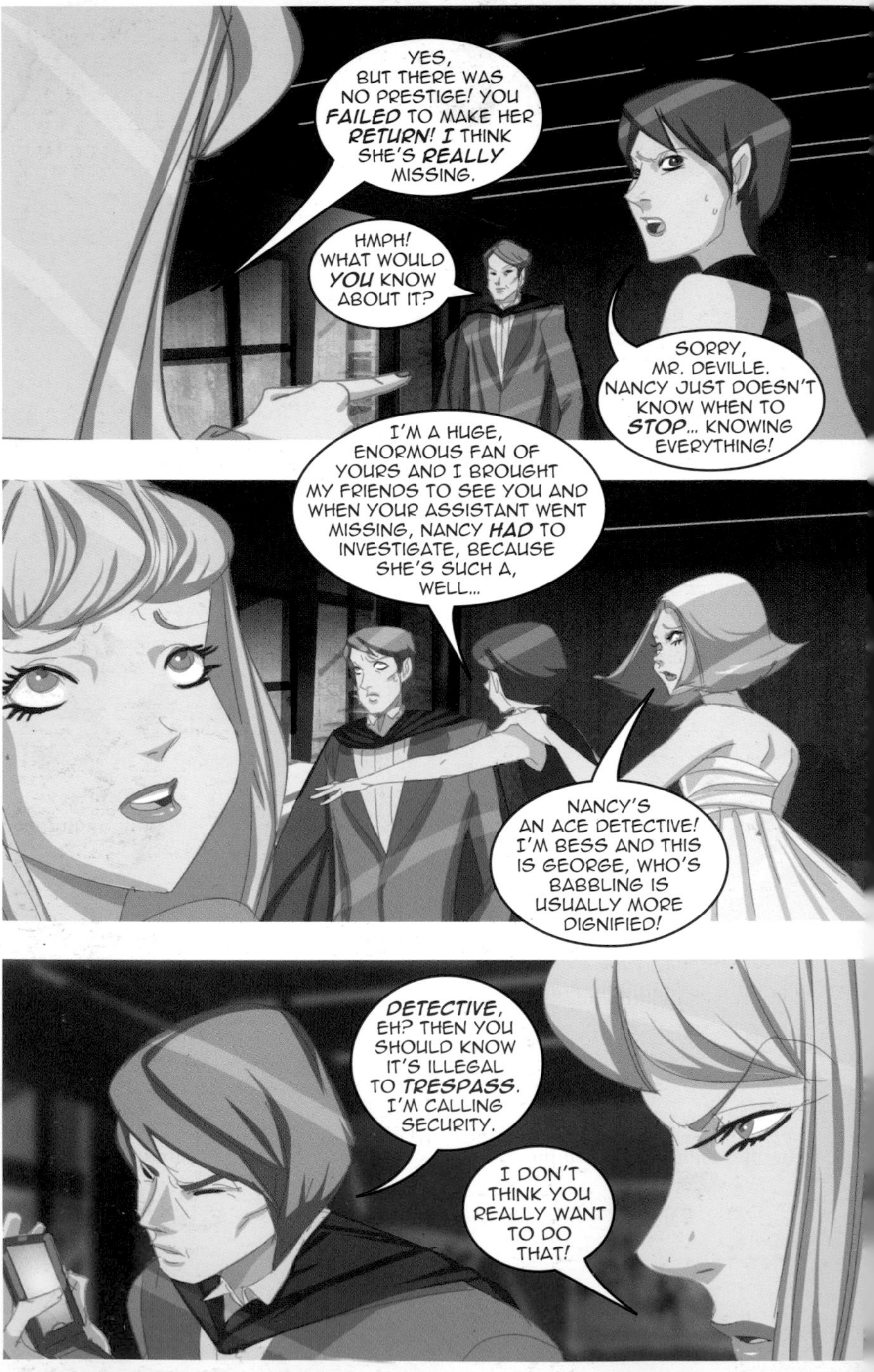

YES, BUT THERE WAS NO PRESTIGE! YOU *FAILED* TO MAKE HER *RETURN*! *I* THINK SHE'S *REALLY* MISSING.
HMPH! WHAT WOULD *YOU* KNOW ABOUT IT?
SORRY, MR. DEVILLE. NANCY JUST DOESN'T KNOW WHEN TO *STOP*... KNOWING EVERYTHING!
I'M A HUGE, ENORMOUS FAN OF YOURS AND I BROUGHT MY FRIENDS TO SEE YOU AND WHEN YOUR ASSISTANT WENT MISSING, NANCY *HAD* TO INVESTIGATE, BECAUSE SHE'S SUCH A, WELL...
NANCY'S AN ACE DETECTIVE! I'M BESS AND THIS IS GEORGE, WHO'S BABBLING IS USUALLY MORE DIGNIFIED!
DETECTIVE, EH? THEN YOU SHOULD KNOW IT'S ILLEGAL TO *TRESPASS*. I'M CALLING SECURITY.
I DON'T THINK YOU REALLY WANT TO DO THAT!

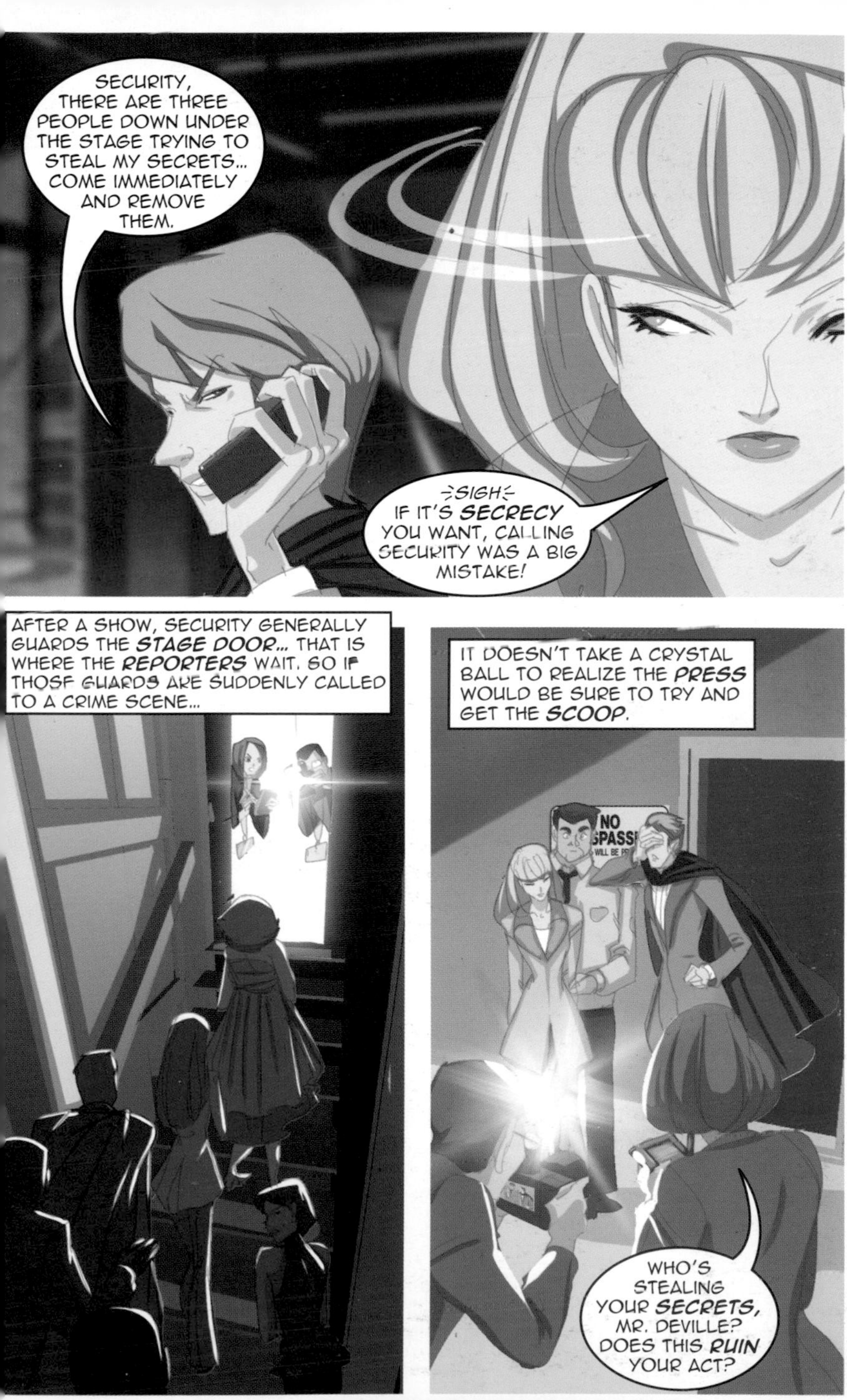
SECURITY, THERE ARE THREE PEOPLE DOWN UNDER THE STAGE TRYING TO STEAL MY SECRETS... COME IMMEDIATELY AND REMOVE THEM.
=SIGH= IF IT'S SECRECY YOU WANT, CALLING SECURITY WAS A BIG MISTAKE!
AFTER A SHOW, SECURITY GENERALLY GUARDS THE STAGE DOOR... THAT IS WHERE THE REPORTERS WAIT. SO IF THOSE GUARDS ARE SUDDENLY CALLED TO A CRIME SCENE...
IT DOESN'T TAKE A CRYSTAL BALL TO REALIZE THE PRESS WOULD BE SURE TO TRY AND GET THE SCOOP.
WHO'S STEALING YOUR SECRETS, MR. DEVILLE? DOES THIS RUIN YOUR ACT?

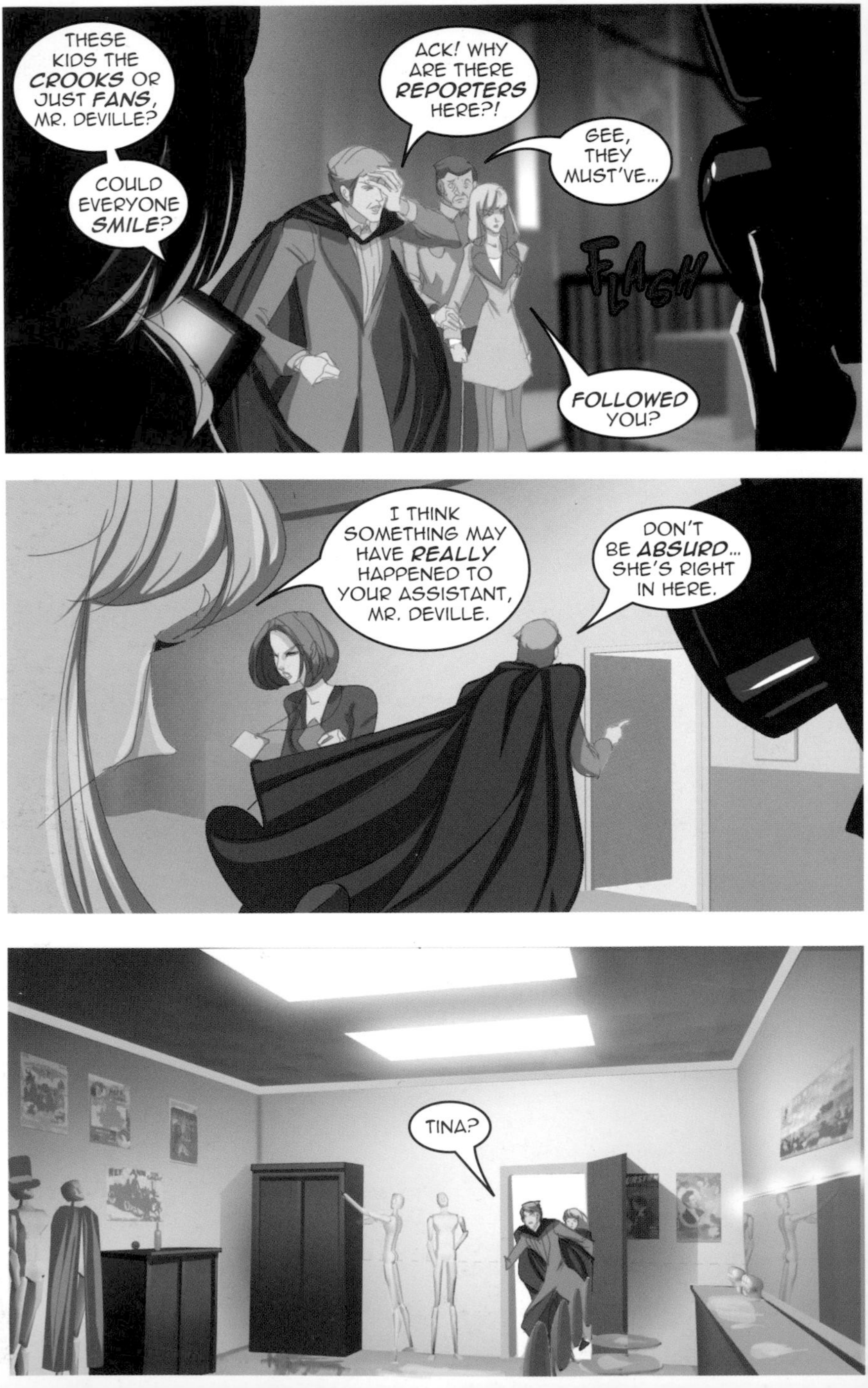
THESE KIDS THE CROOKS OR JUST FANS, MR. DEVILLE?
COULD EVERYONE SMILE?
ACK! WHY ARE THERE REPORTERS HERE?!
GEE, THEY MUST'VE...
FLASH
FOLLOWED YOU?
I THINK SOMETHING MAY HAVE REALLY HAPPENED TO YOUR ASSISTANT, MR. DEVILLE.
DON'T BE ABSURD... SHE'S RIGHT IN HERE.
TINA?

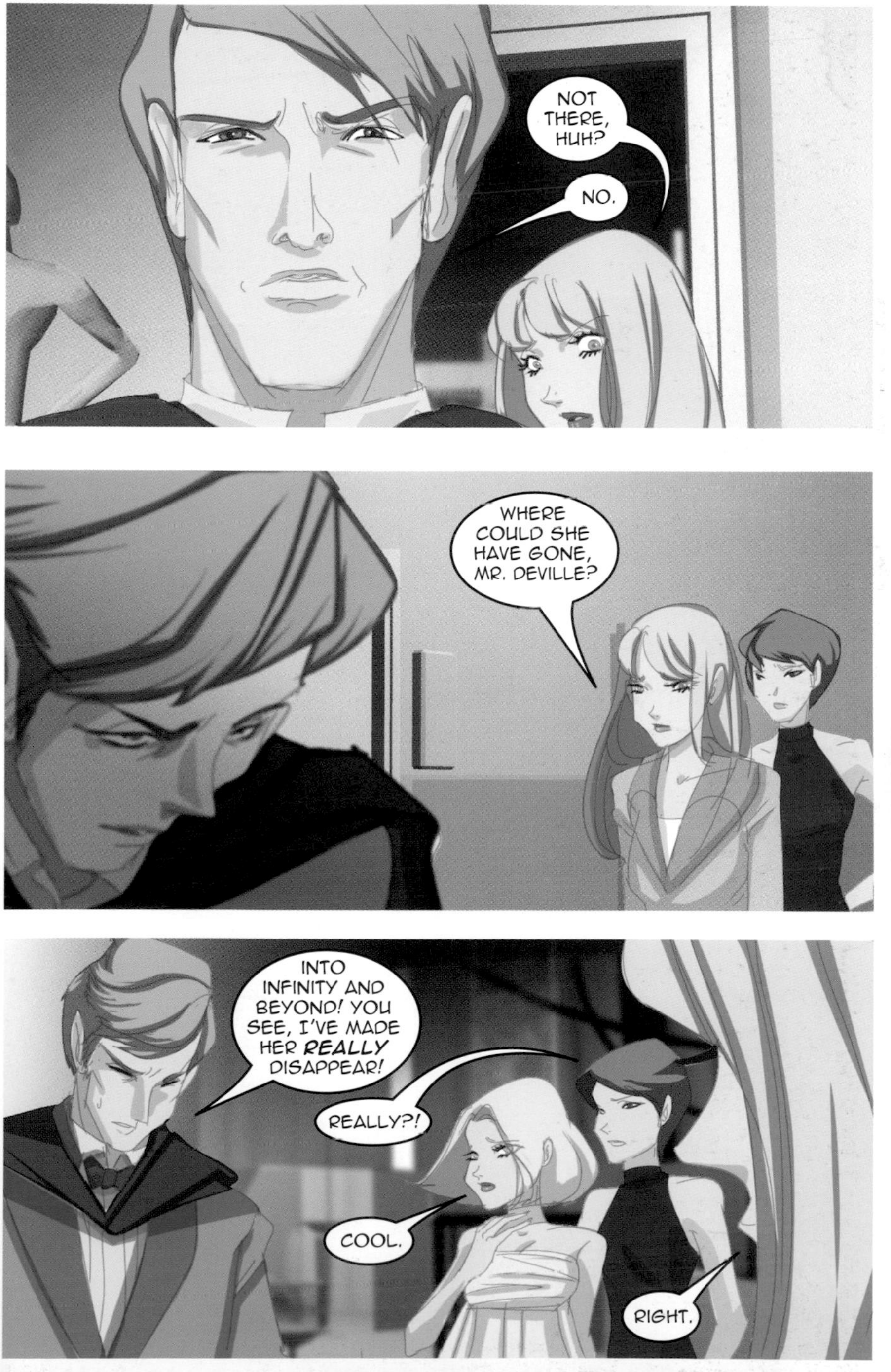
NOT THERE, HUH?
NO.
WHERE COULD SHE HAVE GONE, MR. DEVILLE?
INTO INFINITY AND BEYOND! YOU SEE, I'VE MADE HER **REALLY** DISAPPEAR!
REALLY?!
COOL.
RIGHT.

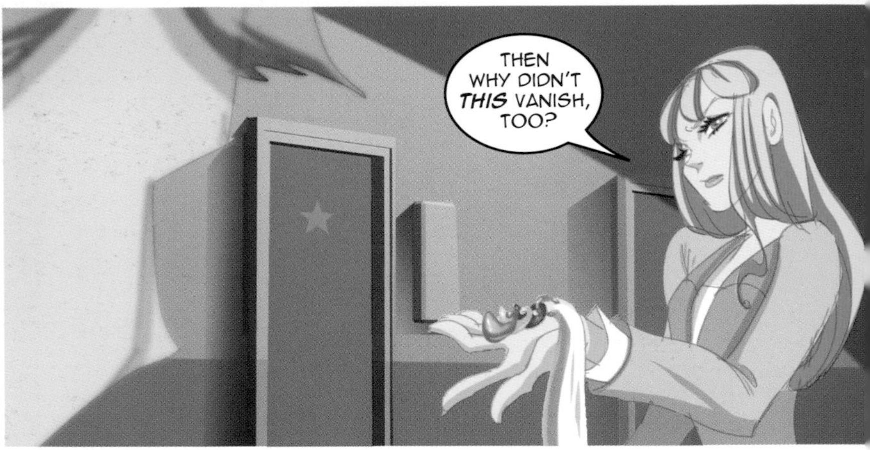
THEN WHY DIDN'T *THIS* VANISH, TOO?

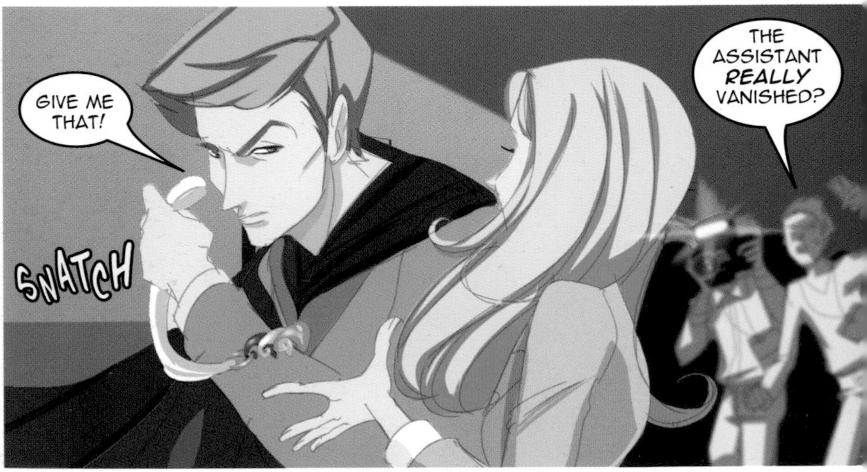
GIVE ME THAT!
SNATCH
THE ASSISTANT *REALLY* VANISHED?

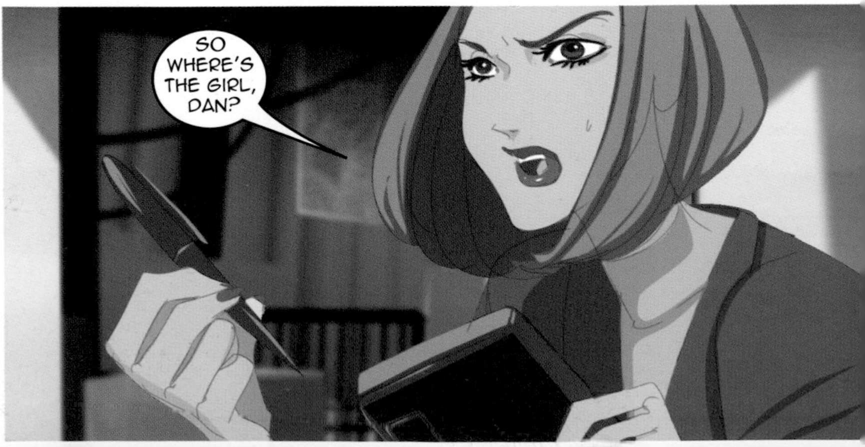
SO WHERE'S THE GIRL, DAN?

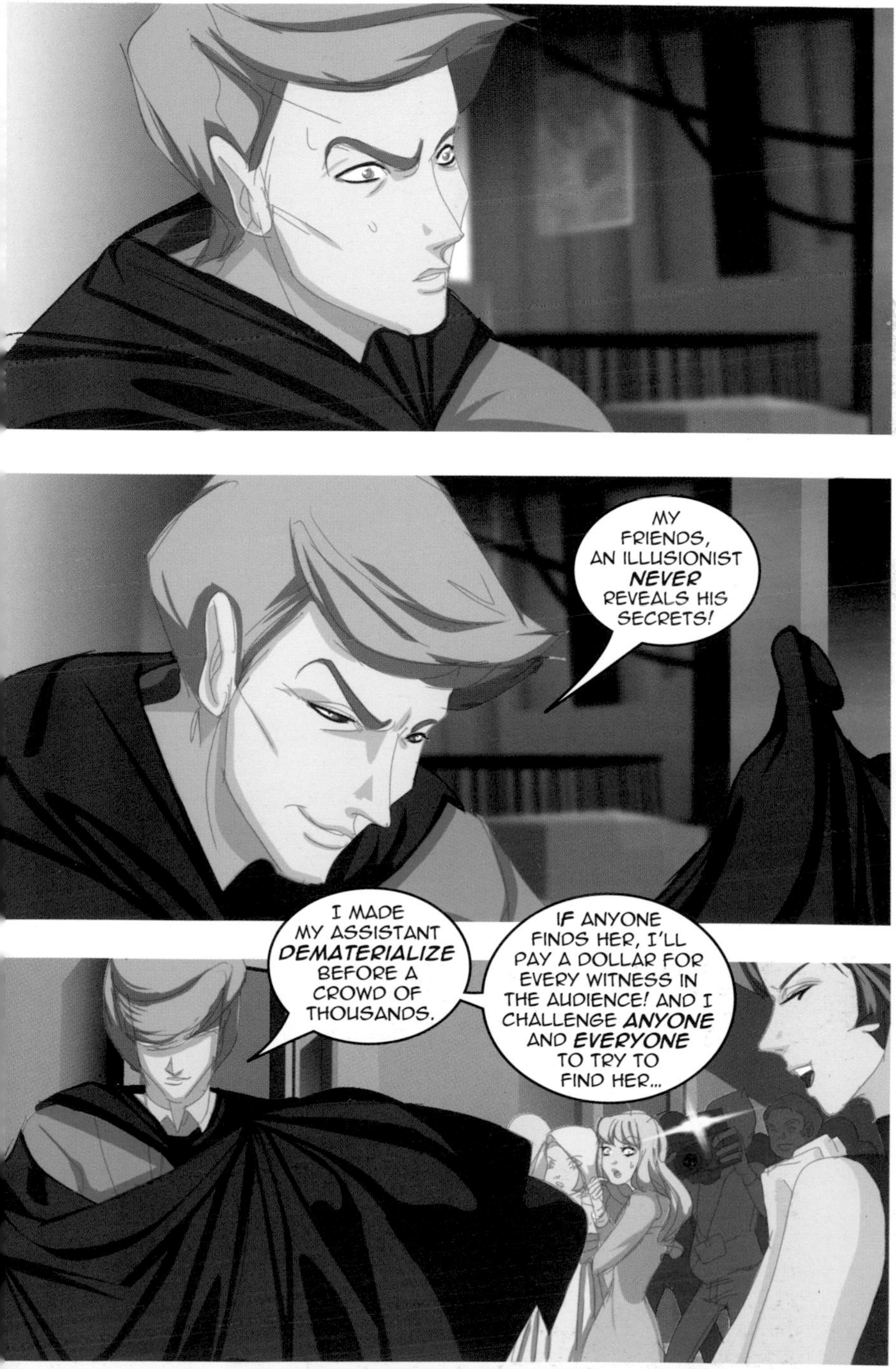
MY FRIENDS, AN ILLUSIONIST ***NEVER*** REVEALS HIS SECRETS!
I MADE MY ASSISTANT ***DEMATERIALIZE*** BEFORE A CROWD OF THOUSANDS.
IF ANYONE FINDS HER, I'LL PAY A DOLLAR FOR EVERY WITNESS IN THE AUDIENCE! AND I CHALLENGE ***ANYONE*** AND ***EVERYONE*** TO TRY TO FIND HER...

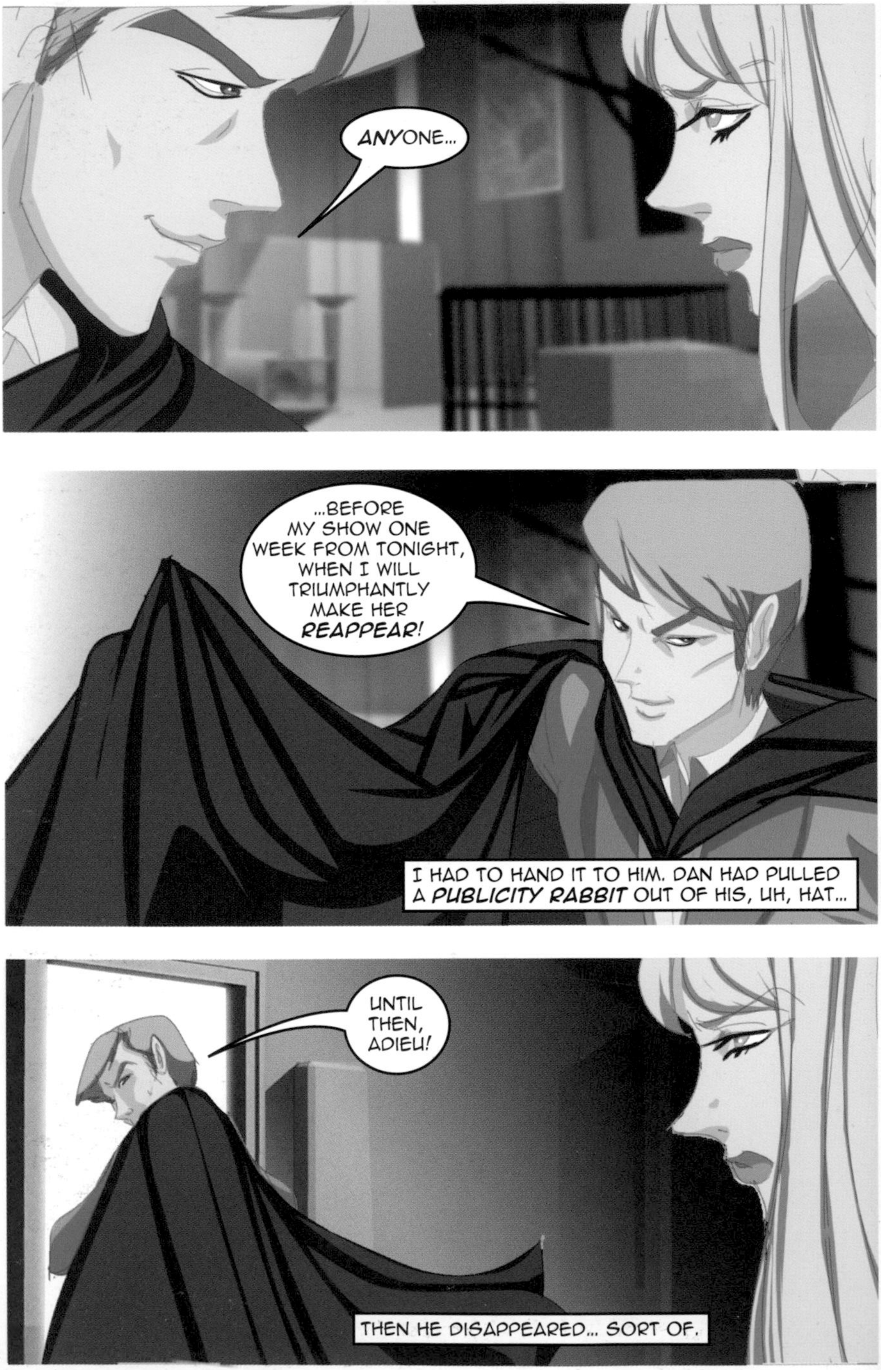
ANYONE...
...BEFORE MY SHOW ONE WEEK FROM TONIGHT, WHEN I WILL TRIUMPHANTLY MAKE HER REAPPEAR!
I HAD TO HAND IT TO HIM. DAN HAD PULLED A PUBLICITY RABBIT OUT OF HIS, UH, HAT...
UNTIL THEN, ADIEU!
THEN HE DISAPPEARED... SORT OF.

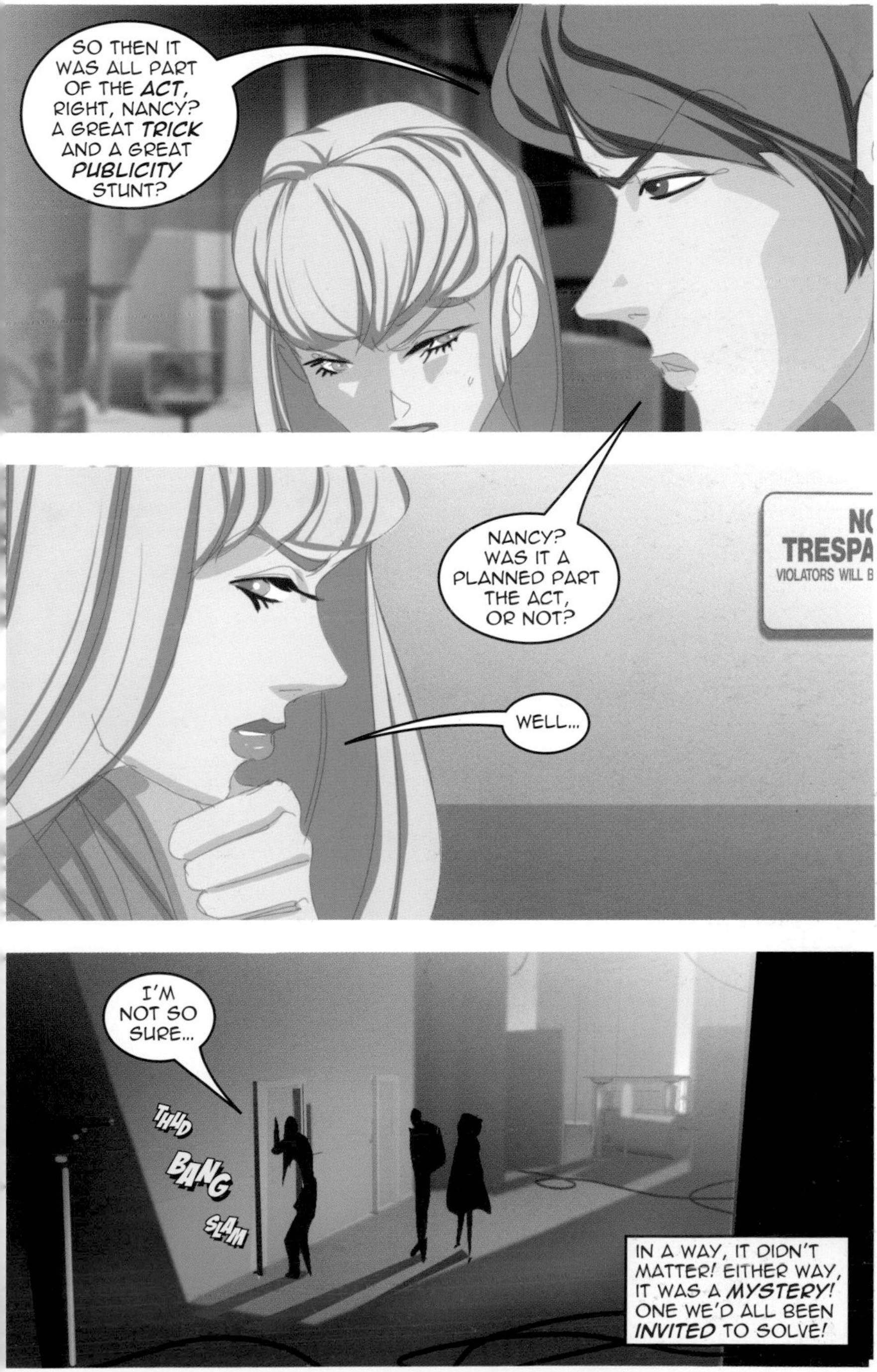
SO THEN IT WAS ALL PART OF THE ACT, RIGHT, NANCY? A GREAT TRICK AND A GREAT PUBLICITY STUNT?
NANCY? WAS IT A PLANNED PART THE ACT, OR NOT?
TRESPA
VIOLATORS WILL B
WELL...
I'M NOT SO SURE...
THUD
BANG
SLAM
IN A WAY, IT DIDN'T MATTER! EITHER WAY, IT WAS A MYSTERY! ONE WE'D ALL BEEN INVITED TO SOLVE!

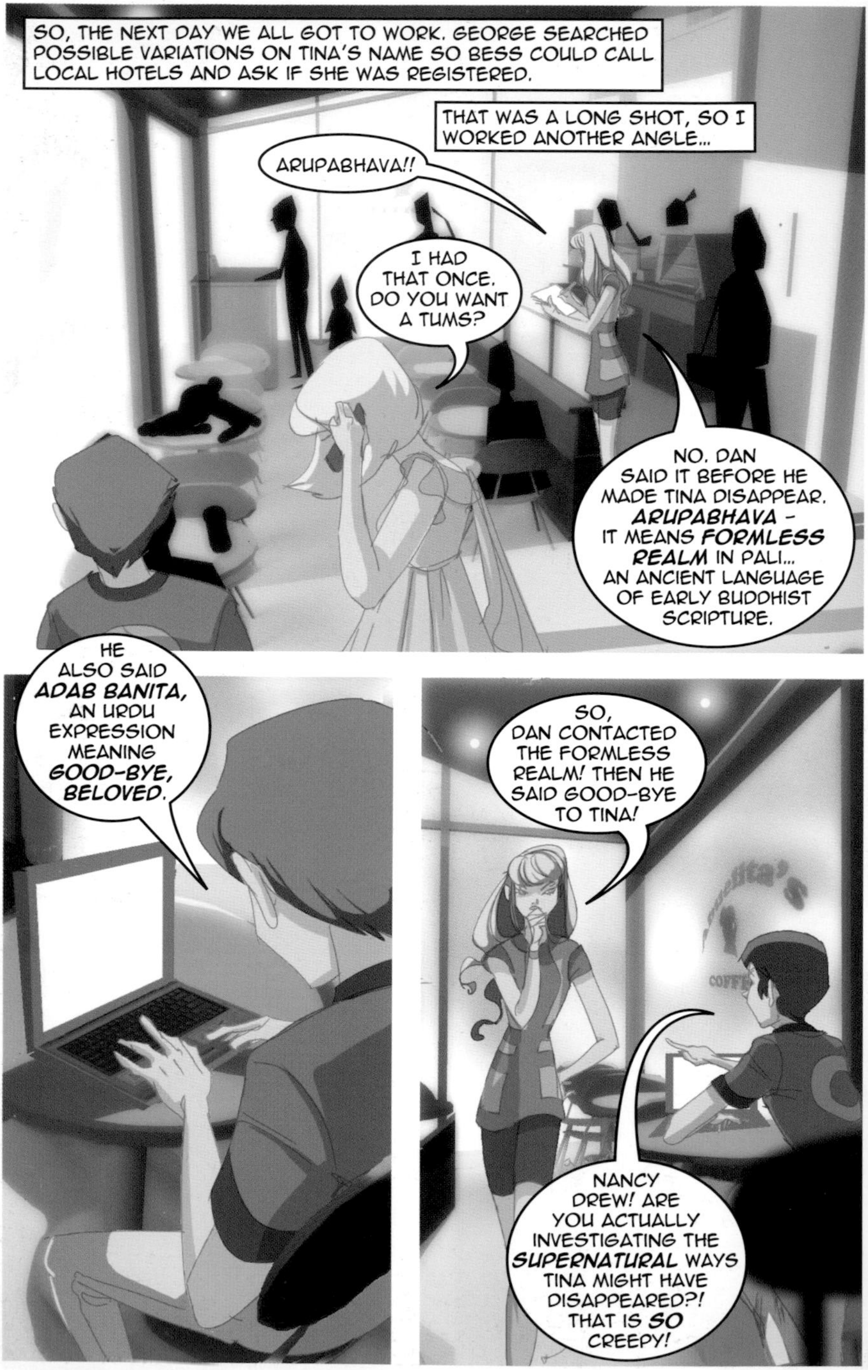

SO, THE NEXT DAY WE ALL GOT TO WORK. GEORGE SEARCHED POSSIBLE VARIATIONS ON TINA'S NAME SO BESS COULD CALL LOCAL HOTELS AND ASK IF SHE WAS REGISTERED.
THAT WAS A LONG SHOT, SO I WORKED ANOTHER ANGLE...
ARUPABHAVA!!
I HAD THAT ONCE. DO YOU WANT A TUMS?
NO. DAN SAID IT BEFORE HE MADE TINA DISAPPEAR. ***ARUPABHAVA*** – IT MEANS ***FORMLESS REALM*** IN PALI... AN ANCIENT LANGUAGE OF EARLY BUDDHIST SCRIPTURE.
HE ALSO SAID ***ADAB BANITA,*** AN URDU EXPRESSION MEANING ***GOOD-BYE, BELOVED.***
SO, DAN CONTACTED THE FORMLESS REALM! THEN HE SAID GOOD-BYE TO TINA!
NANCY DREW! ARE YOU ACTUALLY INVESTIGATING THE ***SUPERNATURAL*** WAYS TINA MIGHT HAVE DISAPPEARED?! THAT IS ***SO*** CREEPY!

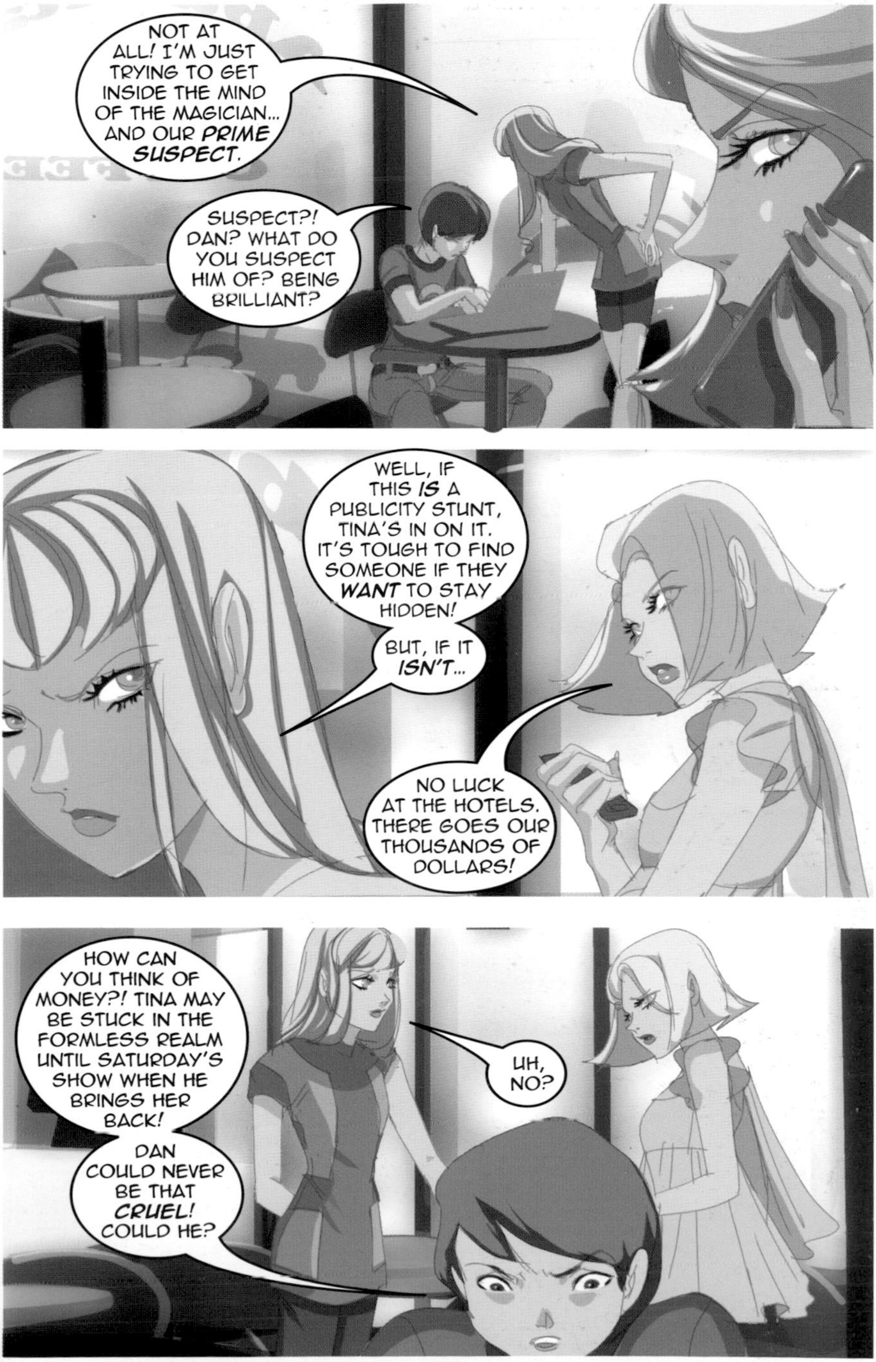
NOT AT ALL! I'M JUST TRYING TO GET INSIDE THE MIND OF THE MAGICIAN... AND OUR PRIME SUSPECT.
SUSPECT?! DAN? WHAT DO YOU SUSPECT HIM OF? BEING BRILLIANT?
WELL, IF THIS IS A PUBLICITY STUNT, TINA'S IN ON IT. IT'S TOUGH TO FIND SOMEONE IF THEY WANT TO STAY HIDDEN!
BUT, IF IT ISN'T...
NO LUCK AT THE HOTELS. THERE GOES OUR THOUSANDS OF DOLLARS!
HOW CAN YOU THINK OF MONEY?! TINA MAY BE STUCK IN THE FORMLESS REALM UNTIL SATURDAY'S SHOW WHEN HE BRINGS HER BACK!
DAN COULD NEVER BE THAT CRUEL! COULD HE?
UH, NO?

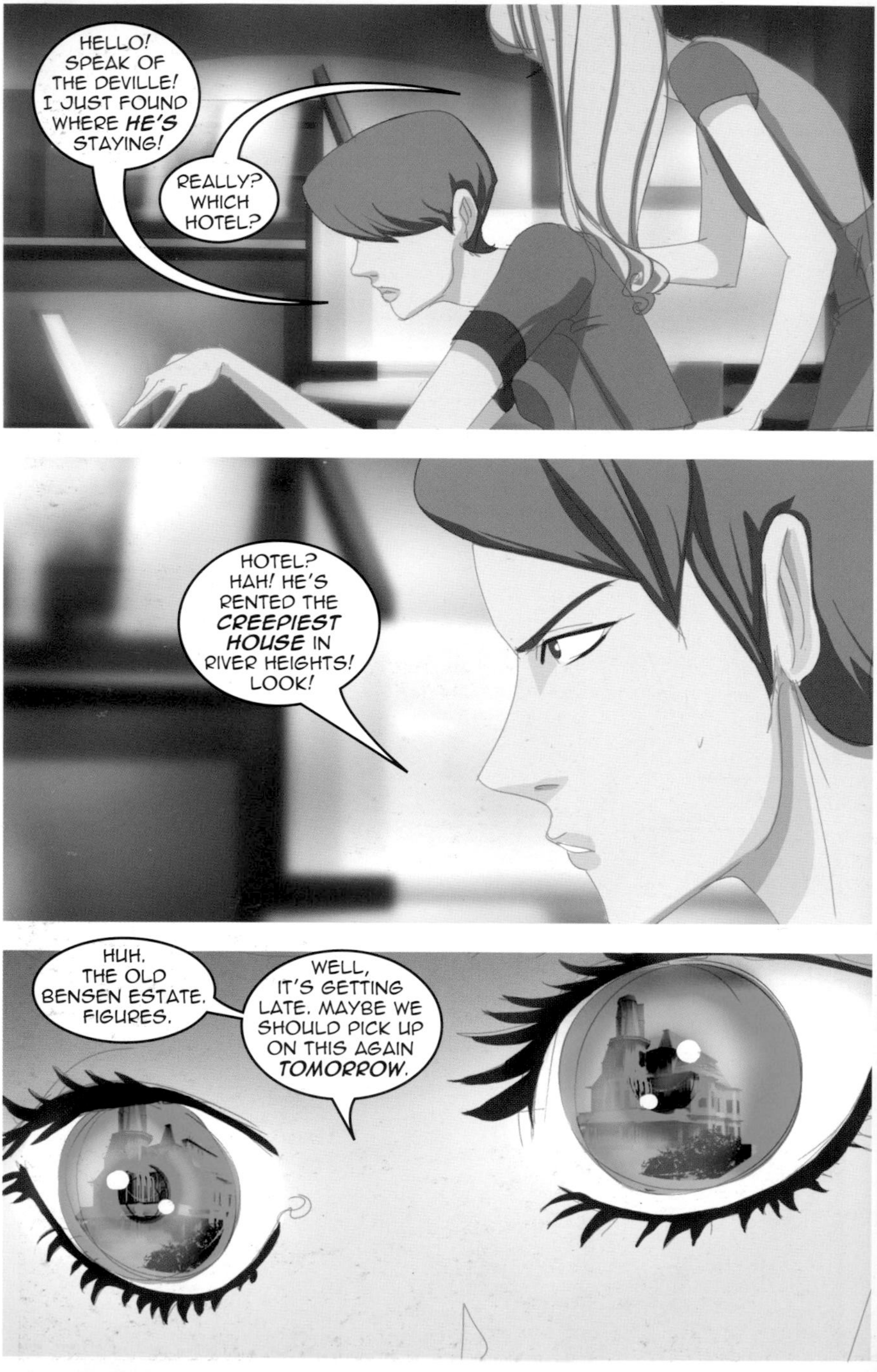
HELLO! SPEAK OF THE DEVILLE! I JUST FOUND WHERE HE'S STAYING!
REALLY? WHICH HOTEL?
HOTEL? HAH! HE'S RENTED THE CREEPIEST HOUSE IN RIVER HEIGHTS! LOOK!
HUH. THE OLD BENSEN ESTATE. FIGURES.
WELL, IT'S GETTING LATE. MAYBE WE SHOULD PICK UP ON THIS AGAIN TOMORROW.

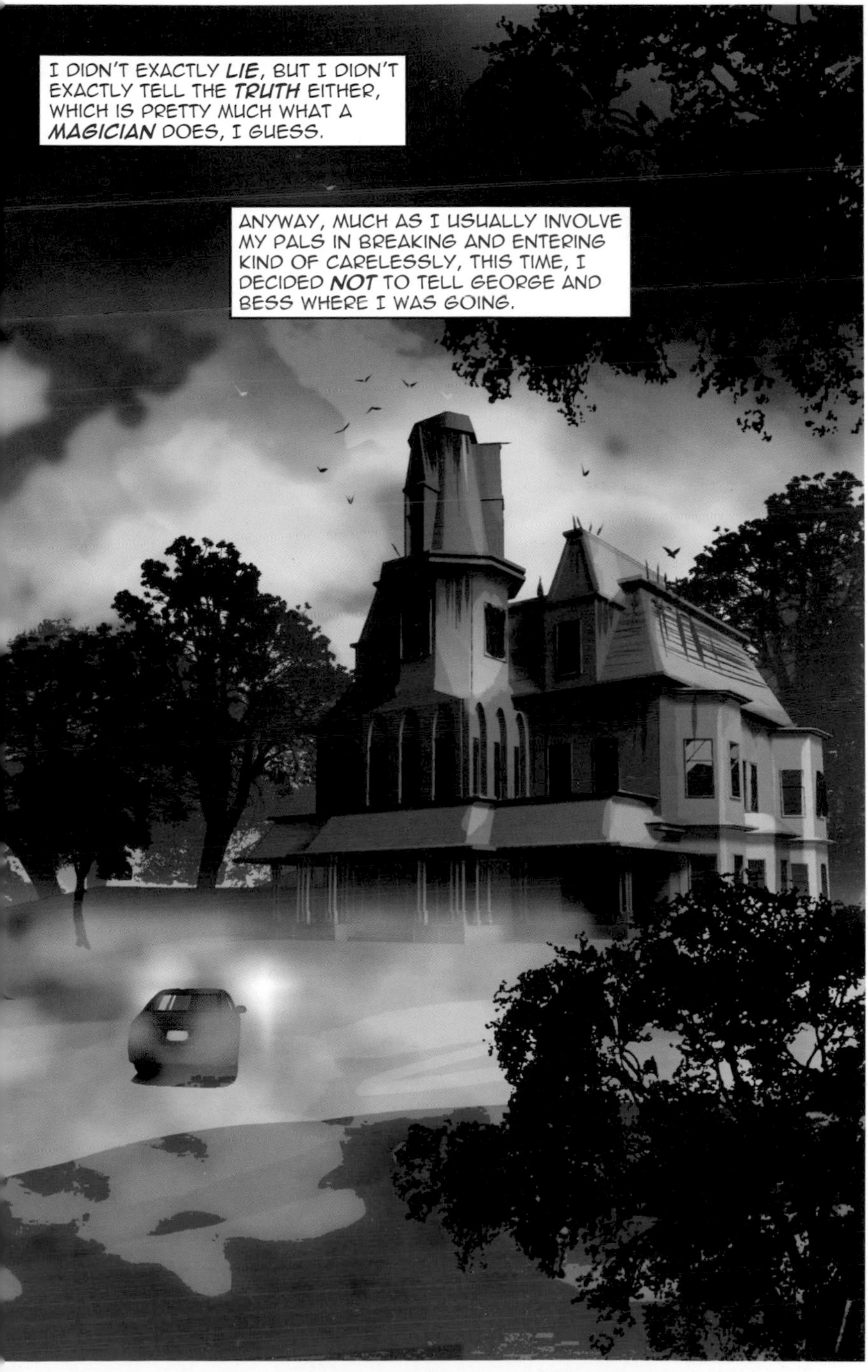
I DIDN'T EXACTLY LIE, BUT I DIDN'T EXACTLY TELL THE TRUTH EITHER, WHICH IS PRETTY MUCH WHAT A MAGICIAN DOES, I GUESS.
ANYWAY, MUCH AS I USUALLY INVOLVE MY PALS IN BREAKING AND ENTERING KIND OF CARELESSLY, THIS TIME, I DECIDED NOT TO TELL GEORGE AND BESS WHERE I WAS GOING.

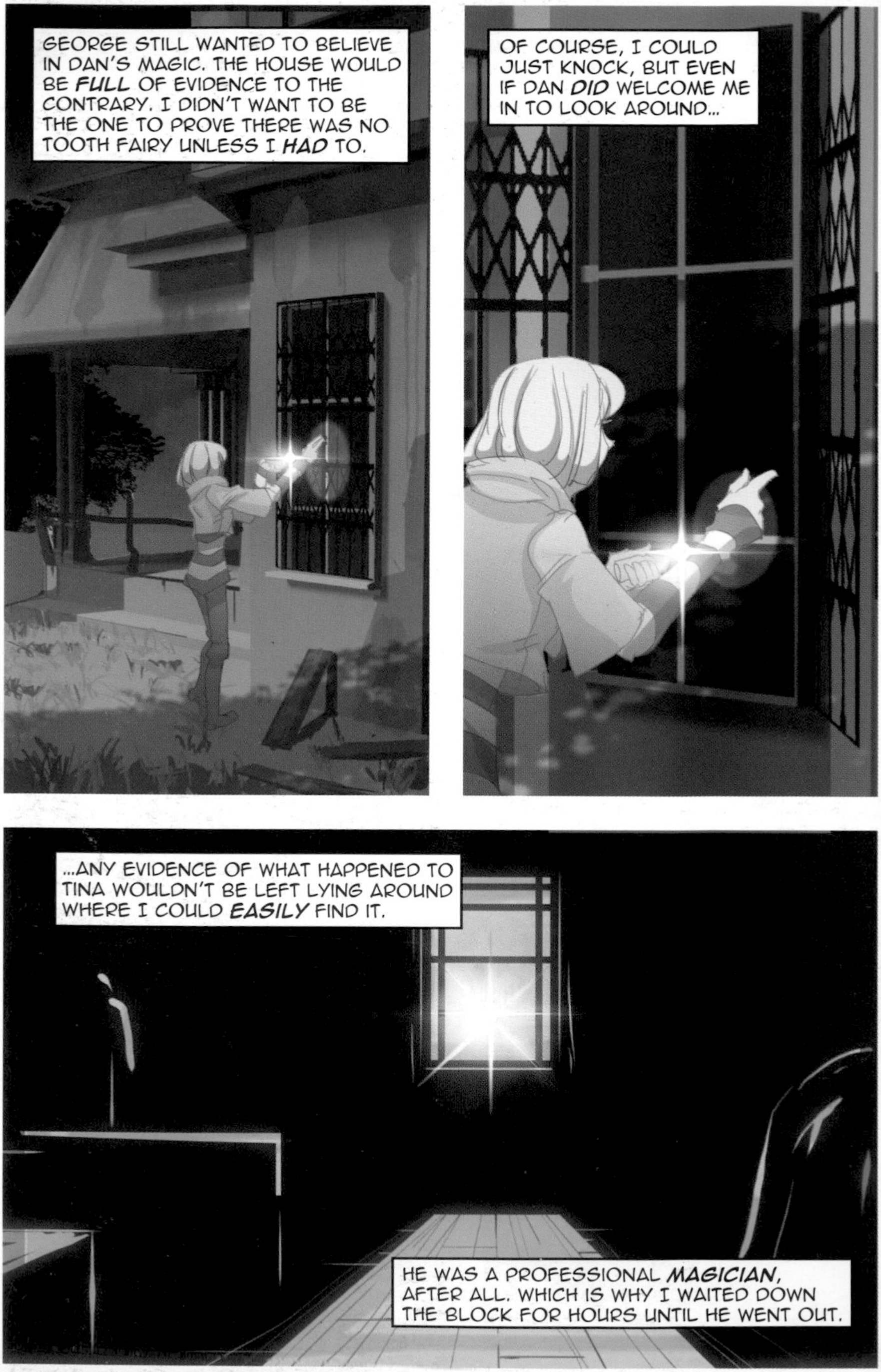
GEORGE STILL WANTED TO BELIEVE IN DAN'S MAGIC. THE HOUSE WOULD BE *FULL* OF EVIDENCE TO THE CONTRARY. I DIDN'T WANT TO BE THE ONE TO PROVE THERE WAS NO TOOTH FAIRY UNLESS I *HAD* TO.
OF COURSE, I COULD JUST KNOCK, BUT EVEN IF DAN *DID* WELCOME ME IN TO LOOK AROUND...
...ANY EVIDENCE OF WHAT HAPPENED TO TINA WOULDN'T BE LEFT LYING AROUND WHERE I COULD *EASILY* FIND IT.
HE WAS A PROFESSIONAL *MAGICIAN*, AFTER ALL. WHICH IS WHY I WAITED DOWN THE BLOCK FOR HOURS UNTIL HE WENT OUT.

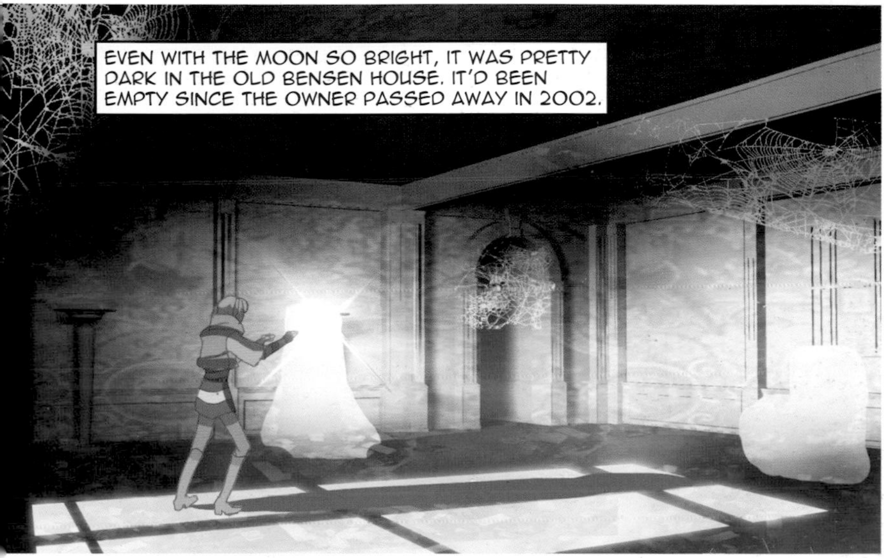
EVEN WITH THE MOON SO BRIGHT, IT WAS PRETTY DARK IN THE OLD BENSEN HOUSE. IT'D BEEN EMPTY SINCE THE OWNER PASSED AWAY IN 2002.

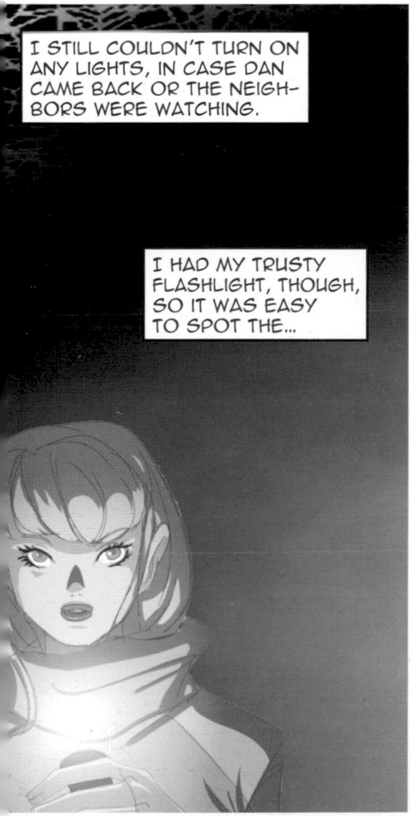
I STILL COULDN'T TURN ON ANY LIGHTS, IN CASE DAN CAME BACK OR THE NEIGHBORS WERE WATCHING.
I HAD MY TRUSTY FLASHLIGHT, THOUGH, SO IT WAS EASY TO SPOT THE...

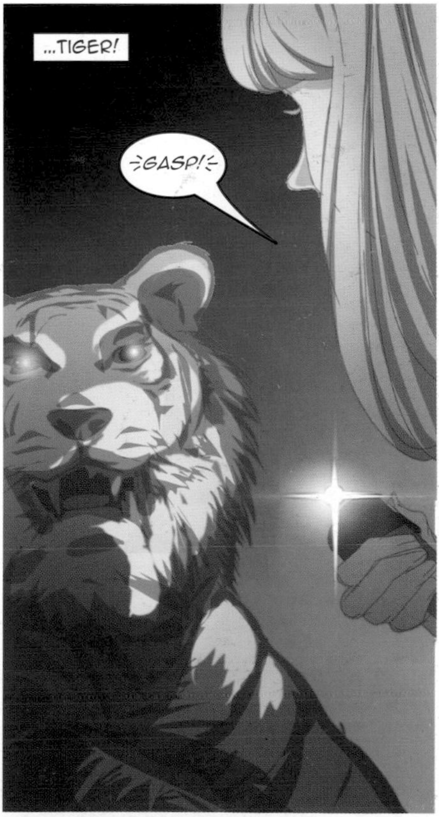
...TIGER!
GASP!

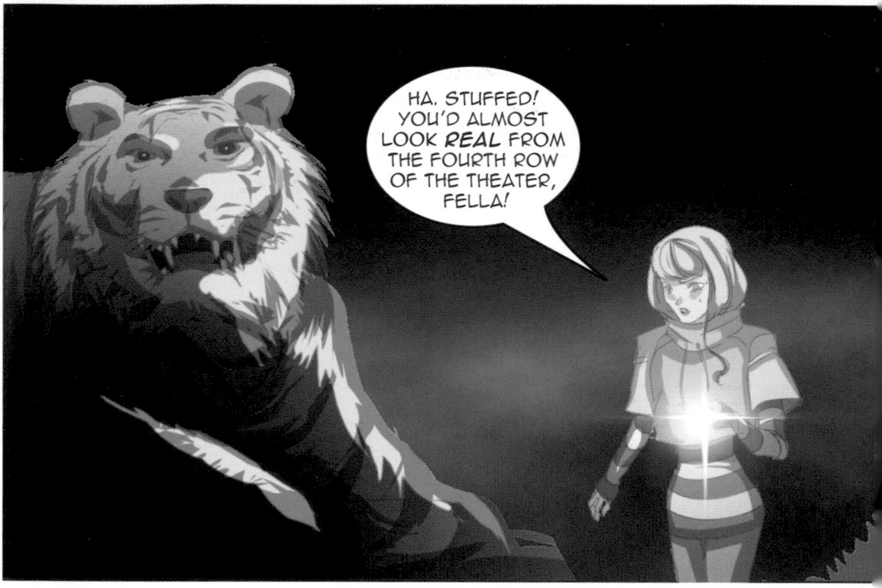
HA. STUFFED! YOU'D ALMOST LOOK *REAL* FROM THE FOURTH ROW OF THE THEATER, FELLA!

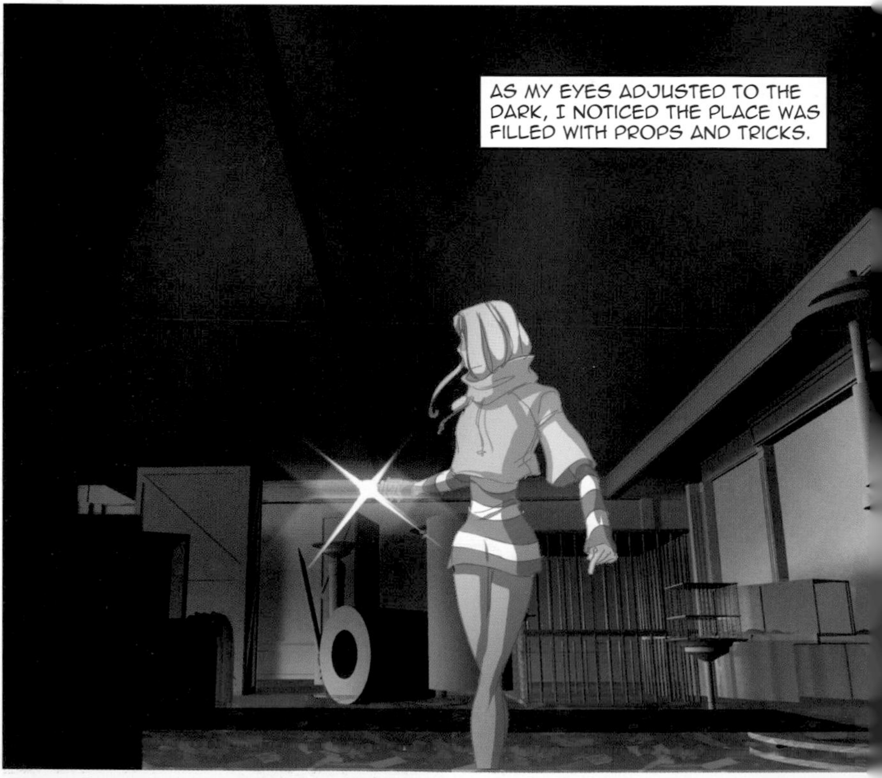
AS MY EYES ADJUSTED TO THE DARK, I NOTICED THE PLACE WAS FILLED WITH PROPS AND TRICKS.

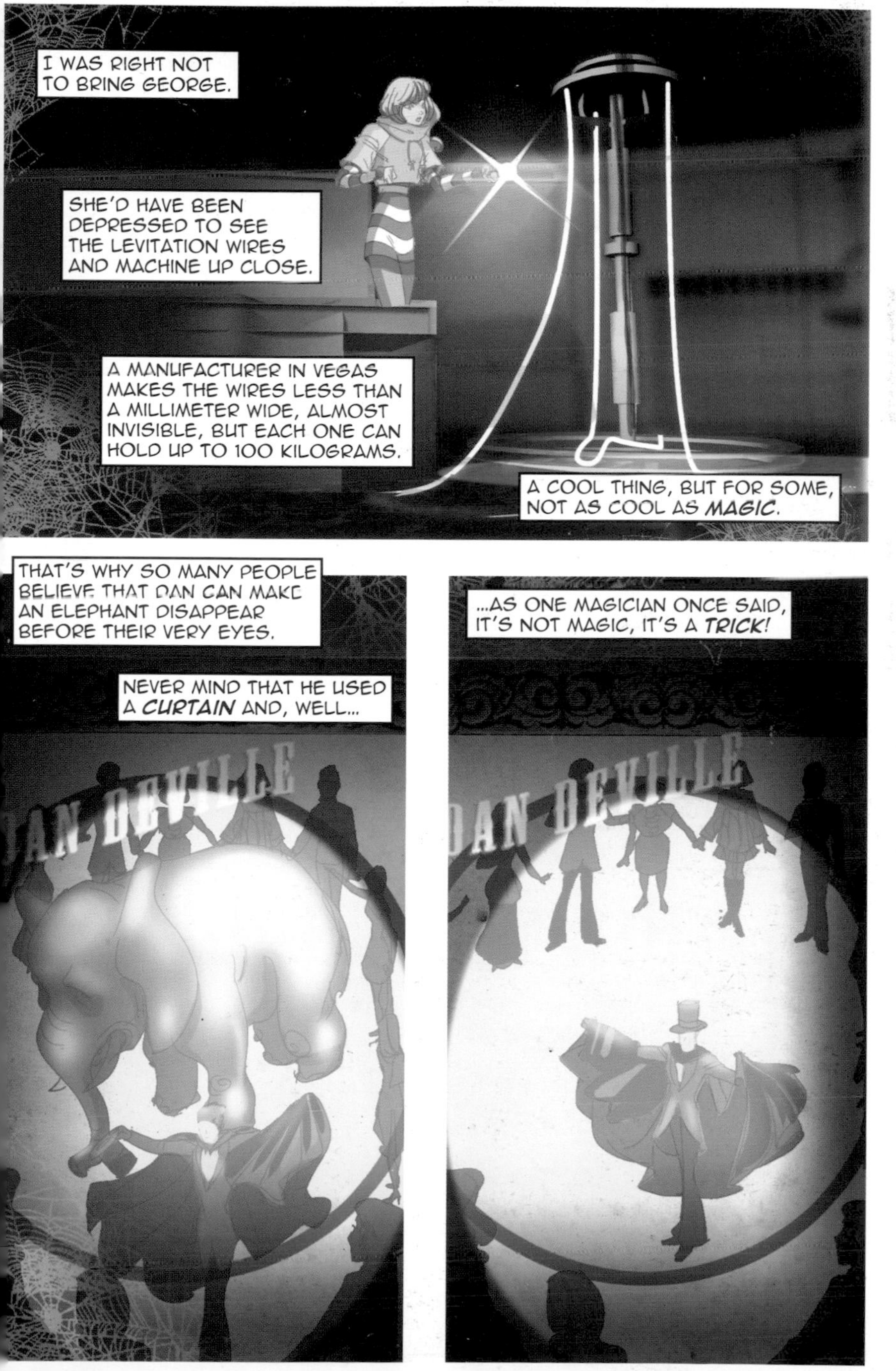
I WAS RIGHT NOT TO BRING GEORGE.
SHE'D HAVE BEEN DEPRESSED TO SEE THE LEVITATION WIRES AND MACHINE UP CLOSE.
A MANUFACTURER IN VEGAS MAKES THE WIRES LESS THAN A MILLIMETER WIDE, ALMOST INVISIBLE, BUT EACH ONE CAN HOLD UP TO 100 KILOGRAMS.
A COOL THING, BUT FOR SOME, NOT AS COOL AS *MAGIC*.
THAT'S WHY SO MANY PEOPLE BELIEVE THAT DAN CAN MAKE AN ELEPHANT DISAPPEAR BEFORE THEIR VERY EYES.
NEVER MIND THAT HE USED A *CURTAIN* AND, WELL...
DAN DEVILLE
...AS ONE MAGICIAN ONCE SAID, IT'S NOT MAGIC, IT'S A *TRICK*!
DAN DEVILLE

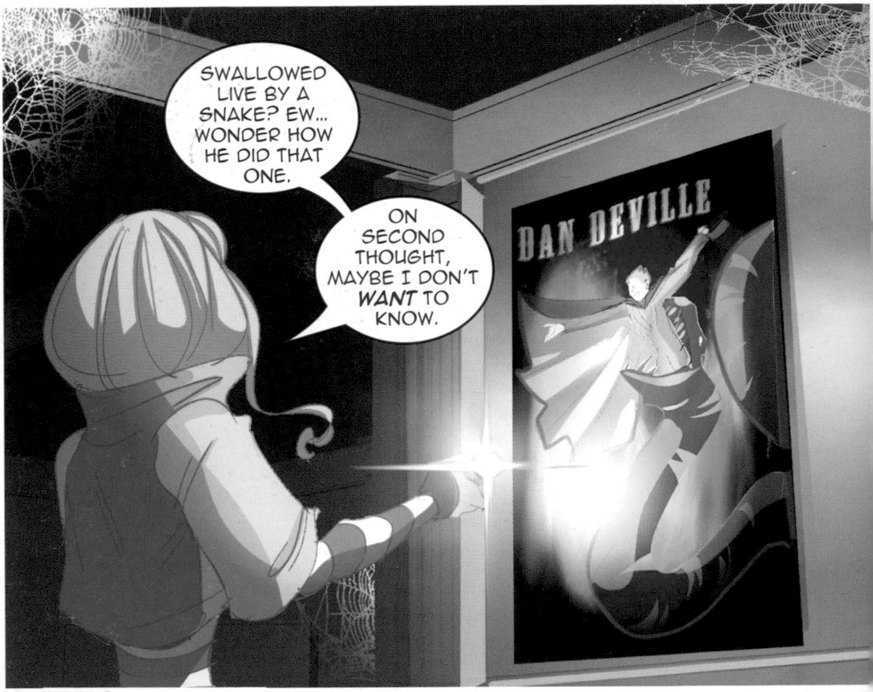
SWALLOWED LIVE BY A SNAKE? EW... WONDER HOW HE DID THAT ONE.
ON SECOND THOUGHT, MAYBE I DON'T *WANT* TO KNOW.
DAN DEVILLE

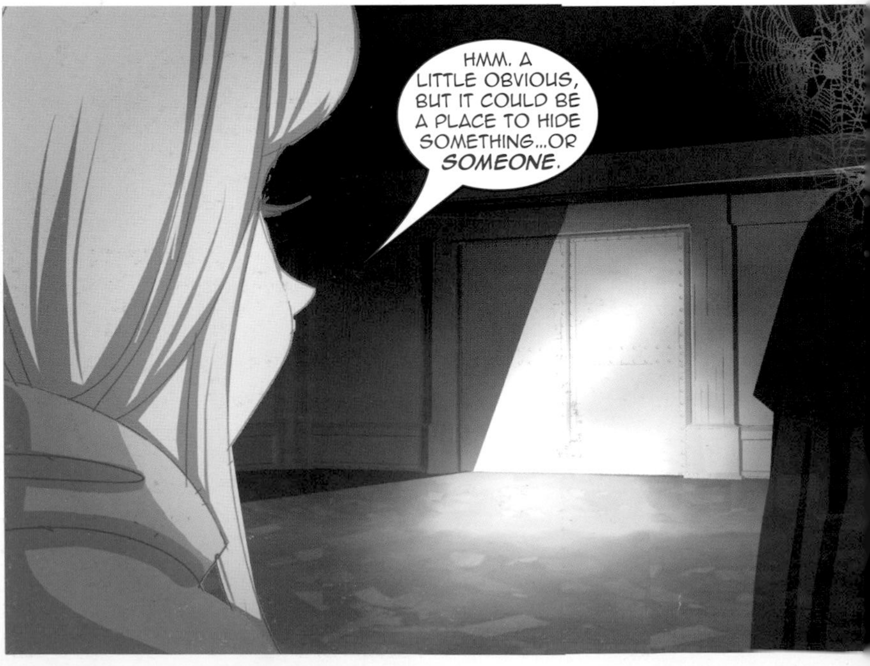
HMM. A LITTLE OBVIOUS, BUT IT COULD BE A PLACE TO HIDE SOMETHING...OR *SOMEONE*.

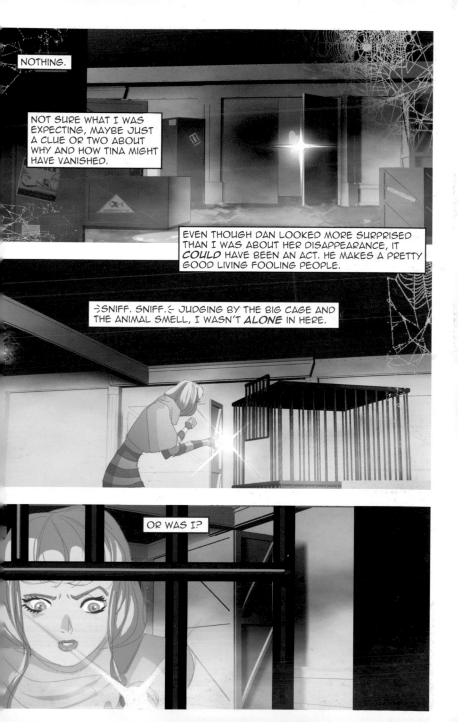

NOTHING.

NOT SURE WHAT I WAS EXPECTING, MAYBE JUST A CLUE OR TWO ABOUT WHY AND HOW TINA MIGHT HAVE VANISHED.

EVEN THOUGH DAN LOOKED MORE SURPRISED THAN I WAS ABOUT HER DISAPPEARANCE, IT *COULD* HAVE BEEN AN ACT. HE MAKES A PRETTY GOOD LIVING FOOLING PEOPLE.

⸰SNIFF. SNIFF.⸰ JUDGING BY THE BIG CAGE AND THE ANIMAL SMELL, I WASN'T *ALONE* IN HERE.

OR WAS I?

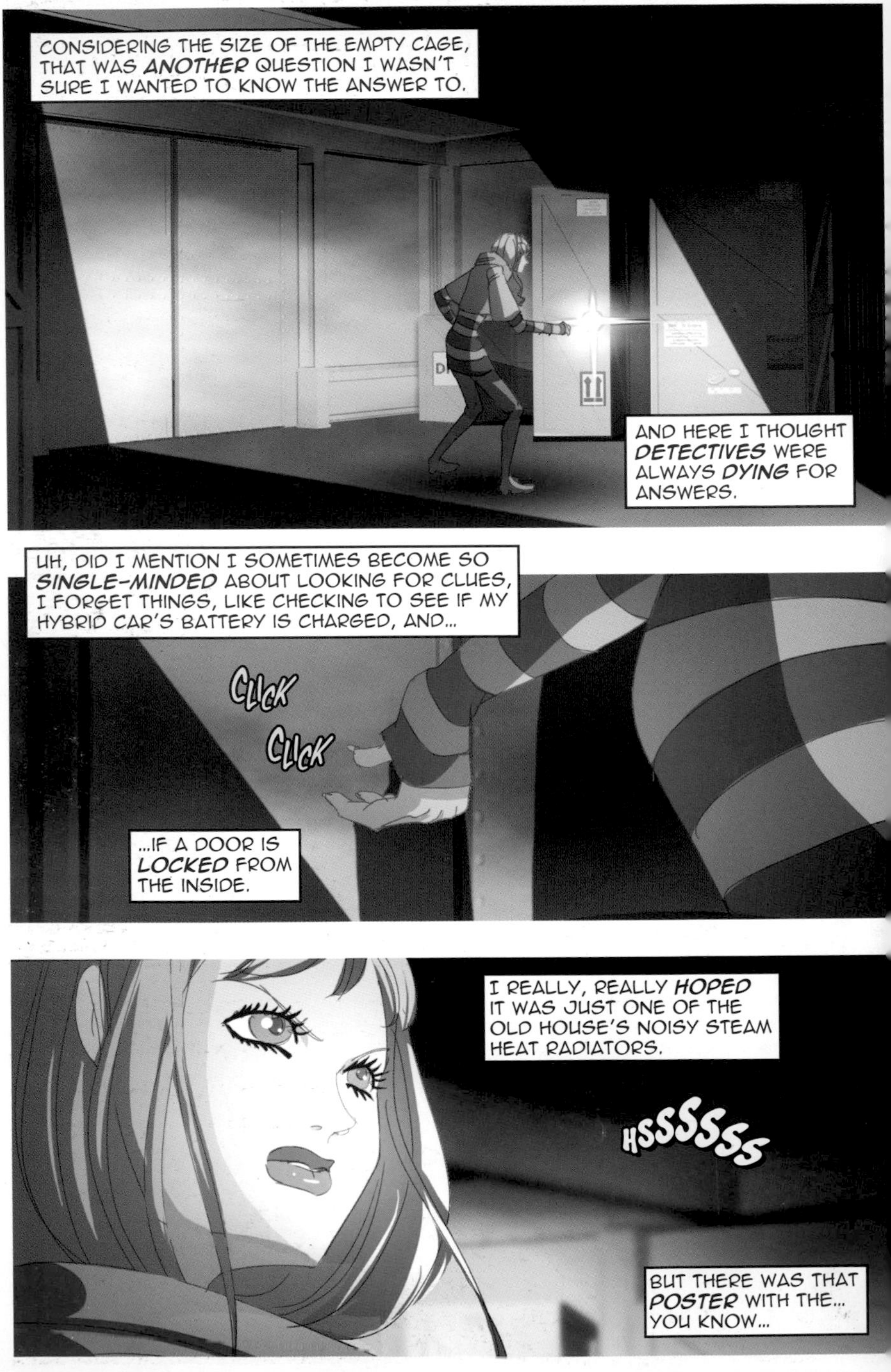
CONSIDERING THE SIZE OF THE EMPTY CAGE, THAT WAS ANOTHER QUESTION I WASN'T SURE I WANTED TO KNOW THE ANSWER TO.
AND HERE I THOUGHT DETECTIVES WERE ALWAYS DYING FOR ANSWERS.
UH, DID I MENTION I SOMETIMES BECOME SO SINGLE-MINDED ABOUT LOOKING FOR CLUES, I FORGET THINGS, LIKE CHECKING TO SEE IF MY HYBRID CAR'S BATTERY IS CHARGED, AND...
CLICK
CLICK
...IF A DOOR IS LOCKED FROM THE INSIDE.
I REALLY, REALLY HOPED IT WAS JUST ONE OF THE OLD HOUSE'S NOISY STEAM HEAT RADIATORS.
HSSSSSS
BUT THERE WAS THAT POSTER WITH THE... YOU KNOW...

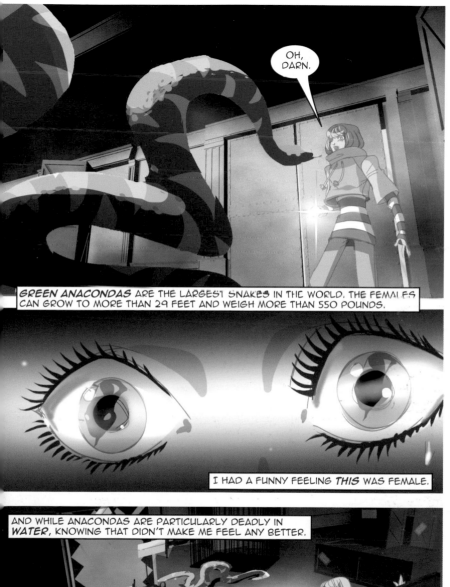

OH, DARN.

GREEN ANACONDAS ARE THE LARGEST SNAKES IN THE WORLD. THE FEMALES CAN GROW TO MORE THAN 29 FEET AND WEIGH MORE THAN 550 POUNDS.

I HAD A FUNNY FEELING *THIS* WAS FEMALE.

AND WHILE ANACONDAS ARE PARTICULARLY DEADLY IN *WATER*, KNOWING THAT DIDN'T MAKE ME FEEL ANY BETTER.

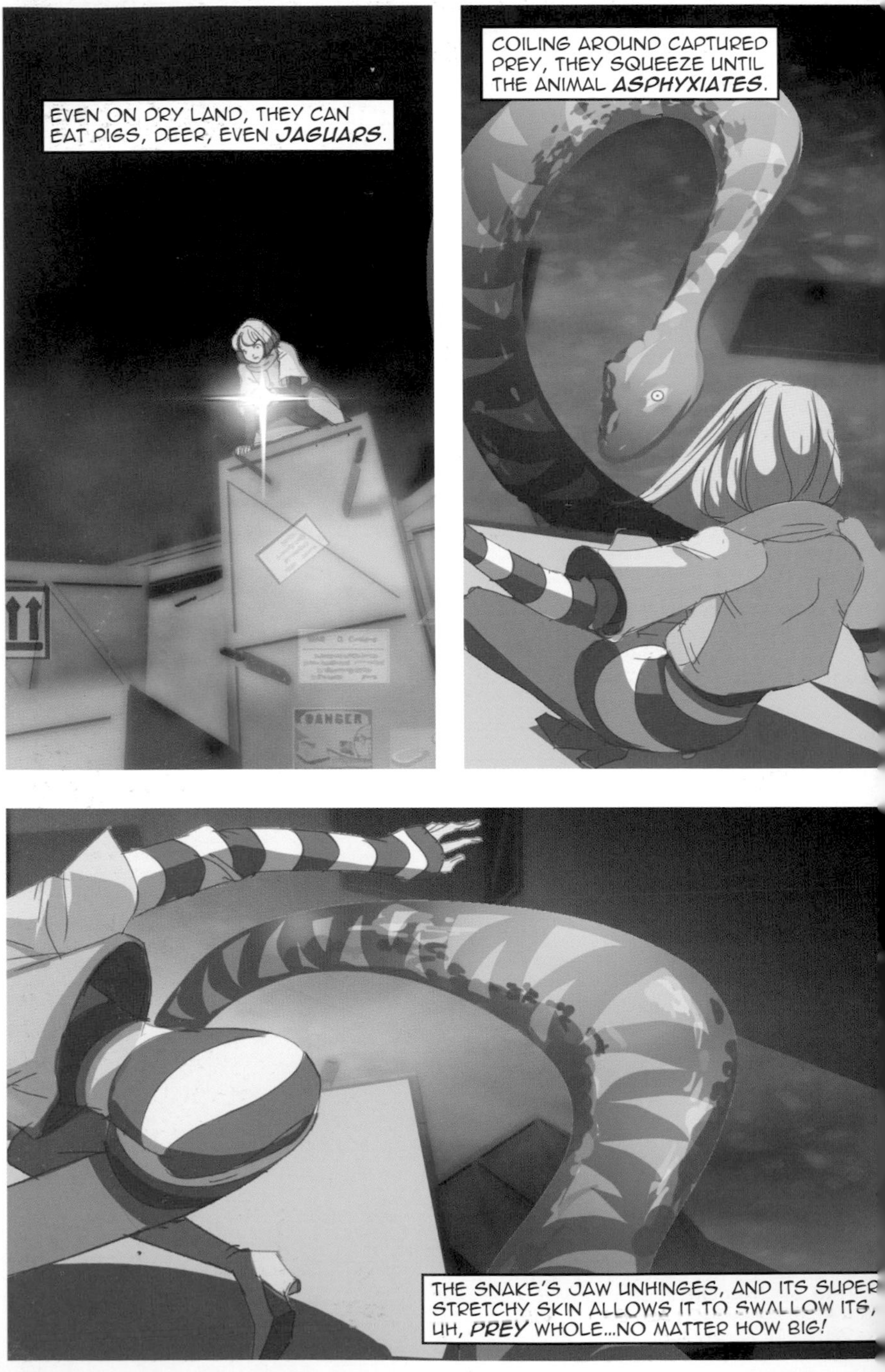
EVEN ON DRY LAND, THEY CAN EAT PIGS, DEER, EVEN *JAGUARS*.
DANGER
COILING AROUND CAPTURED PREY, THEY SQUEEZE UNTIL THE ANIMAL *ASPHYXIATES*.
THE SNAKE'S JAW UNHINGES, AND ITS SUPER STRETCHY SKIN ALLOWS IT TO SWALLOW ITS, UH, *PREY* WHOLE...NO MATTER HOW BIG!

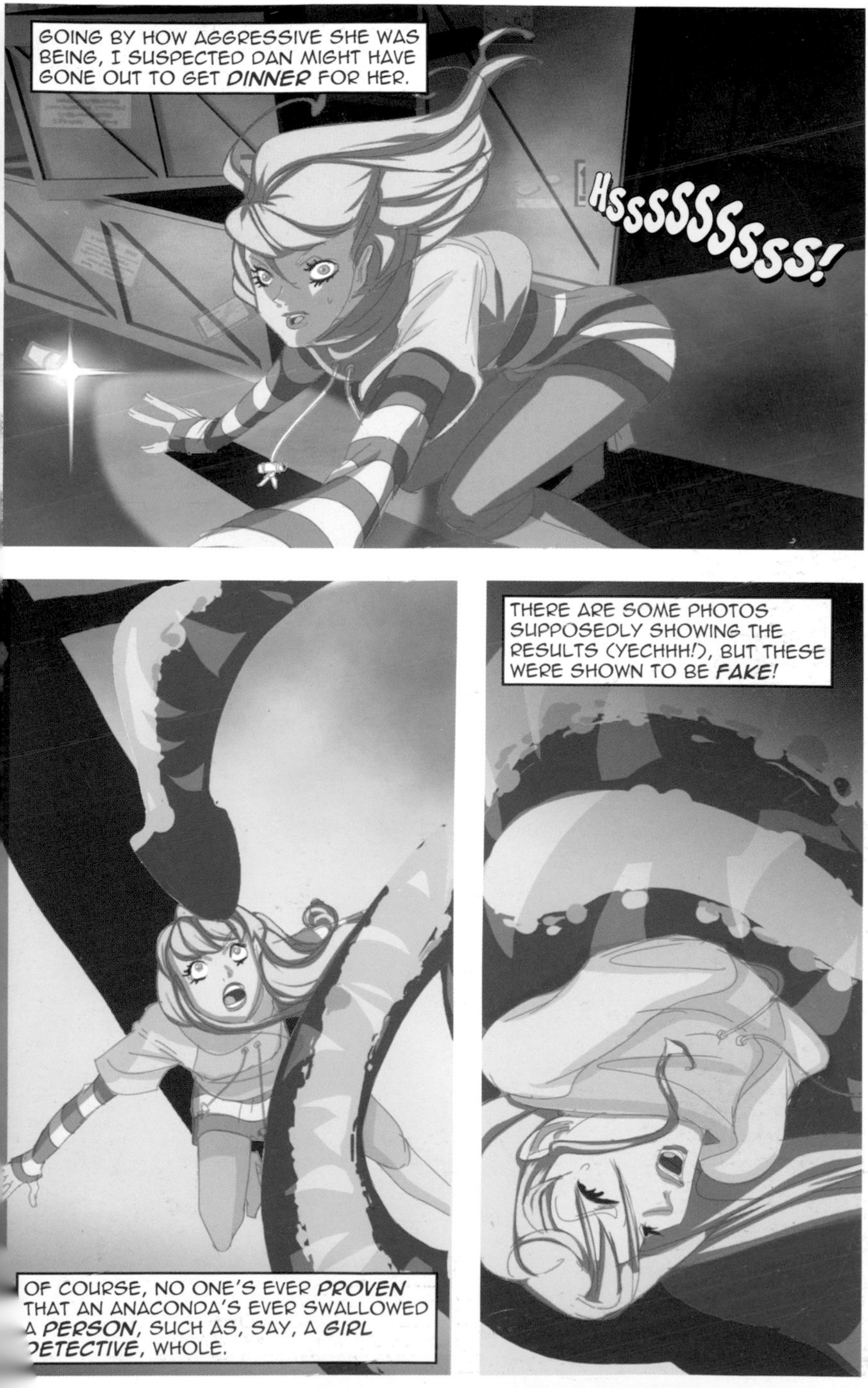
GOING BY HOW AGGRESSIVE SHE WAS BEING, I SUSPECTED DAN MIGHT HAVE GONE OUT TO GET DINNER FOR HER.
HsssSSSSsss!
OF COURSE, NO ONE'S EVER PROVEN THAT AN ANACONDA'S EVER SWALLOWED A PERSON, SUCH AS, SAY, A GIRL DETECTIVE, WHOLE.
THERE ARE SOME PHOTOS SUPPOSEDLY SHOWING THE RESULTS (YECHHH!), BUT THESE WERE SHOWN TO BE FAKE!

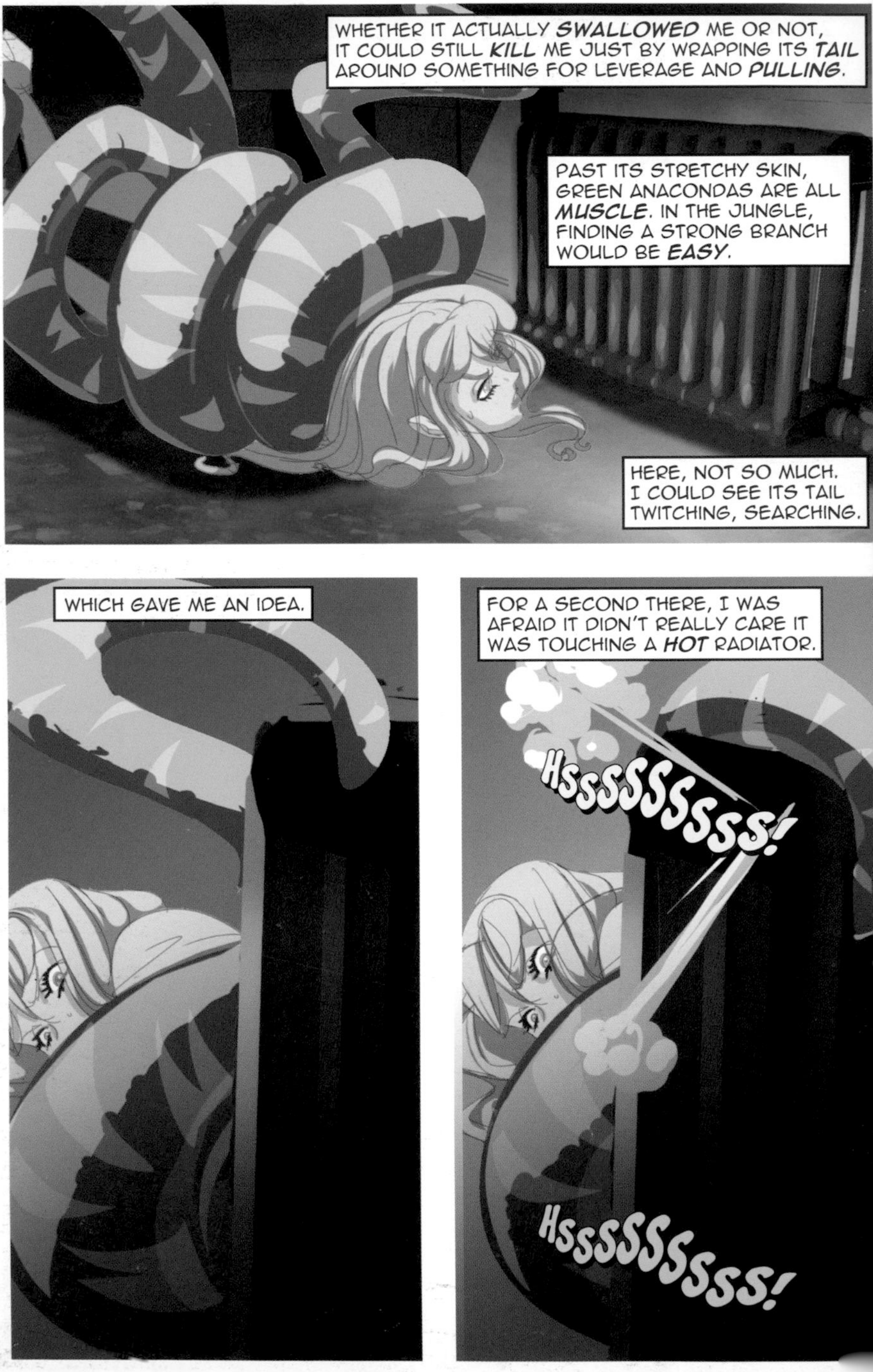
WHETHER IT ACTUALLY SWALLOWED ME OR NOT, IT COULD STILL KILL ME JUST BY WRAPPING ITS TAIL AROUND SOMETHING FOR LEVERAGE AND PULLING.
PAST ITS STRETCHY SKIN, GREEN ANACONDAS ARE ALL MUSCLE. IN THE JUNGLE, FINDING A STRONG BRANCH WOULD BE EASY.
HERE, NOT SO MUCH. I COULD SEE ITS TAIL TWITCHING, SEARCHING.
WHICH GAVE ME AN IDEA.
FOR A SECOND THERE, I WAS AFRAID IT DIDN'T REALLY CARE IT WAS TOUCHING A HOT RADIATOR.
HsSSSSSSSS!
HsSSSSSSSSS!

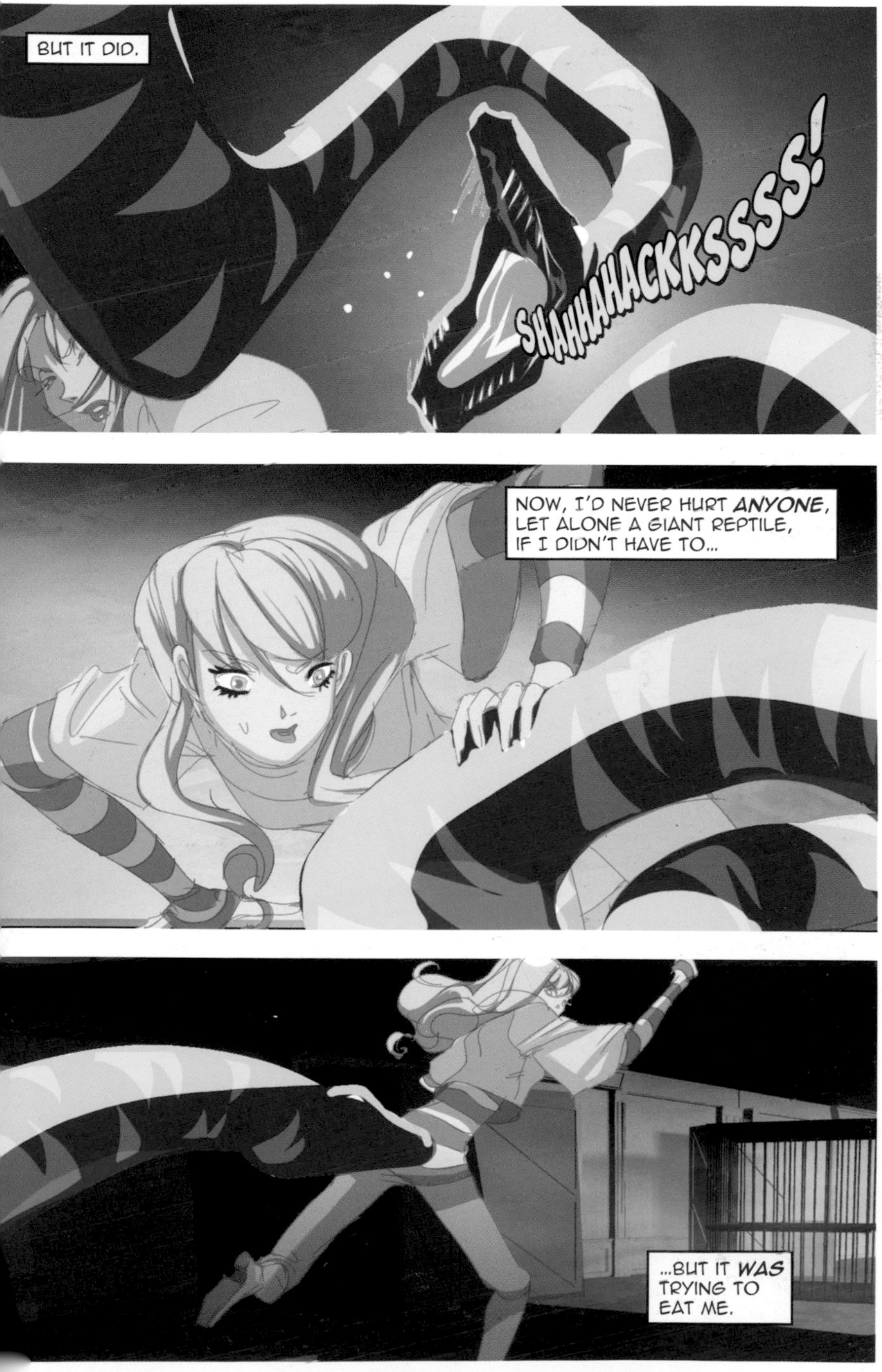
BUT IT DID.
SHAHHAHACKKSSSSS!
NOW, I'D NEVER HURT ANYONE, LET ALONE A GIANT REPTILE, IF I DIDN'T HAVE TO...
...BUT IT WAS TRYING TO EAT ME.

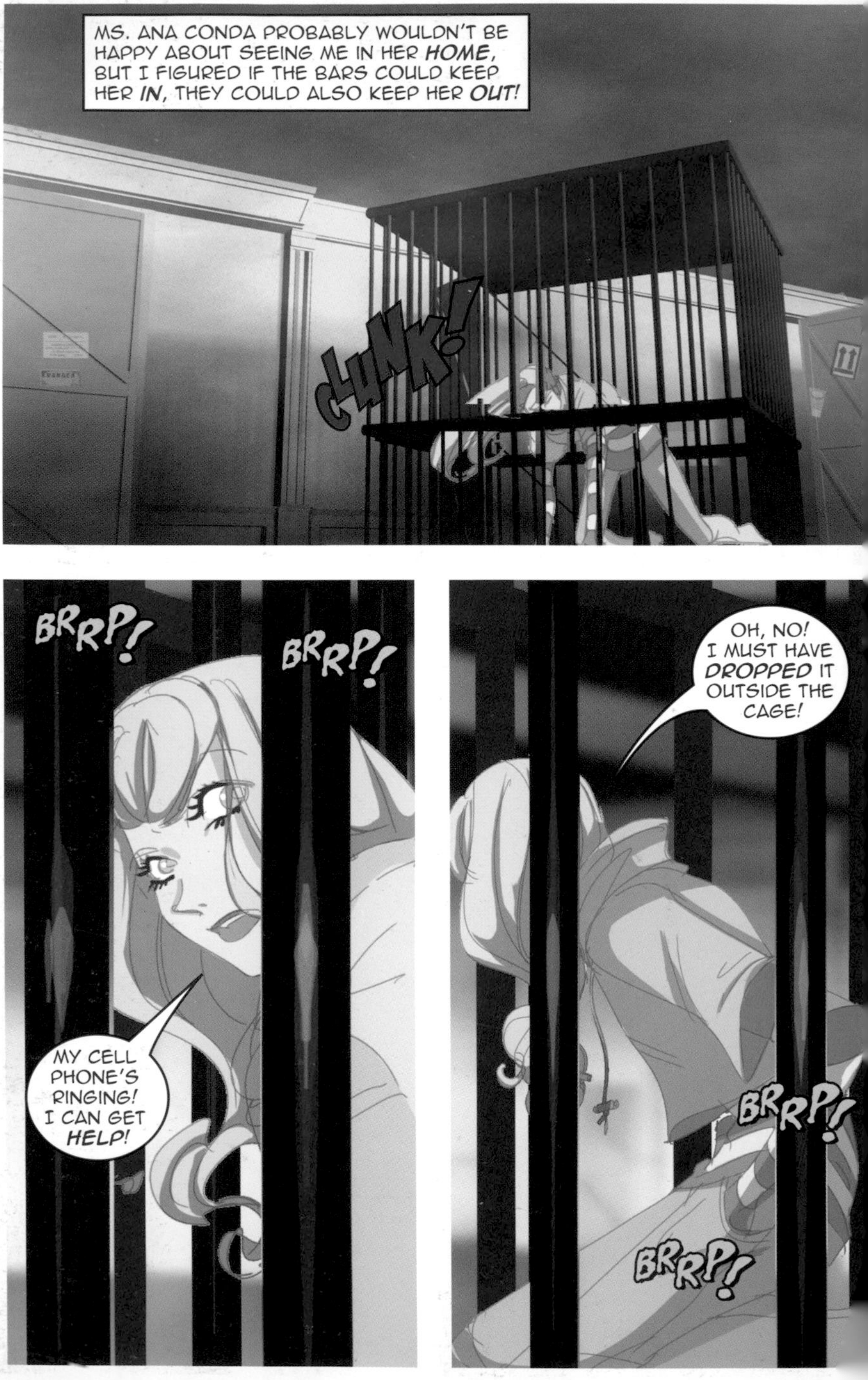
MS. ANA CONDA PROBABLY WOULDN'T BE HAPPY ABOUT SEEING ME IN HER HOME, BUT I FIGURED IF THE BARS COULD KEEP HER IN, THEY COULD ALSO KEEP HER OUT!
CLUNK!
BRRP!
BRRP!
MY CELL PHONE'S RINGING! I CAN GET HELP!
OH, NO! I MUST HAVE DROPPED IT OUTSIDE THE CAGE!
BRRP!
BRRP!

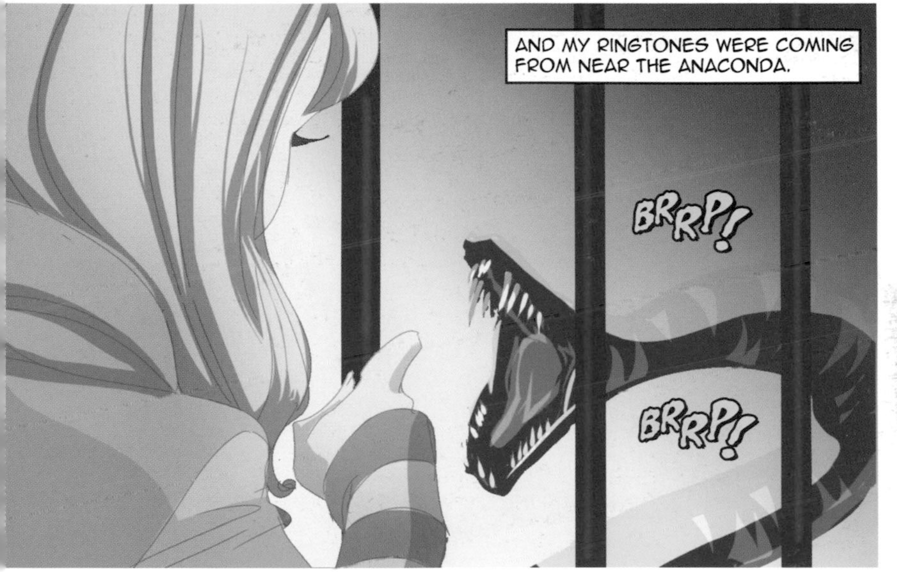
AND MY RINGTONES WERE COMING FROM NEAR THE ANACONDA.
BRRP!
BRRP!

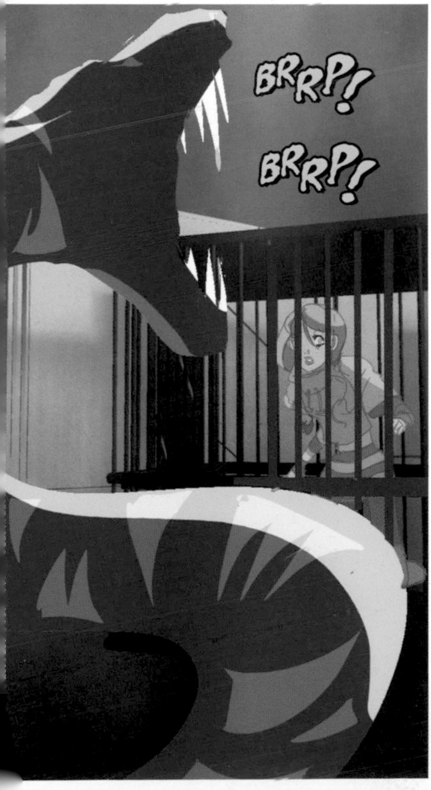
BRRP!
BRRP!

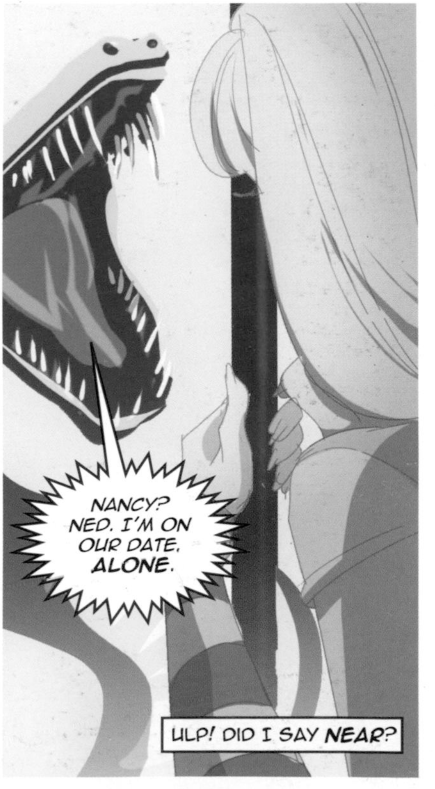
NANCY? NED. I'M ON OUR DATE. **ALONE**.
ULP! DID I SAY **NEAR**?

I MEANT INSIDE!
JUST FOR ONCE, CAN'T YOU BE WHERE YOU'RE SUPPOSED TO BE, HERE WITH ME?
IT'S NICE AND DARK AND ROMANTIC! YOU'D LOVE IT!
END CHAPTER TWO.

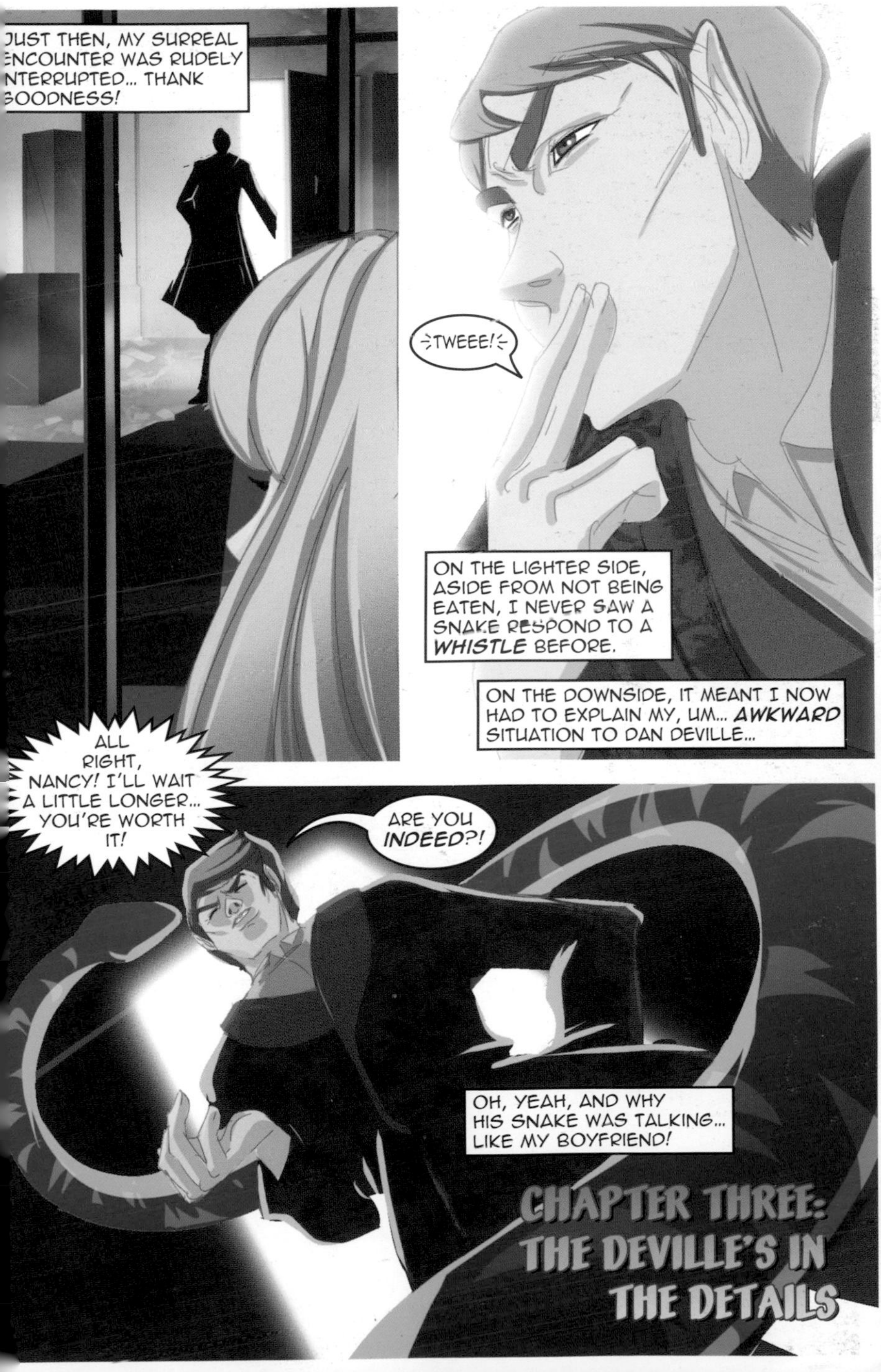
JUST THEN, MY SURREAL ENCOUNTER WAS RUDELY INTERRUPTED... THANK GOODNESS!
TWEEE!
ON THE LIGHTER SIDE, ASIDE FROM NOT BEING EATEN, I NEVER SAW A SNAKE RESPOND TO A WHISTLE BEFORE.
ON THE DOWNSIDE, IT MEANT I NOW HAD TO EXPLAIN MY, UM... AWKWARD SITUATION TO DAN DEVILLE...
ALL RIGHT, NANCY! I'LL WAIT A LITTLE LONGER... YOU'RE WORTH IT!
ARE YOU INDEED?!
OH, YEAH, AND WHY HIS SNAKE WAS TALKING... LIKE MY BOYFRIEND!
CHAPTER THREE: THE DEVILLE'S IN THE DETAILS

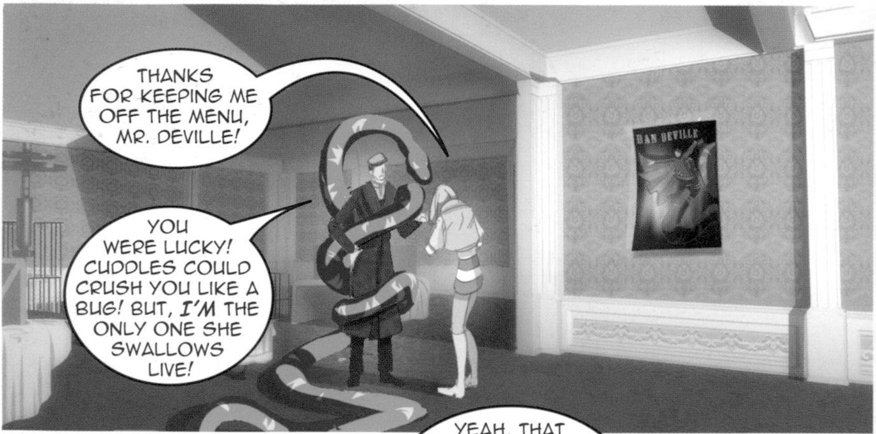
THANKS FOR KEEPING ME OFF THE MENU, MR. DEVILLE!
DAN DEVILLE
YOU WERE LUCKY! CUDDLES COULD CRUSH YOU LIKE A BUG! BUT, ***I'M*** THE ONLY ONE SHE SWALLOWS LIVE!

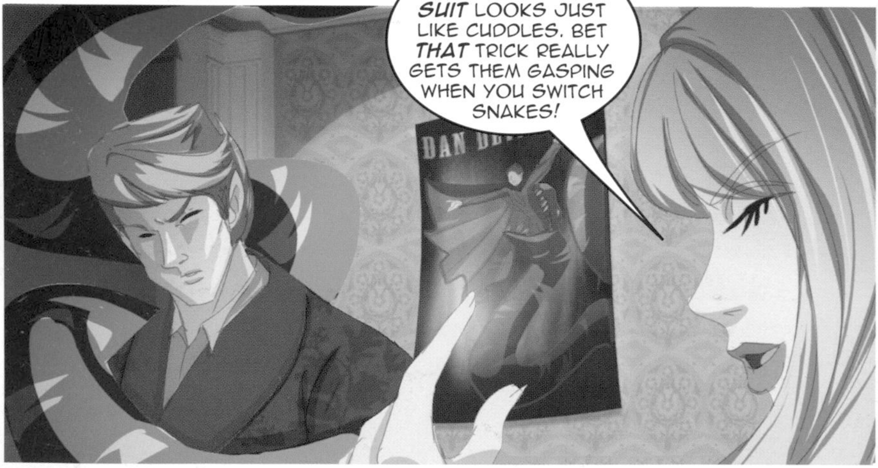
YEAH, THAT ***RUBBER SNAKE SUIT*** LOOKS JUST LIKE CUDDLES. BET ***THAT*** TRICK REALLY GETS THEM GASPING WHEN YOU SWITCH SNAKES!

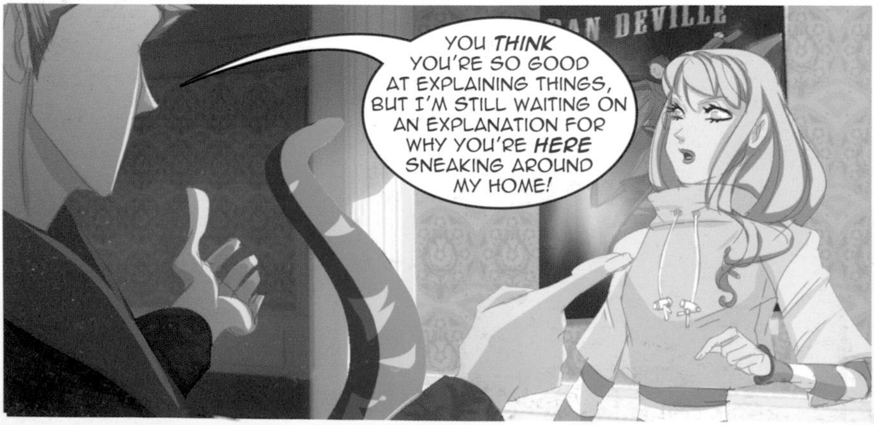
DAN DEVILLE
YOU ***THINK*** YOU'RE SO GOOD AT EXPLAINING THINGS, BUT I'M STILL WAITING ON AN EXPLANATION FOR WHY YOU'RE ***HERE*** SNEAKING AROUND MY HOME!

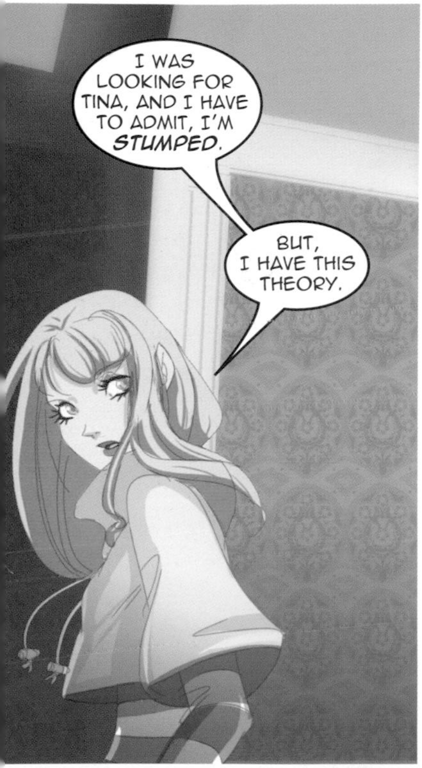
I WAS LOOKING FOR TINA, AND I HAVE TO ADMIT, I'M **STUMPED**.
BUT, I HAVE THIS THEORY.

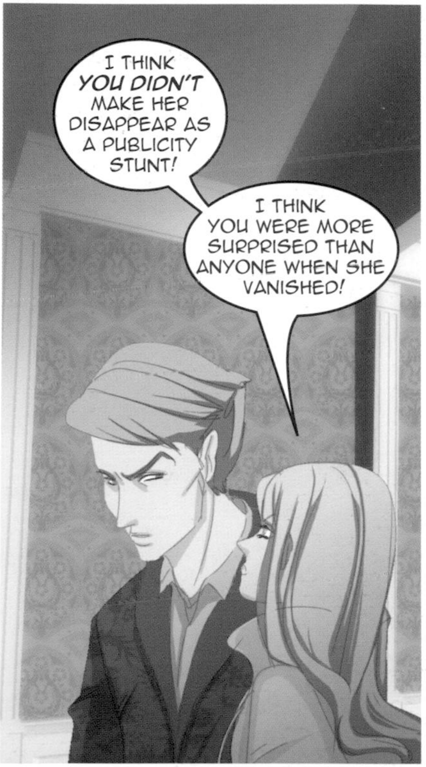
I THINK ***YOU DIDN'T*** MAKE HER DISAPPEAR AS A PUBLICITY STUNT!
I THINK YOU WERE MORE SURPRISED THAN ANYONE WHEN SHE VANISHED!

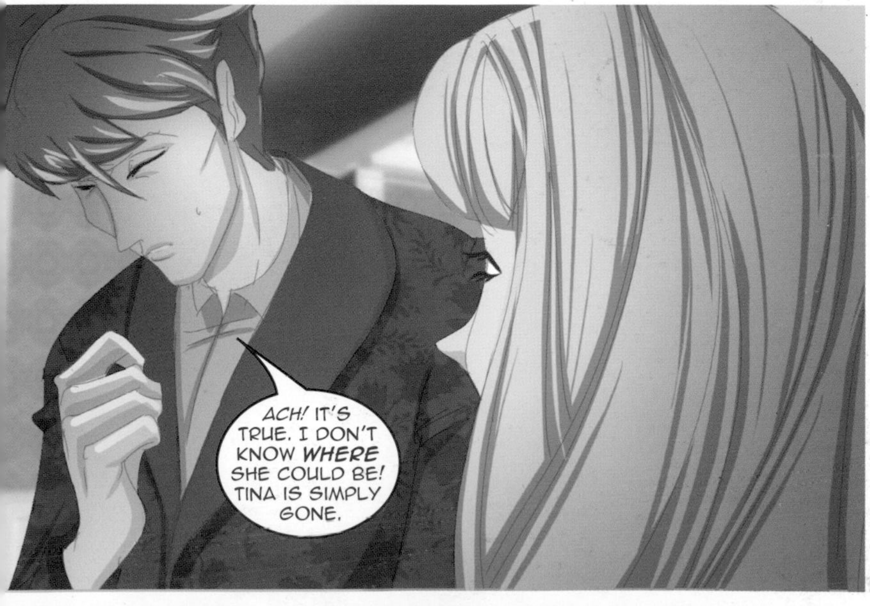
ACH! IT'S TRUE. I DON'T KNOW ***WHERE*** SHE COULD BE! TINA IS SIMPLY GONE.

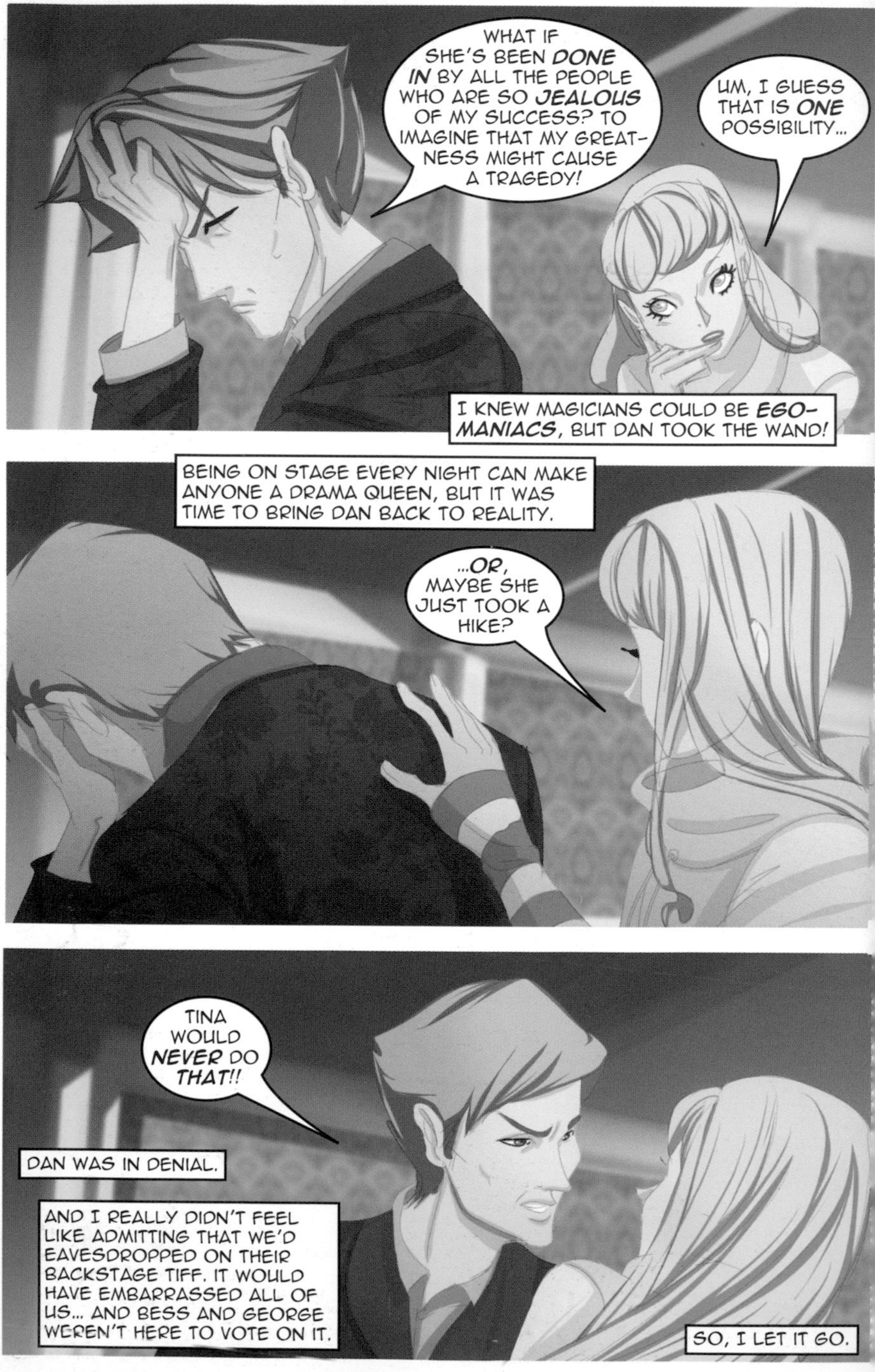
WHAT IF SHE'S BEEN DONE IN BY ALL THE PEOPLE WHO ARE SO JEALOUS OF MY SUCCESS? TO IMAGINE THAT MY GREAT-NESS MIGHT CAUSE A TRAGEDY!
UM, I GUESS THAT IS ONE POSSIBILITY...
I KNEW MAGICIANS COULD BE EGO-MANIACS, BUT DAN TOOK THE WAND!
BEING ON STAGE EVERY NIGHT CAN MAKE ANYONE A DRAMA QUEEN, BUT IT WAS TIME TO BRING DAN BACK TO REALITY.
...OR, MAYBE SHE JUST TOOK A HIKE?
TINA WOULD NEVER DO THAT!!
DAN WAS IN DENIAL.
AND I REALLY DIDN'T FEEL LIKE ADMITTING THAT WE'D EAVESDROPPED ON THEIR BACKSTAGE TIFF. IT WOULD HAVE EMBARRASSED ALL OF US... AND BESS AND GEORGE WEREN'T HERE TO VOTE ON IT.
SO, I LET IT GO.

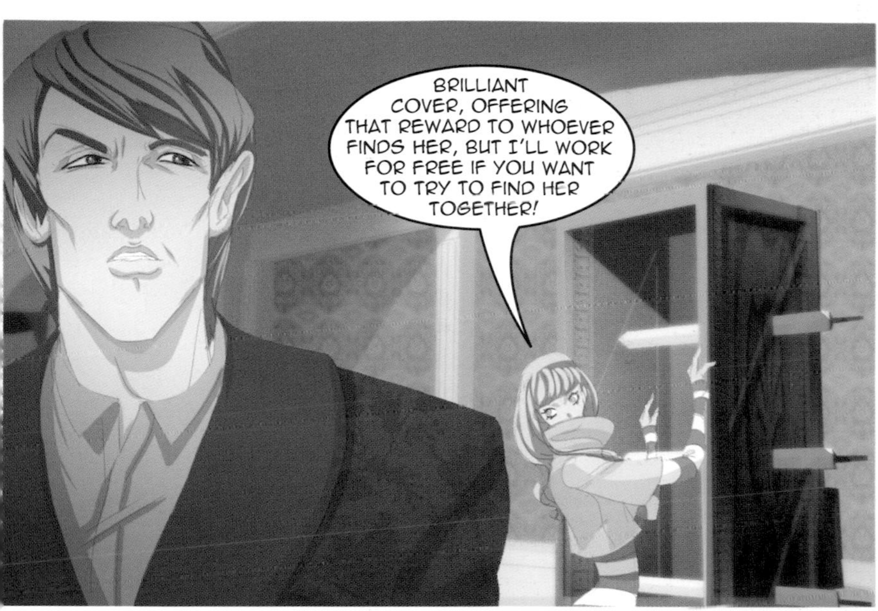
BRILLIANT COVER, OFFERING THAT REWARD TO WHOEVER FINDS HER, BUT I'LL WORK FOR FREE IF YOU WANT TO TRY TO FIND HER TOGETHER!

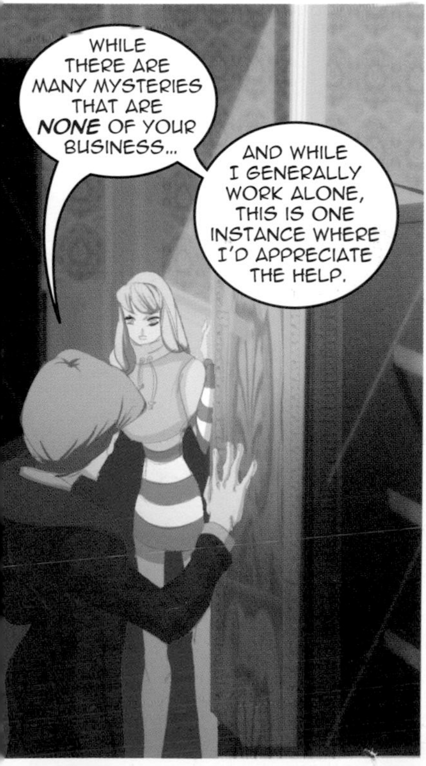
WHILE THERE ARE MANY MYSTERIES THAT ARE ***NONE*** OF YOUR BUSINESS...
AND WHILE I GENERALLY WORK ALONE, THIS IS ONE INSTANCE WHERE I'D APPRECIATE THE HELP.

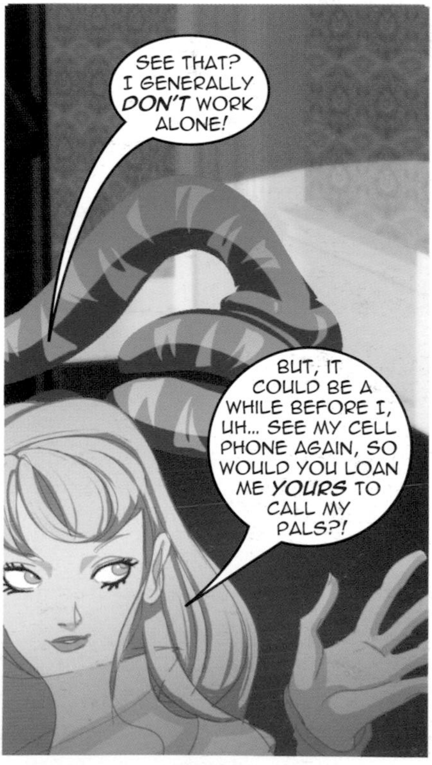
SEE THAT? I GENERALLY ***DON'T*** WORK ALONE!
BUT, IT COULD BE A WHILE BEFORE I, UH... SEE MY CELL PHONE AGAIN, SO WOULD YOU LOAN ME ***YOURS*** TO CALL MY PALS?!

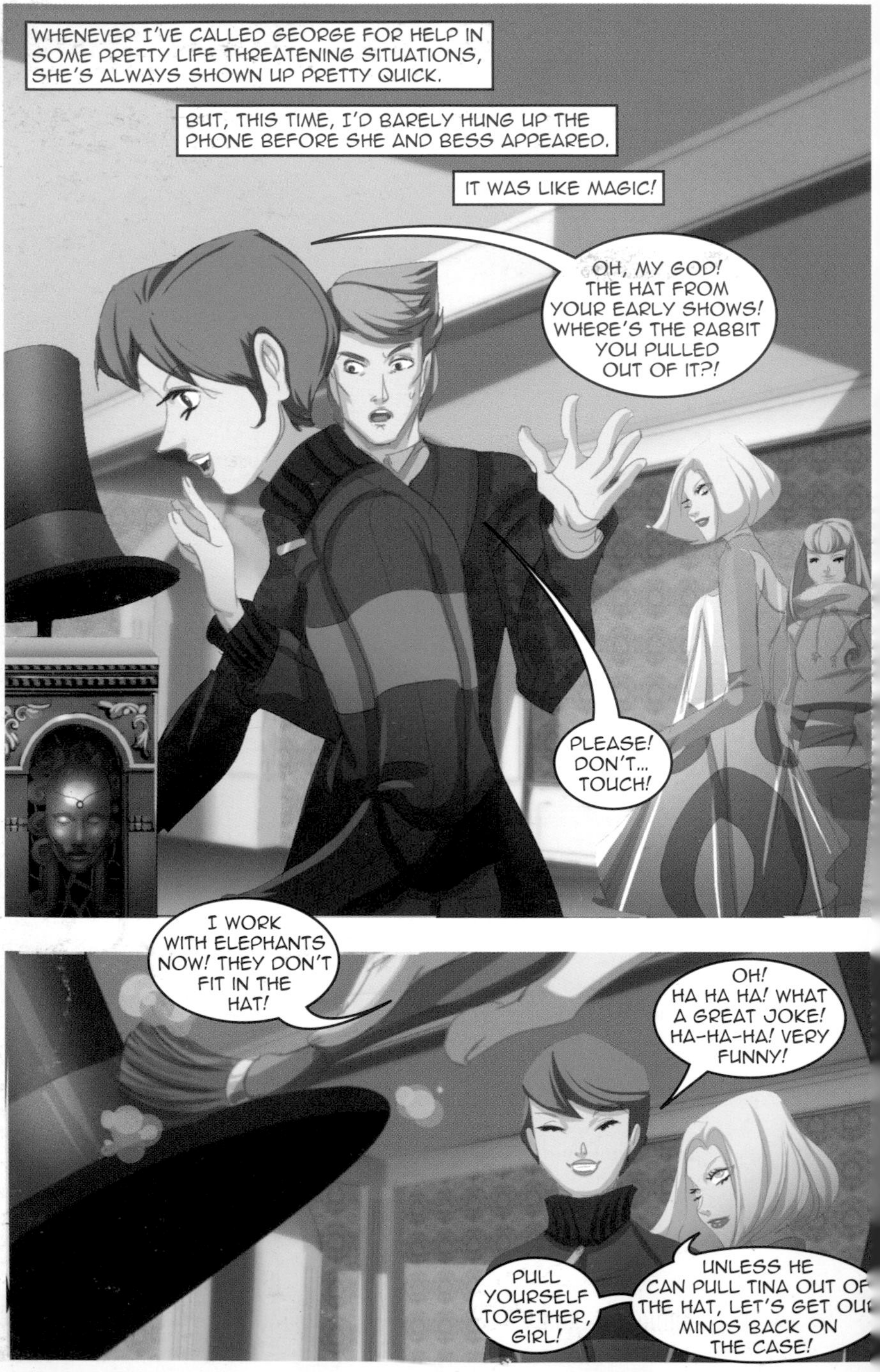
WHENEVER I'VE CALLED GEORGE FOR HELP IN SOME PRETTY LIFE THREATENING SITUATIONS, SHE'S ALWAYS SHOWN UP PRETTY QUICK.
BUT, THIS TIME, I'D BARELY HUNG UP THE PHONE BEFORE SHE AND BESS APPEARED.
IT WAS LIKE MAGIC!
OH, MY GOD! THE HAT FROM YOUR EARLY SHOWS! WHERE'S THE RABBIT YOU PULLED OUT OF IT?!
PLEASE! DON'T... TOUCH!
I WORK WITH ELEPHANTS NOW! THEY DON'T FIT IN THE HAT!
OH! HA HA HA! WHAT A GREAT JOKE! HA-HA-HA! VERY FUNNY!
PULL YOURSELF TOGETHER, GIRL!
UNLESS HE CAN PULL TINA OUT OF THE HAT, LET'S GET OUR MINDS BACK ON THE CASE!

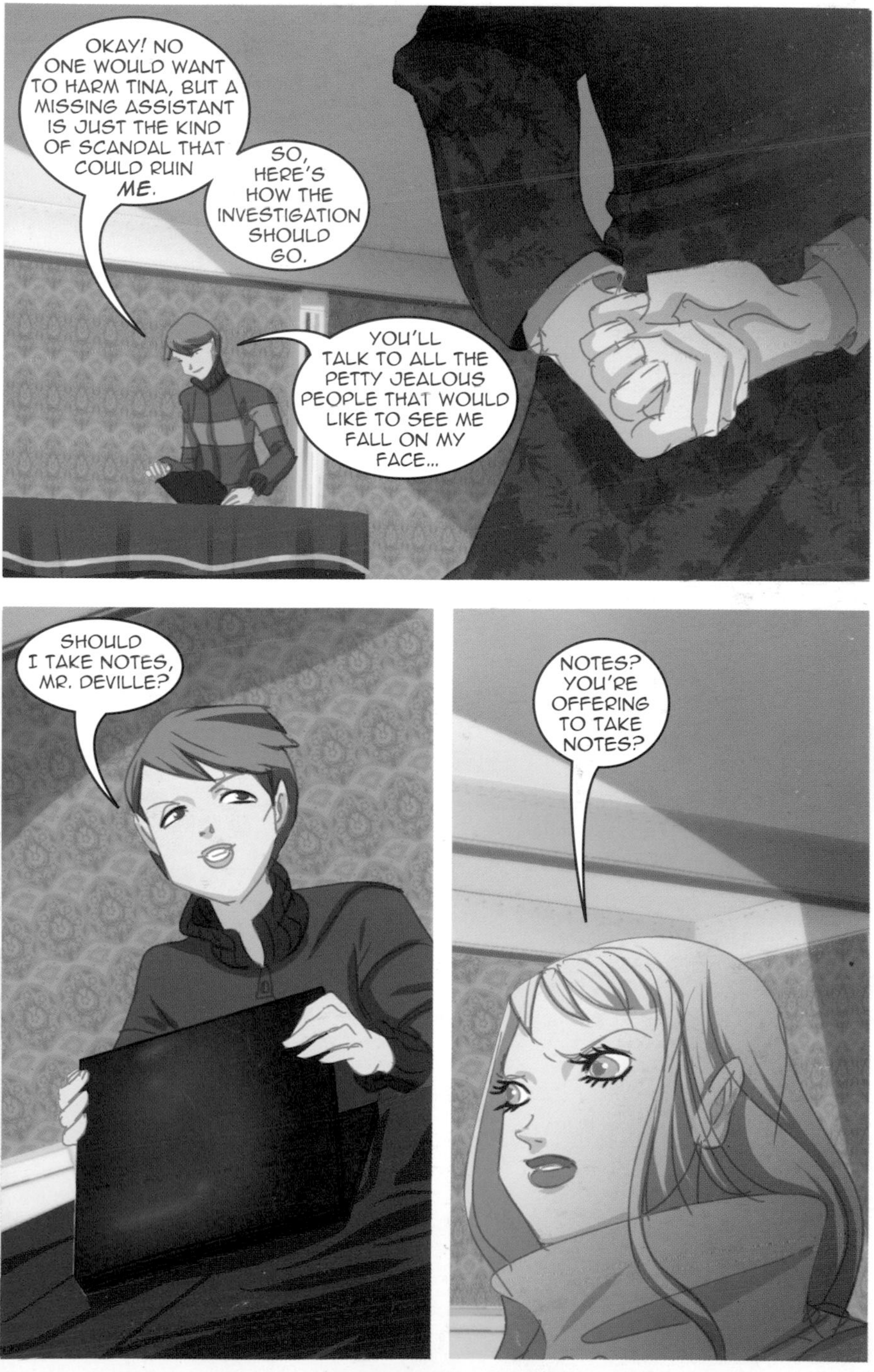
OKAY! NO ONE WOULD WANT TO HARM TINA, BUT A MISSING ASSISTANT IS JUST THE KIND OF SCANDAL THAT COULD RUIN *ME*.
SO, HERE'S HOW THE INVESTIGATION SHOULD GO.
YOU'LL TALK TO ALL THE PETTY JEALOUS PEOPLE THAT WOULD LIKE TO SEE ME FALL ON MY FACE...
SHOULD I TAKE NOTES, MR. DEVILLE?
NOTES? YOU'RE OFFERING TO TAKE NOTES?

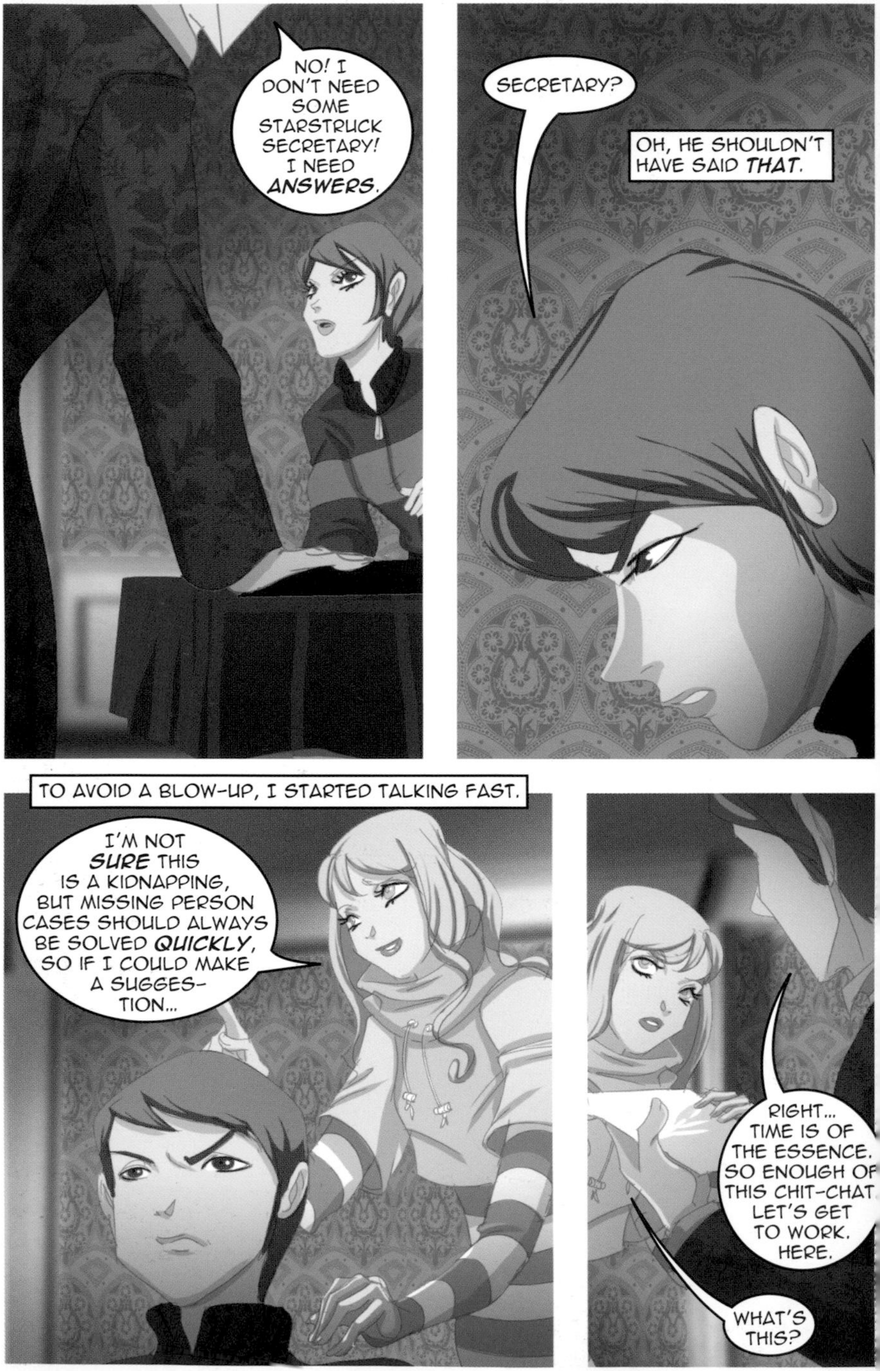
NO! I DON'T NEED SOME STARSTRUCK SECRETARY! I NEED ANSWERS.
SECRETARY?
OH, HE SHOULDN'T HAVE SAID THAT.
TO AVOID A BLOW-UP, I STARTED TALKING FAST.
I'M NOT SURE THIS IS A KIDNAPPING, BUT MISSING PERSON CASES SHOULD ALWAYS BE SOLVED QUICKLY, SO IF I COULD MAKE A SUGGES-TION...
RIGHT... TIME IS OF THE ESSENCE. SO ENOUGH OF THIS CHIT-CHAT. LET'S GET TO WORK. HERE.
WHAT'S THIS?

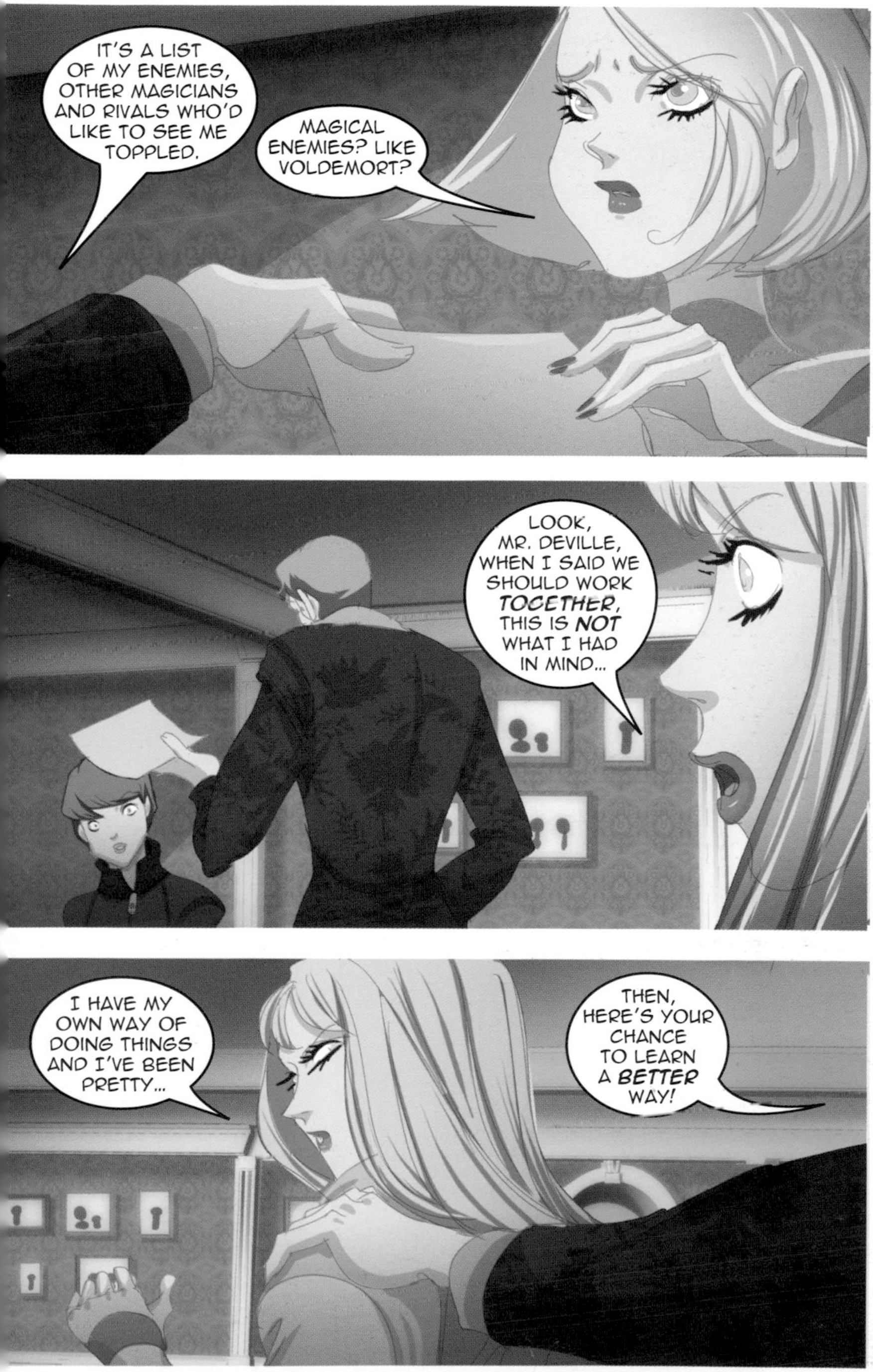
IT'S A LIST OF MY ENEMIES, OTHER MAGICIANS AND RIVALS WHO'D LIKE TO SEE ME TOPPLED.
MAGICAL ENEMIES? LIKE VOLDEMORT?
LOOK, MR. DEVILLE, WHEN I SAID WE SHOULD WORK **TOGETHER**, THIS IS **NOT** WHAT I HAD IN MIND...
I HAVE MY OWN WAY OF DOING THINGS AND I'VE BEEN PRETTY...
THEN, HERE'S YOUR CHANCE TO LEARN A **BETTER** WAY!

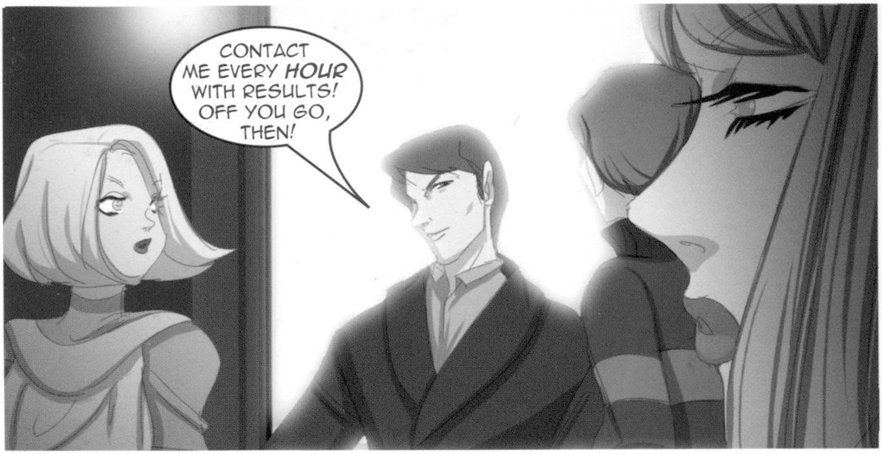
CONTACT ME EVERY HOUR WITH RESULTS! OFF YOU GO, THEN!

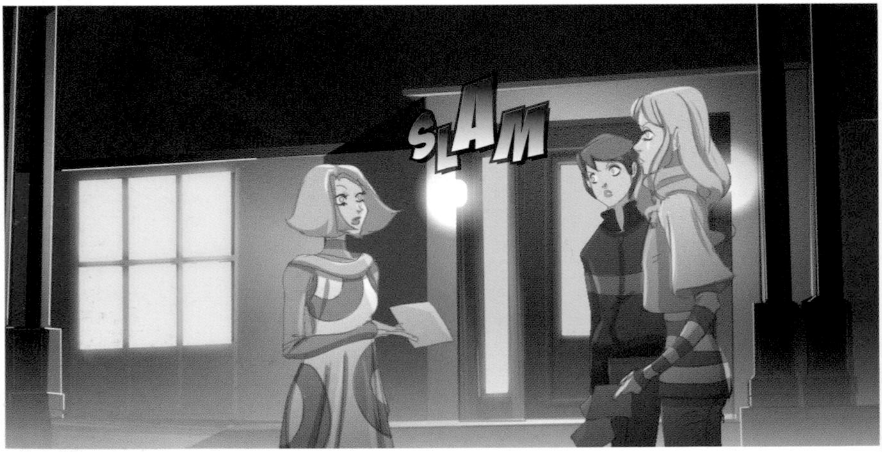
SLAM

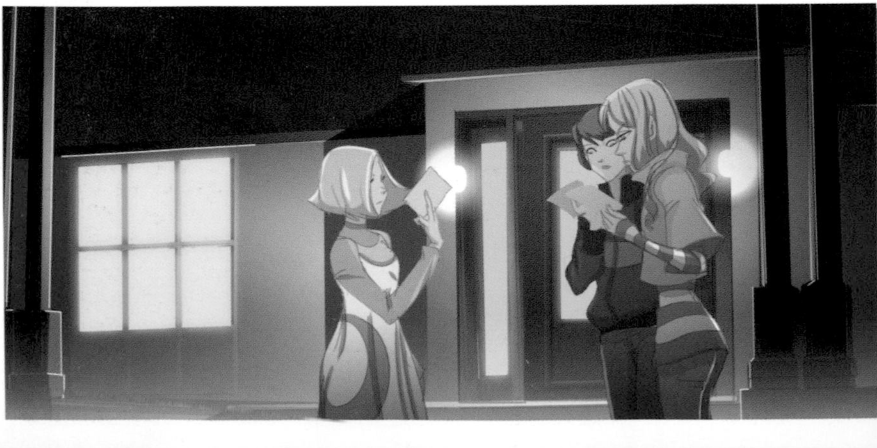

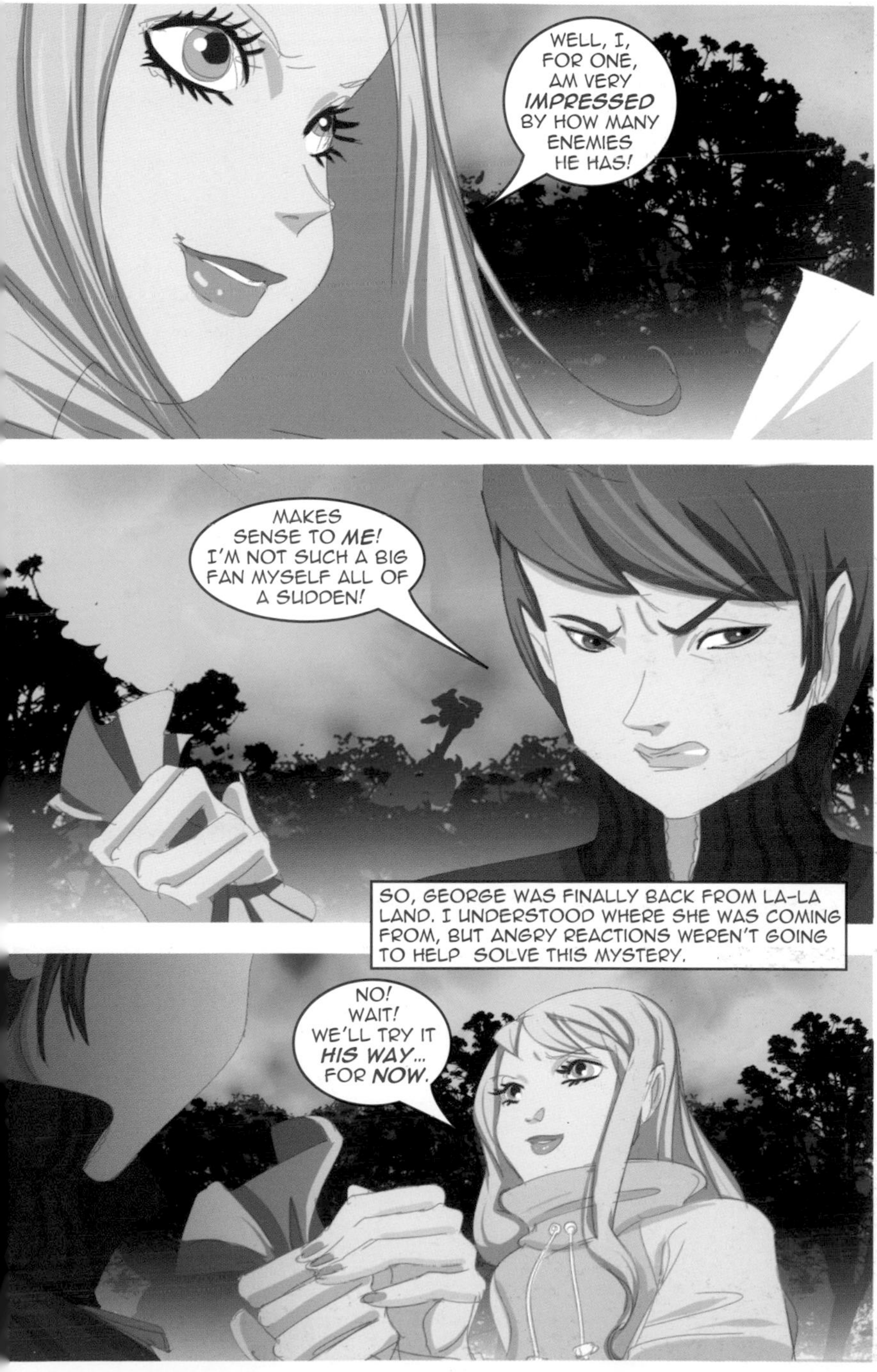
WELL, I, FOR ONE, AM VERY IMPRESSED BY HOW MANY ENEMIES HE HAS!
MAKES SENSE TO ME! I'M NOT SUCH A BIG FAN MYSELF ALL OF A SUDDEN!
SO, GEORGE WAS FINALLY BACK FROM LA-LA LAND. I UNDERSTOOD WHERE SHE WAS COMING FROM, BUT ANGRY REACTIONS WEREN'T GOING TO HELP SOLVE THIS MYSTERY.
NO! WAIT! WE'LL TRY IT HIS WAY... FOR NOW.

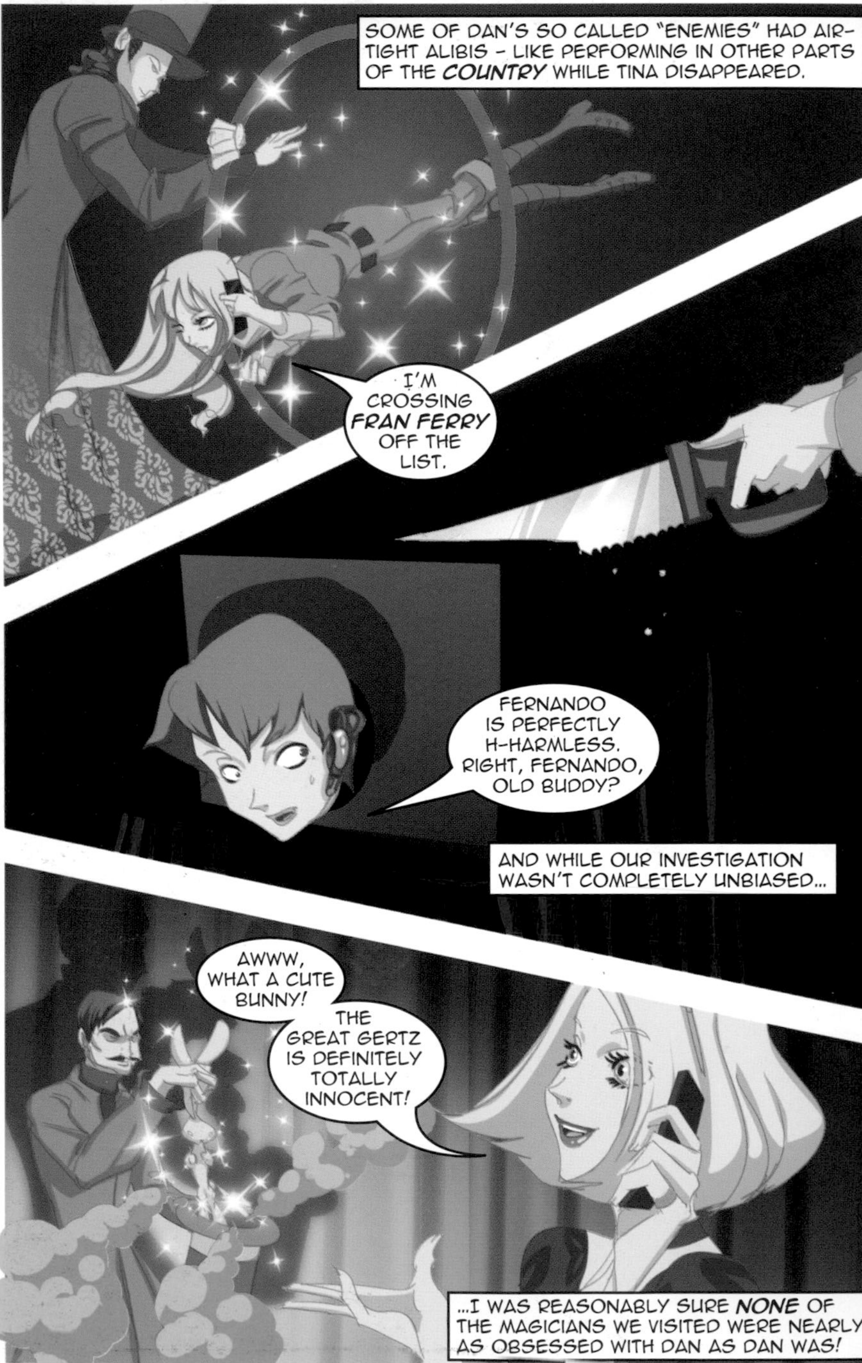
SOME OF DAN'S SO CALLED "ENEMIES" HAD AIR-TIGHT ALIBIS - LIKE PERFORMING IN OTHER PARTS OF THE COUNTRY WHILE TINA DISAPPEARED.
I'M CROSSING FRAN FERRY OFF THE LIST.
FERNANDO IS PERFECTLY H-HARMLESS. RIGHT, FERNANDO, OLD BUDDY?
AND WHILE OUR INVESTIGATION WASN'T COMPLETELY UNBIASED...
AWWW, WHAT A CUTE BUNNY!
THE GREAT GERTZ IS DEFINITELY TOTALLY INNOCENT!
...I WAS REASONABLY SURE NONE OF THE MAGICIANS WE VISITED WERE NEARLY AS OBSESSED WITH DAN AS DAN WAS!

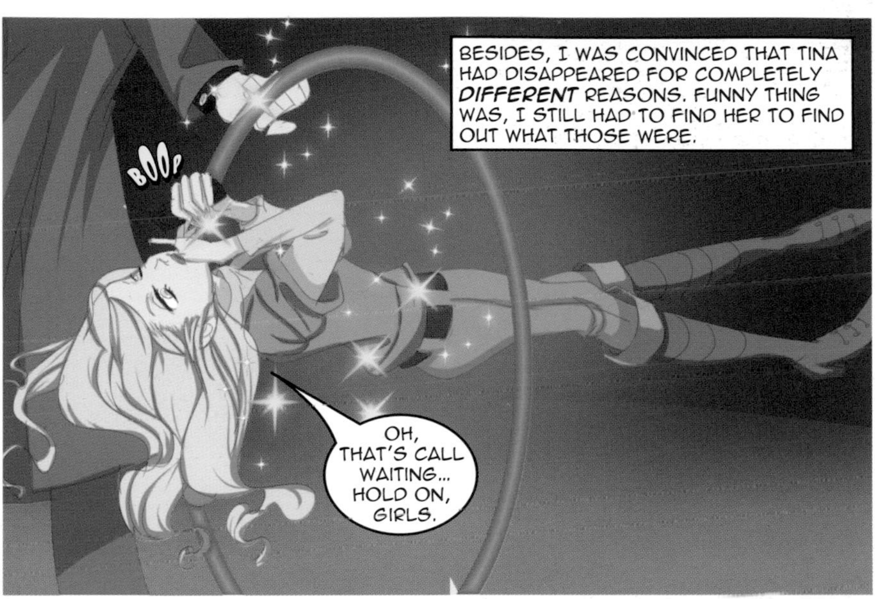
BESIDES, I WAS CONVINCED THAT TINA HAD DISAPPEARED FOR COMPLETELY DIFFERENT REASONS. FUNNY THING WAS, I STILL HAD TO FIND HER TO FIND OUT WHAT THOSE WERE.
BOOP
OH, THAT'S CALL WAITING... HOLD ON, GIRLS.

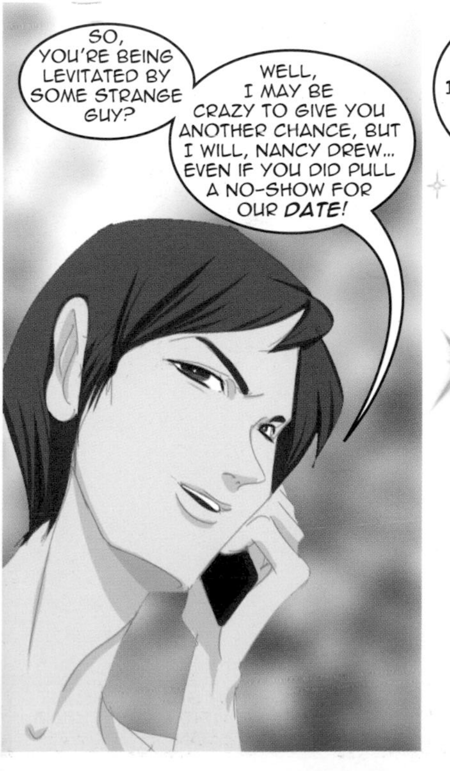
SO, YOU'RE BEING LEVITATED BY SOME STRANGE GUY?
WELL, I MAY BE CRAZY TO GIVE YOU ANOTHER CHANCE, BUT I WILL, NANCY DREW... EVEN IF YOU DID PULL A NO-SHOW FOR OUR DATE!

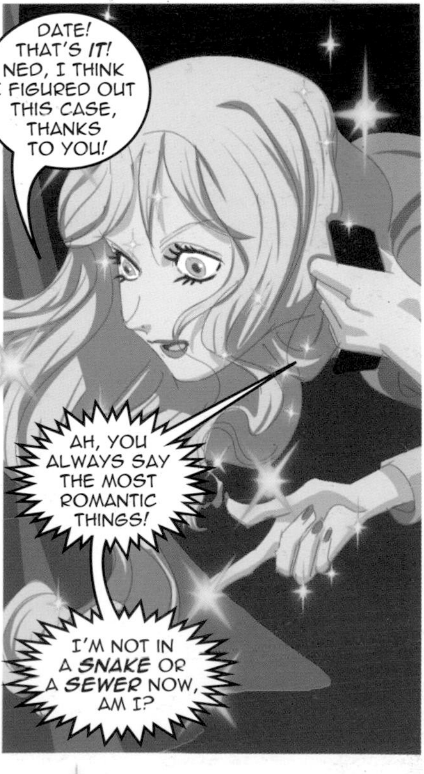
DATE! THAT'S IT! NED, I THINK I FIGURED OUT THIS CASE, THANKS TO YOU!
AH, YOU ALWAYS SAY THE MOST ROMANTIC THINGS!
I'M NOT IN A SNAKE OR A SEWER NOW, AM I?

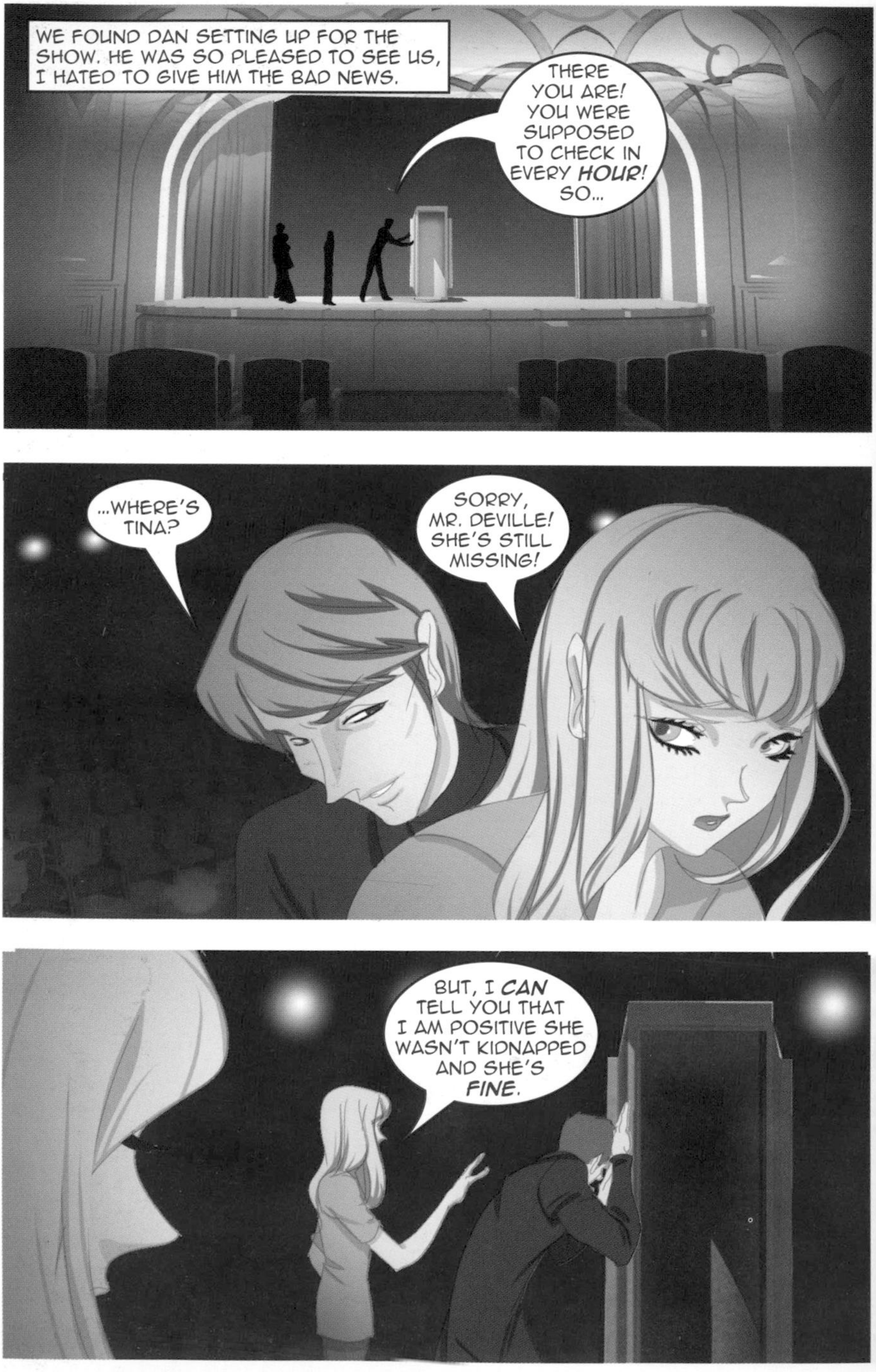
WE FOUND DAN SETTING UP FOR THE SHOW. HE WAS SO PLEASED TO SEE US, I HATED TO GIVE HIM THE BAD NEWS.
THERE YOU ARE! YOU WERE SUPPOSED TO CHECK IN EVERY HOUR! SO...
...WHERE'S TINA?
SORRY, MR. DEVILLE! SHE'S STILL MISSING!
BUT, I CAN TELL YOU THAT I AM POSITIVE SHE WASN'T KIDNAPPED AND SHE'S FINE.

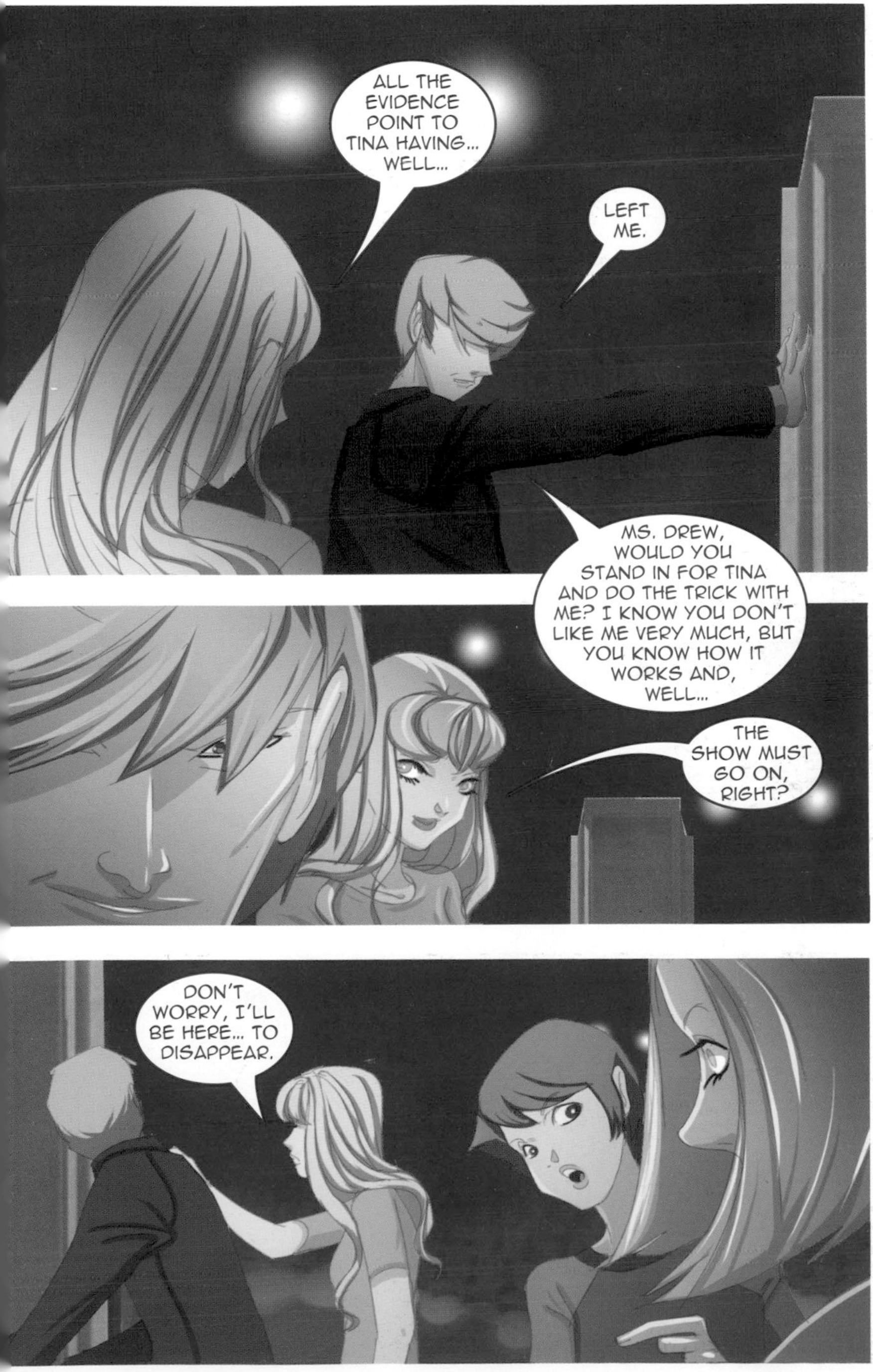
ALL THE EVIDENCE POINT TO TINA HAVING... WELL...
LEFT ME.
MS. DREW, WOULD YOU STAND IN FOR TINA AND DO THE TRICK WITH ME? I KNOW YOU DON'T LIKE ME VERY MUCH, BUT YOU KNOW HOW IT WORKS AND, WELL...
THE SHOW MUST GO ON, RIGHT?
DON'T WORRY, I'LL BE HERE... TO DISAPPEAR.

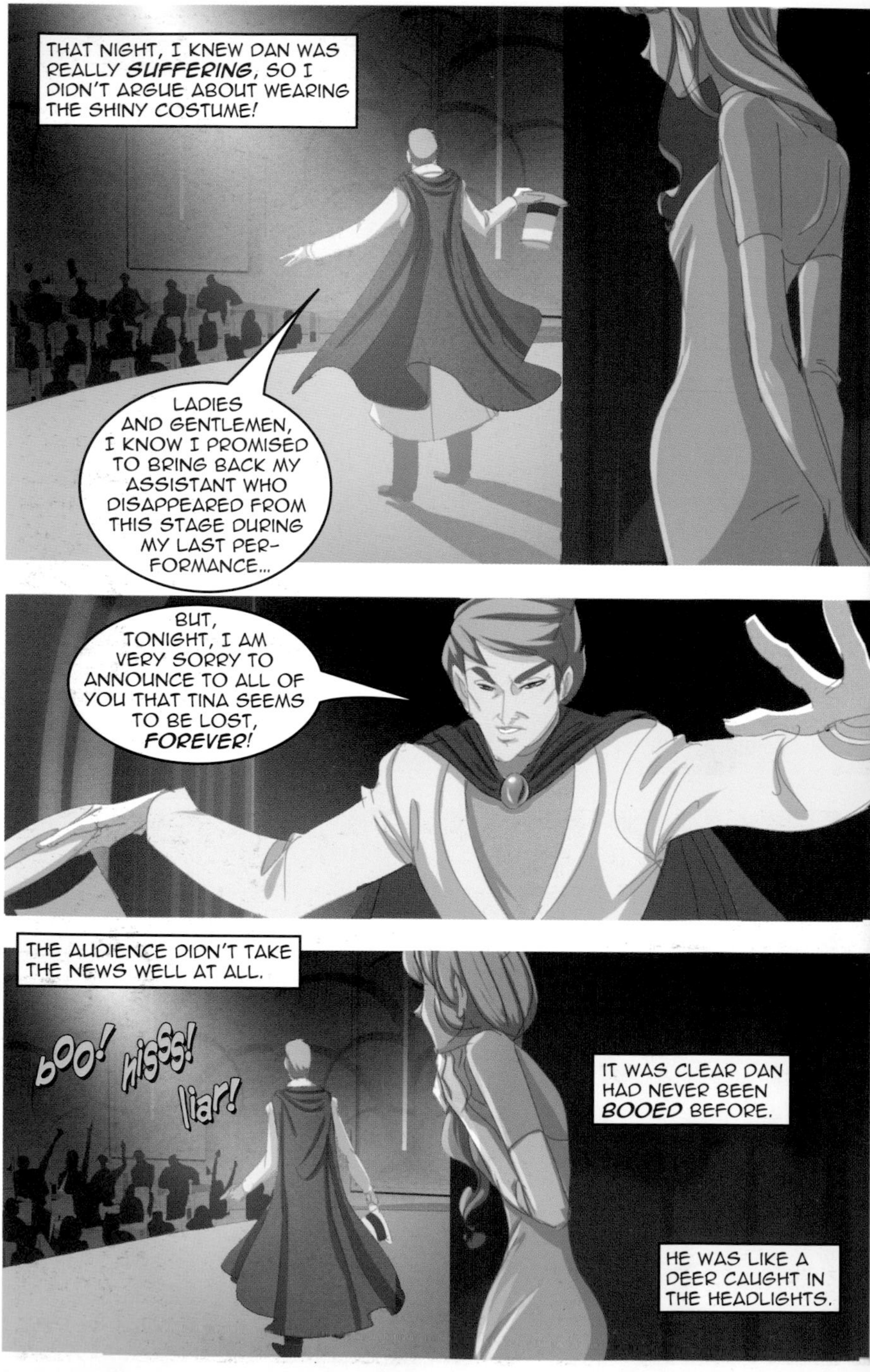
THAT NIGHT, I KNEW DAN WAS REALLY SUFFERING, SO I DIDN'T ARGUE ABOUT WEARING THE SHINY COSTUME!
LADIES AND GENTLEMEN, I KNOW I PROMISED TO BRING BACK MY ASSISTANT WHO DISAPPEARED FROM THIS STAGE DURING MY LAST PER-FORMANCE...
BUT, TONIGHT, I AM VERY SORRY TO ANNOUNCE TO ALL OF YOU THAT TINA SEEMS TO BE LOST, FOREVER!
THE AUDIENCE DIDN'T TAKE THE NEWS WELL AT ALL.
bOO! hisss! liar!
IT WAS CLEAR DAN HAD NEVER BEEN BOOED BEFORE.
HE WAS LIKE A DEER CAUGHT IN THE HEADLIGHTS.

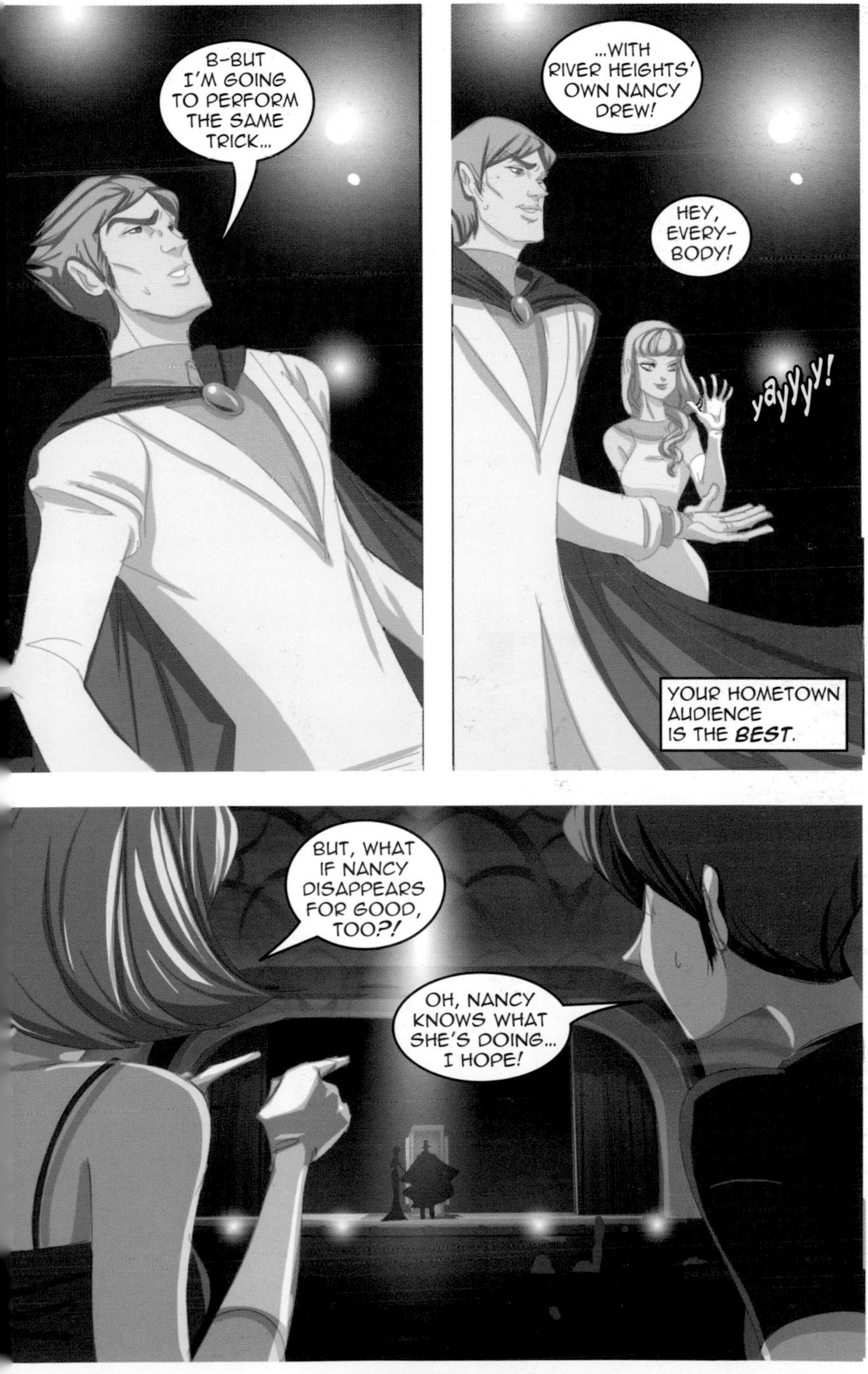
B-BUT I'M GOING TO PERFORM THE SAME TRICK...
...WITH RIVER HEIGHTS' OWN NANCY DREW!
HEY, EVERY-BODY!
yayyyy!
YOUR HOMETOWN AUDIENCE IS THE **BEST**.
BUT, WHAT IF NANCY DISAPPEARS FOR GOOD, TOO?!
OH, NANCY KNOWS WHAT SHE'S DOING... I HOPE!

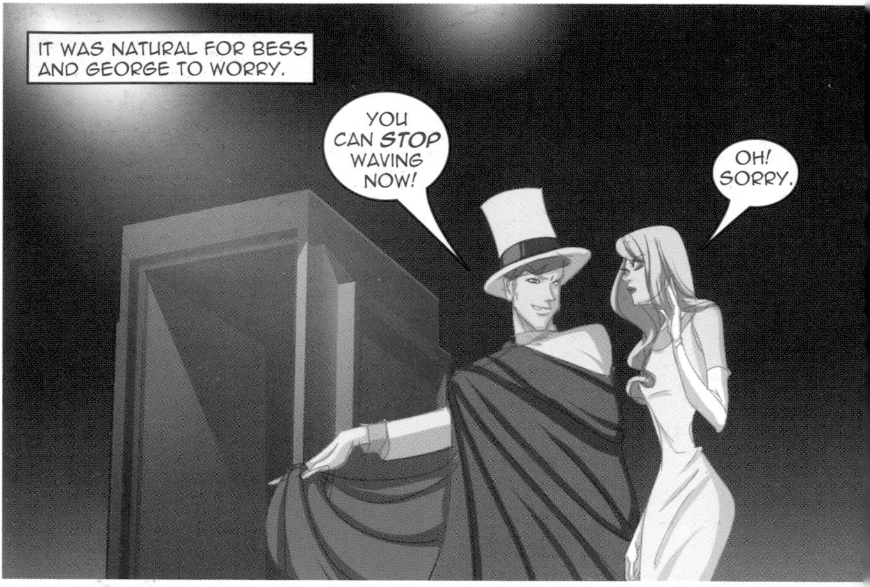
IT WAS NATURAL FOR BESS AND GEORGE TO WORRY.
YOU CAN STOP WAVING NOW!
OH! SORRY.

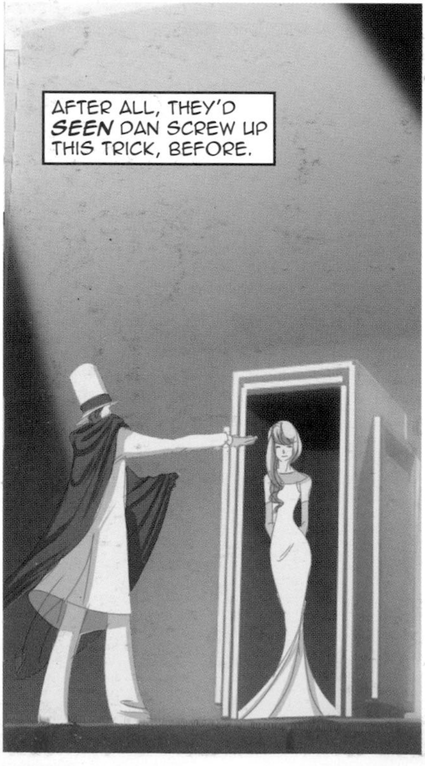
AFTER ALL, THEY'D SEEN DAN SCREW UP THIS TRICK, BEFORE.

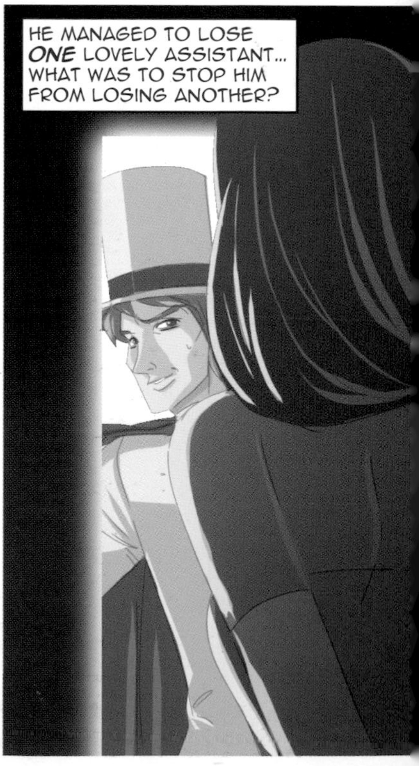
HE MANAGED TO LOSE ONE LOVELY ASSISTANT... WHAT WAS TO STOP HIM FROM LOSING ANOTHER?

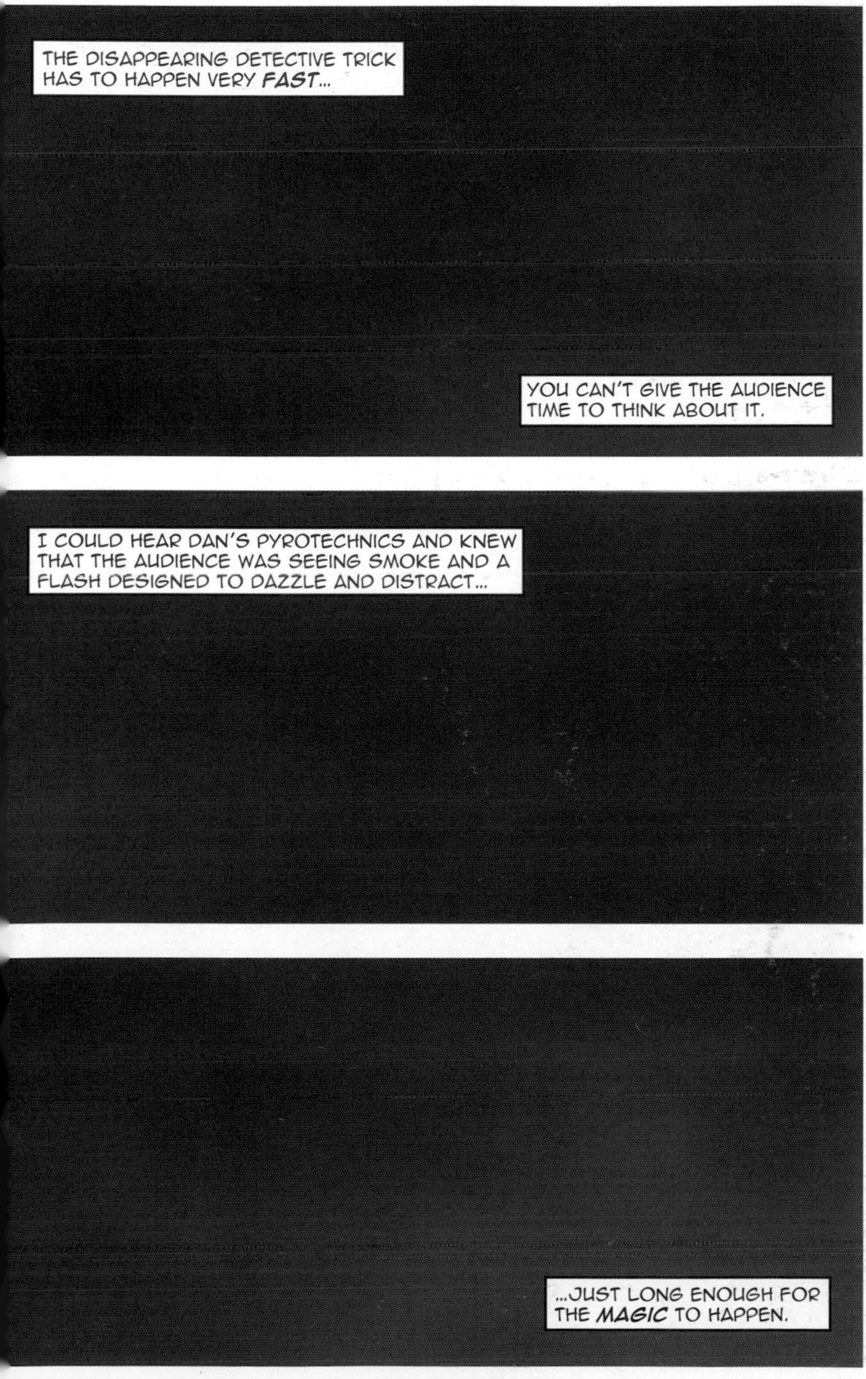
THE DISAPPEARING DETECTIVE TRICK HAS TO HAPPEN VERY FAST...
YOU CAN'T GIVE THE AUDIENCE TIME TO THINK ABOUT IT.
I COULD HEAR DAN'S PYROTECHNICS AND KNEW THAT THE AUDIENCE WAS SEEING SMOKE AND A FLASH DESIGNED TO DAZZLE AND DISTRACT...
...JUST LONG ENOUGH FOR THE MAGIC TO HAPPEN.

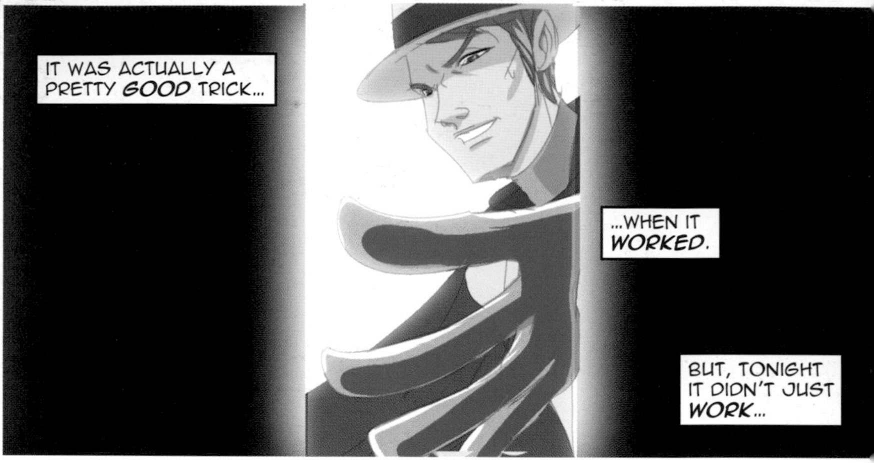
IT WAS ACTUALLY A PRETTY GOOD TRICK...
...WHEN IT WORKED.
BUT, TONIGHT IT DIDN'T JUST WORK...

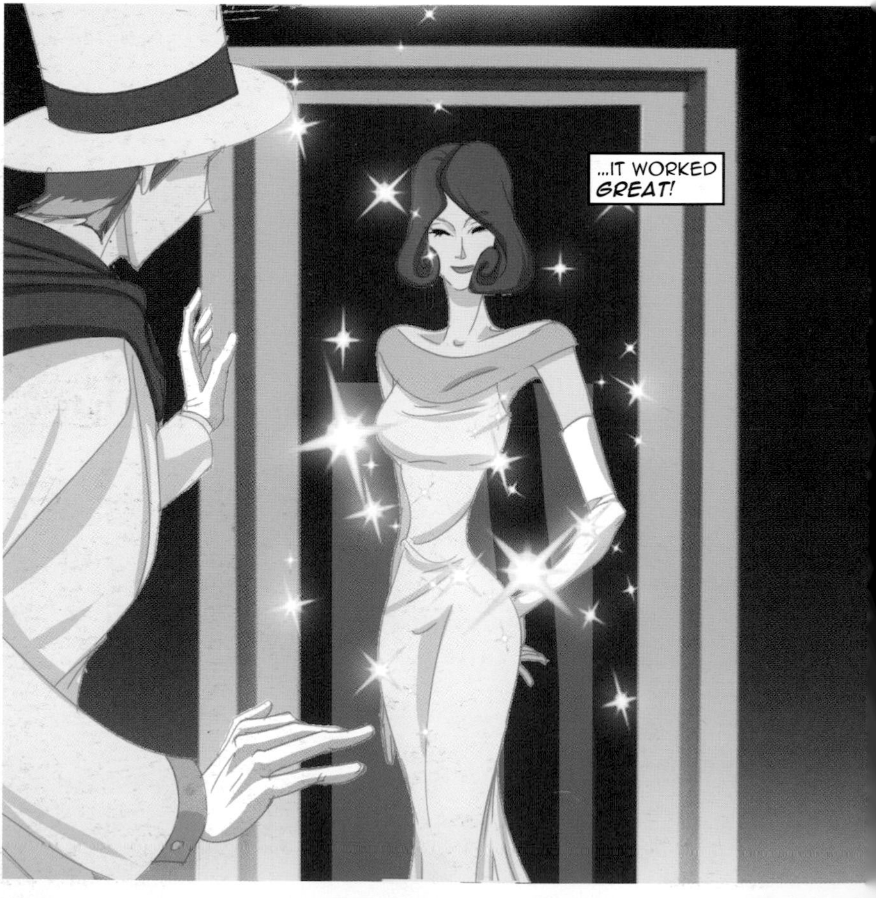
...IT WORKED GREAT!

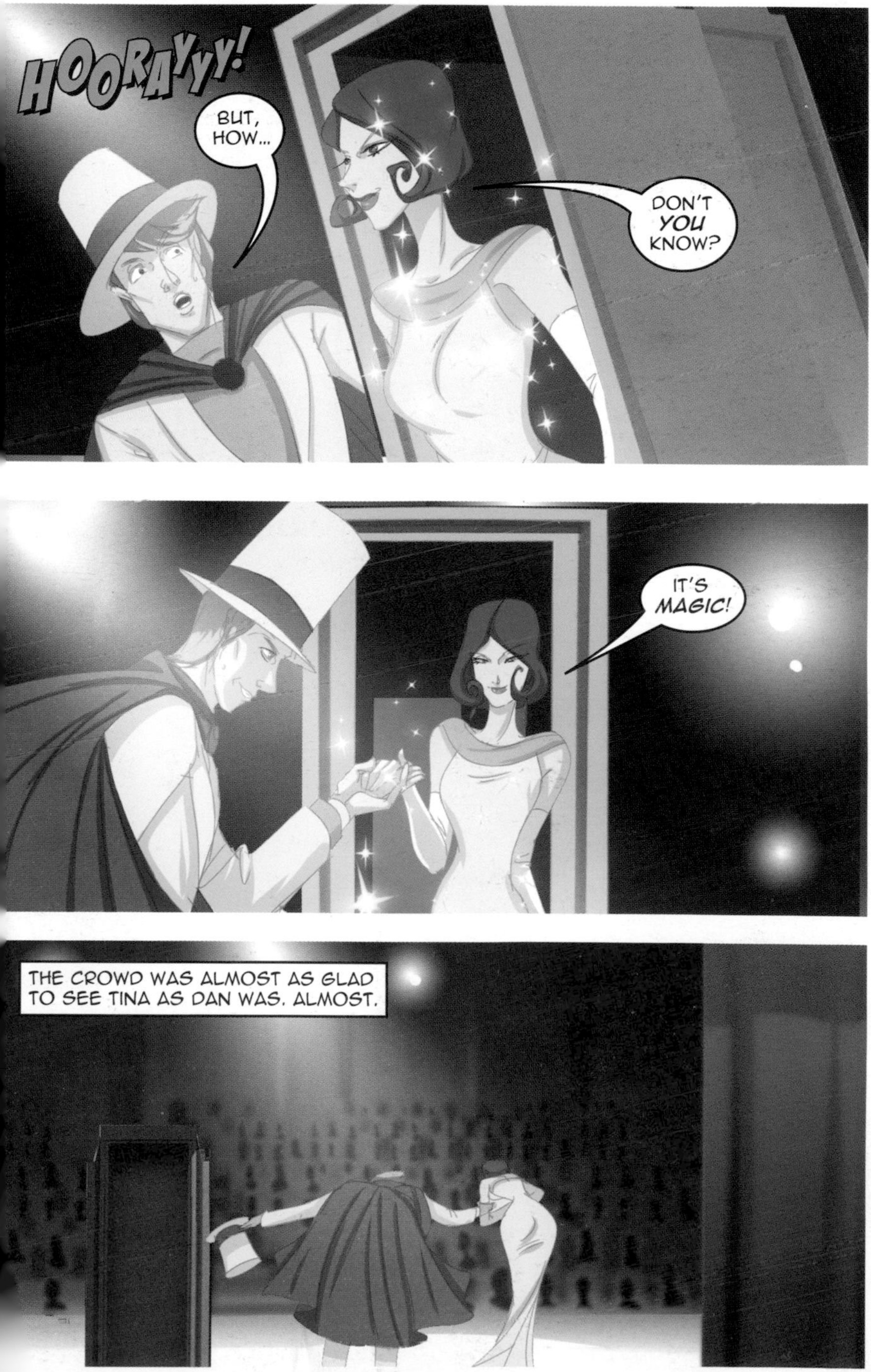
HOORAYYY!
BUT, HOW...
DON'T YOU KNOW?
IT'S MAGIC!
THE CROWD WAS ALMOST AS GLAD TO SEE TINA AS DAN WAS. ALMOST.

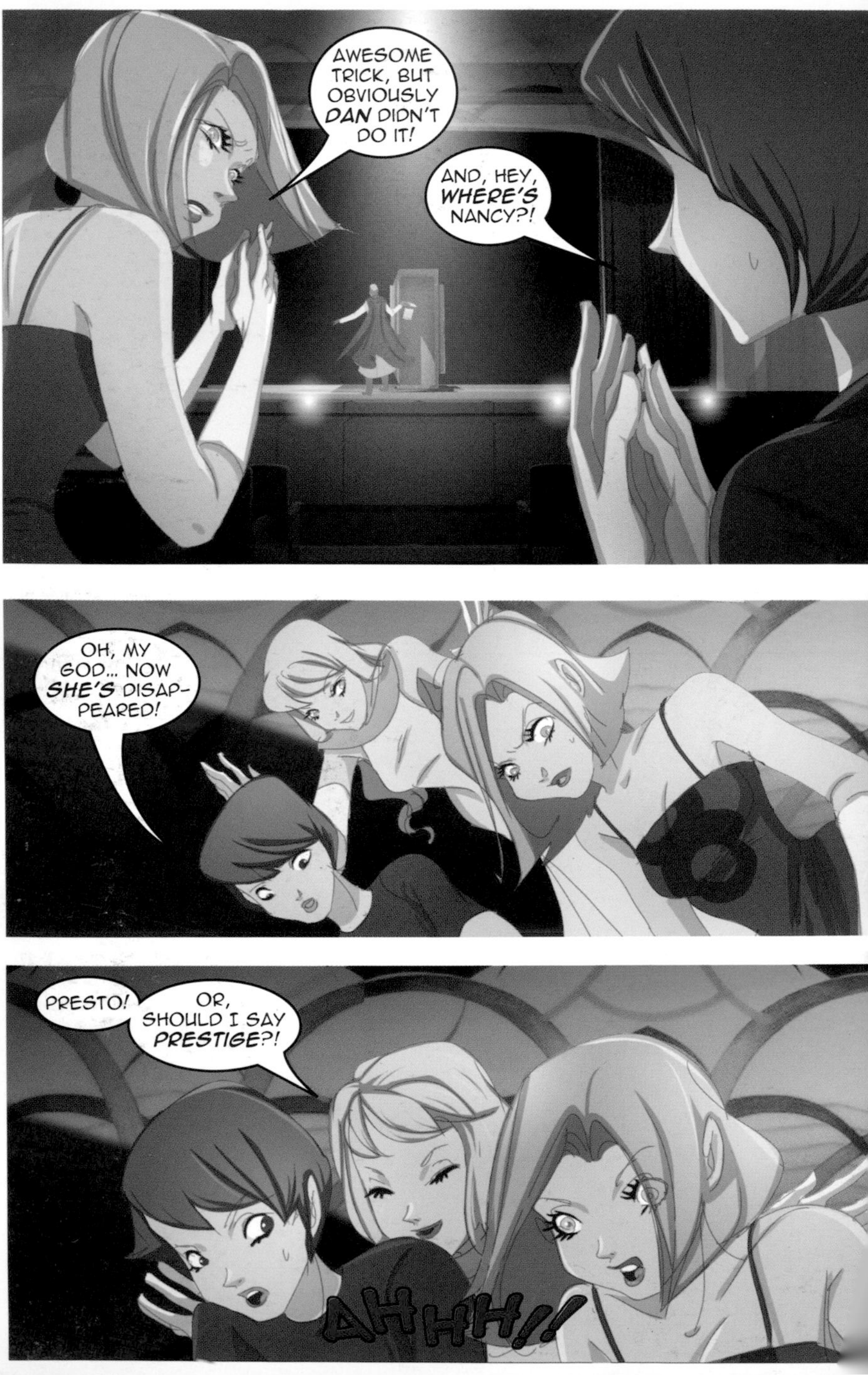
AWESOME TRICK, BUT OBVIOUSLY DAN DIDN'T DO IT!
AND, HEY, WHERE'S NANCY?!
OH, MY GOD... NOW SHE'S DISAP-PEARED!
PRESTO!
OR, SHOULD I SAY PRESTIGE?!
AHHH!!

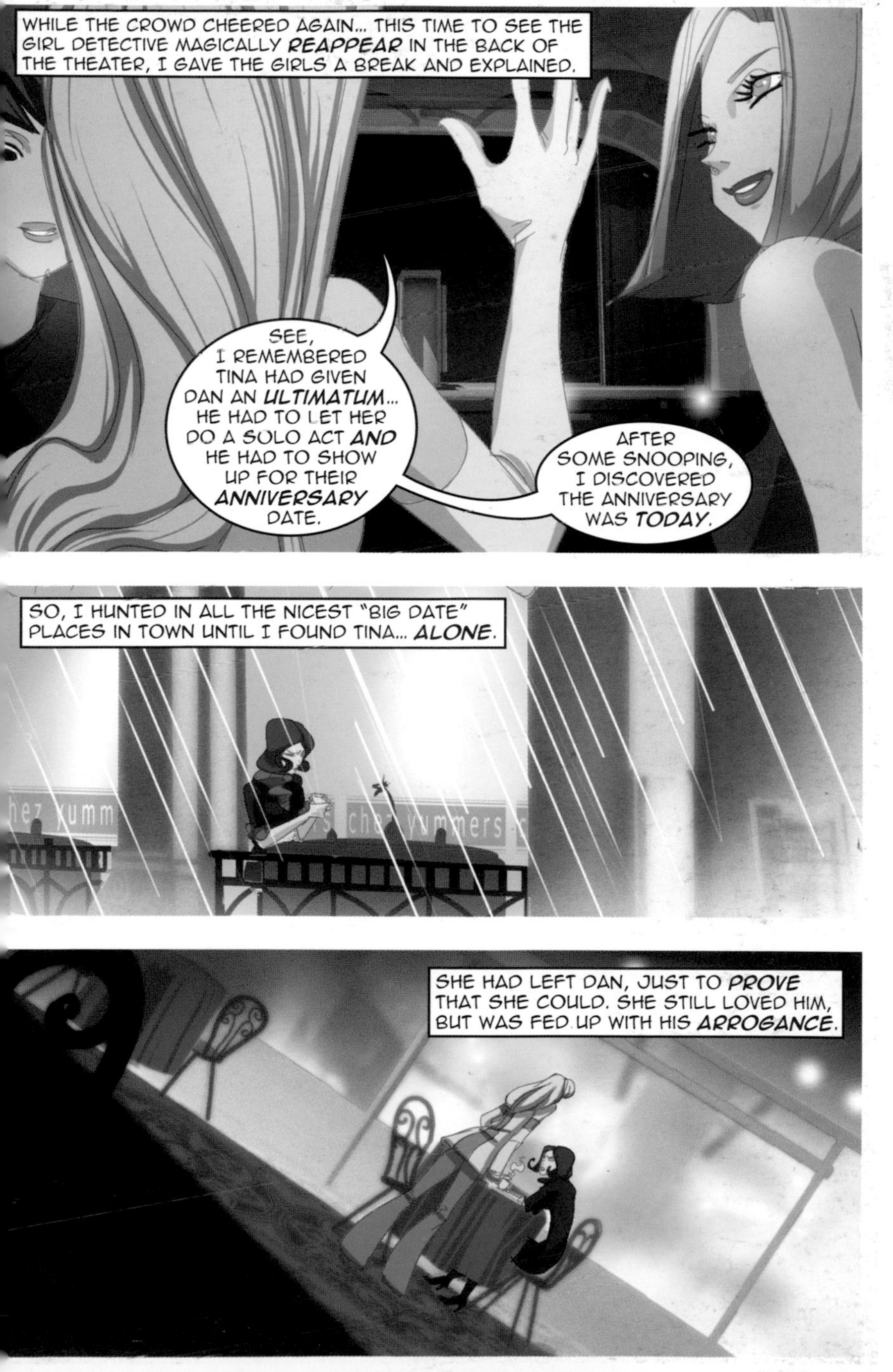
WHILE THE CROWD CHEERED AGAIN... THIS TIME TO SEE THE GIRL DETECTIVE MAGICALLY *REAPPEAR* IN THE BACK OF THE THEATER, I GAVE THE GIRLS A BREAK AND EXPLAINED.
SEE, I REMEMBERED TINA HAD GIVEN DAN AN *ULTIMATUM*... HE HAD TO LET HER DO A SOLO ACT *AND* HE HAD TO SHOW UP FOR THEIR *ANNIVERSARY* DATE.
AFTER SOME SNOOPING, I DISCOVERED THE ANNIVERSARY WAS *TODAY*.
SO, I HUNTED IN ALL THE NICEST "BIG DATE" PLACES IN TOWN UNTIL I FOUND TINA... *ALONE*.
chez yummers
SHE HAD LEFT DAN, JUST TO *PROVE* THAT SHE COULD. SHE STILL LOVED HIM, BUT WAS FED UP WITH HIS *ARROGANCE*.

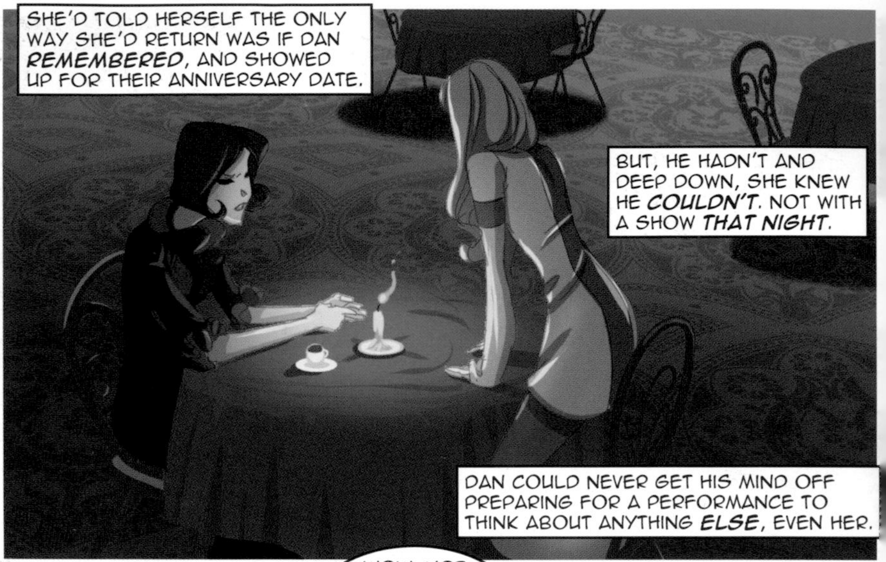
SHE'D TOLD HERSELF THE ONLY WAY SHE'D RETURN WAS IF DAN *REMEMBERED*, AND SHOWED UP FOR THEIR ANNIVERSARY DATE.
BUT, HE HADN'T AND DEEP DOWN, SHE KNEW HE *COULDN'T*. NOT WITH A SHOW *THAT NIGHT*.
DAN COULD NEVER GET HIS MIND OFF PREPARING FOR A PERFORMANCE TO THINK ABOUT ANYTHING *ELSE*, EVEN HER.

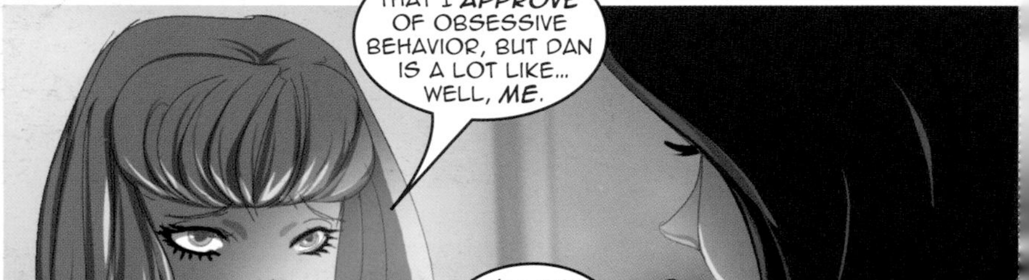
WOW. NOT THAT I *APPROVE* OF OBSESSIVE BEHAVIOR, BUT DAN IS A LOT LIKE... WELL, *ME*.
I'VE GOT THIS GREAT BOYFRIEND, NED...
USING MY OWN STORY, I WAS ABLE TO HELP TINA SEE IT MIGHT TAKE SOME PATIENCE– A *LOT* OF PATIENCE–TO LOVE SOMEONE THAT SINGLE-MINDED...

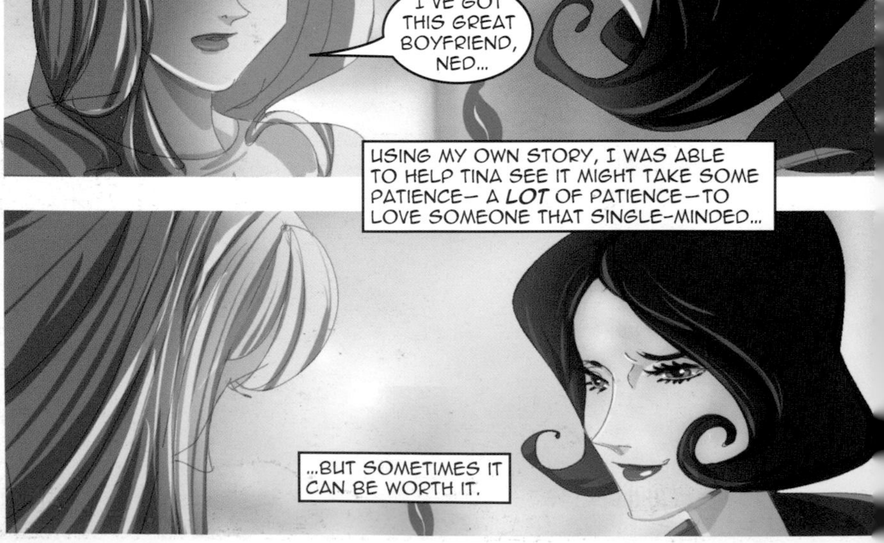
...BUT SOMETIMES IT CAN BE WORTH IT.

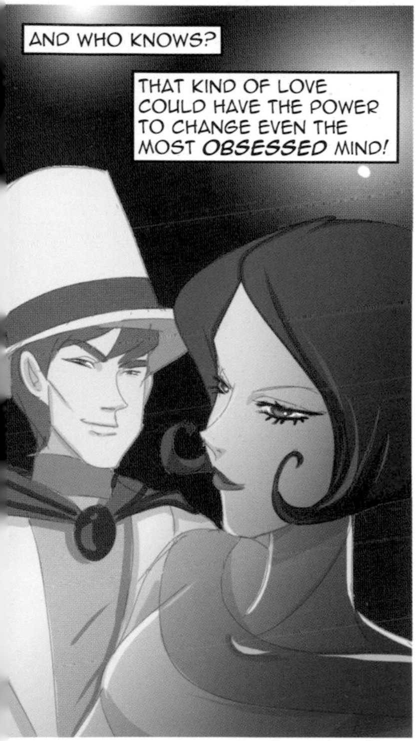
AND WHO KNOWS?
THAT KIND OF LOVE COULD HAVE THE POWER TO CHANGE EVEN THE MOST OBSESSED MIND!
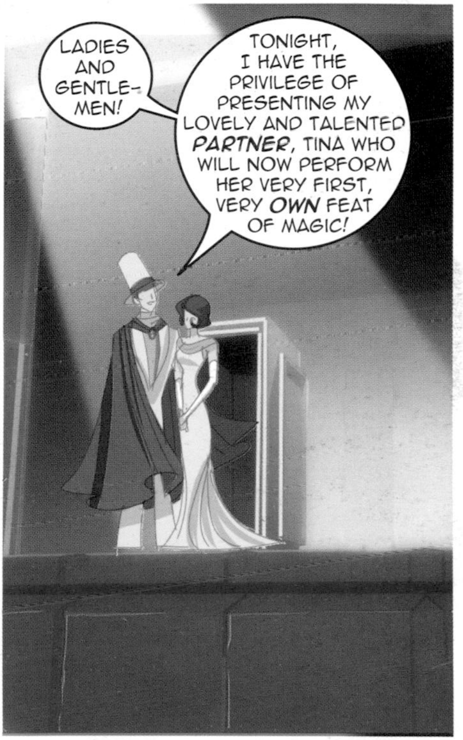
LADIES AND GENTLE-MEN!
TONIGHT, I HAVE THE PRIVILEGE OF PRESENTING MY LOVELY AND TALENTED PARTNER, TINA WHO WILL NOW PERFORM HER VERY FIRST, VERY OWN FEAT OF MAGIC!
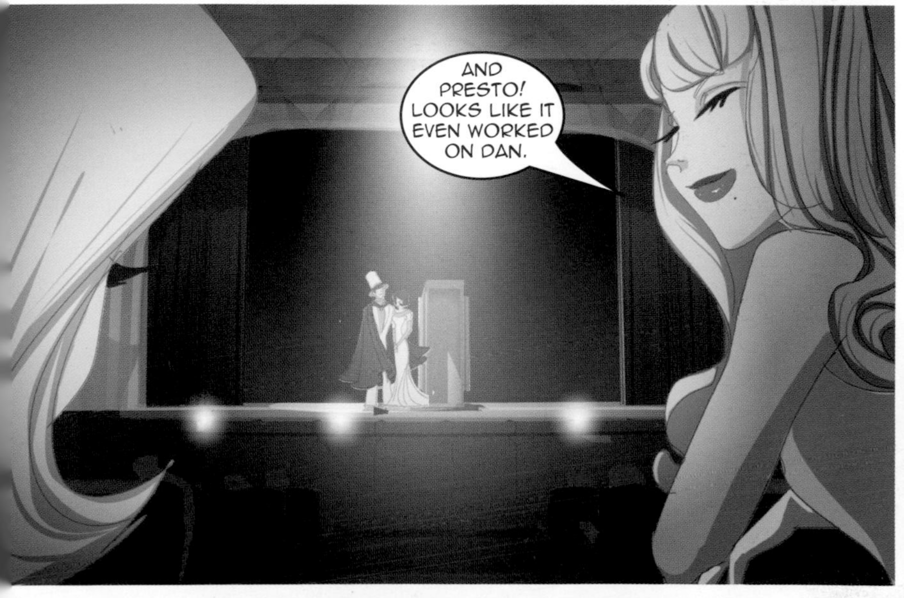
AND PRESTO! LOOKS LIKE IT EVEN WORKED ON DAN.

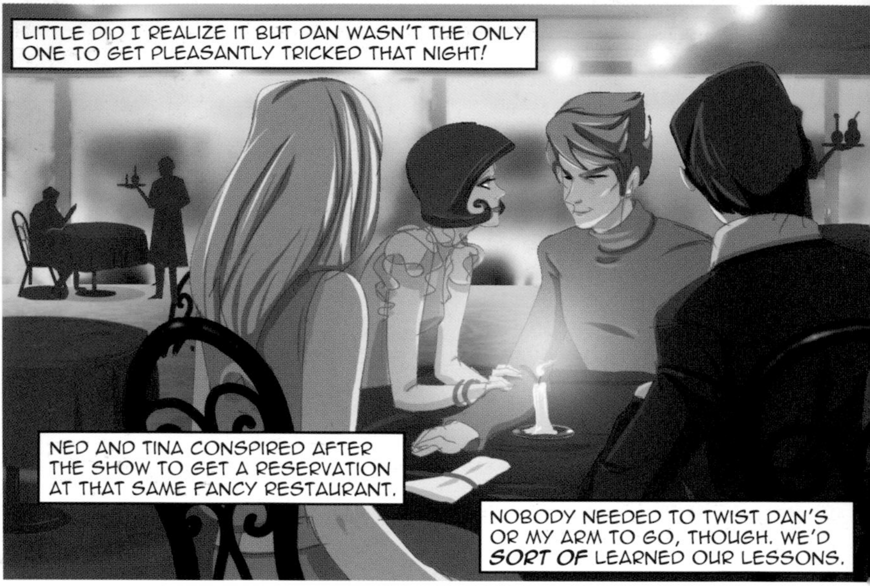
LITTLE DID I REALIZE IT BUT DAN WASN'T THE ONLY ONE TO GET PLEASANTLY TRICKED THAT NIGHT!
NED AND TINA CONSPIRED AFTER THE SHOW TO GET A RESERVATION AT THAT SAME FANCY RESTAURANT.
NOBODY NEEDED TO TWIST DAN'S OR MY ARM TO GO, THOUGH. WE'D SORT OF LEARNED OUR LESSONS.

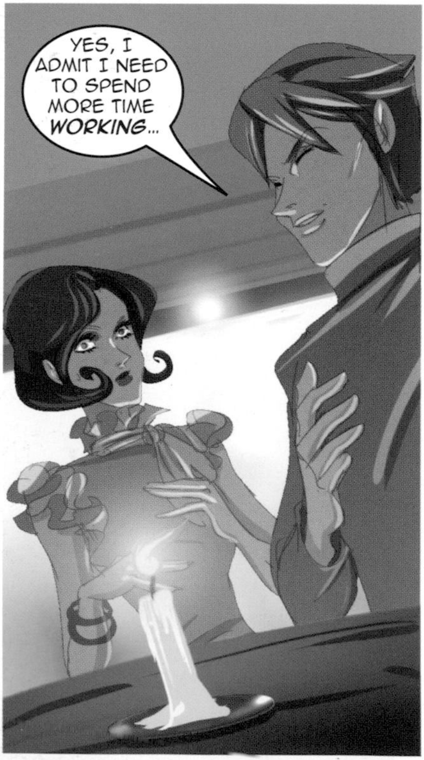
YES, I ADMIT I NEED TO SPEND MORE TIME WORKING...

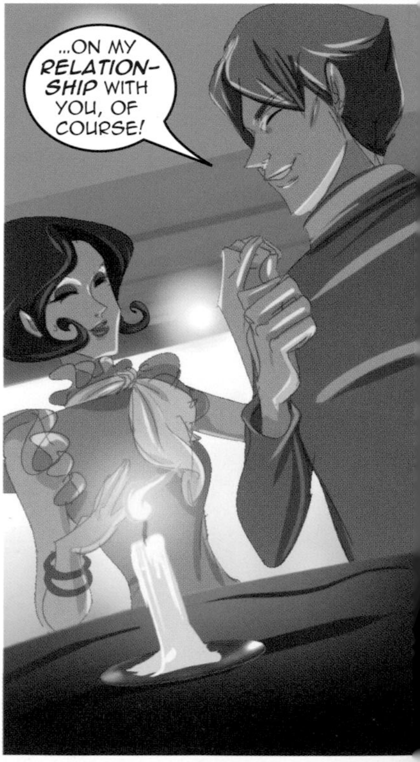
...ON MY RELATIONSHIP WITH YOU, OF COURSE!

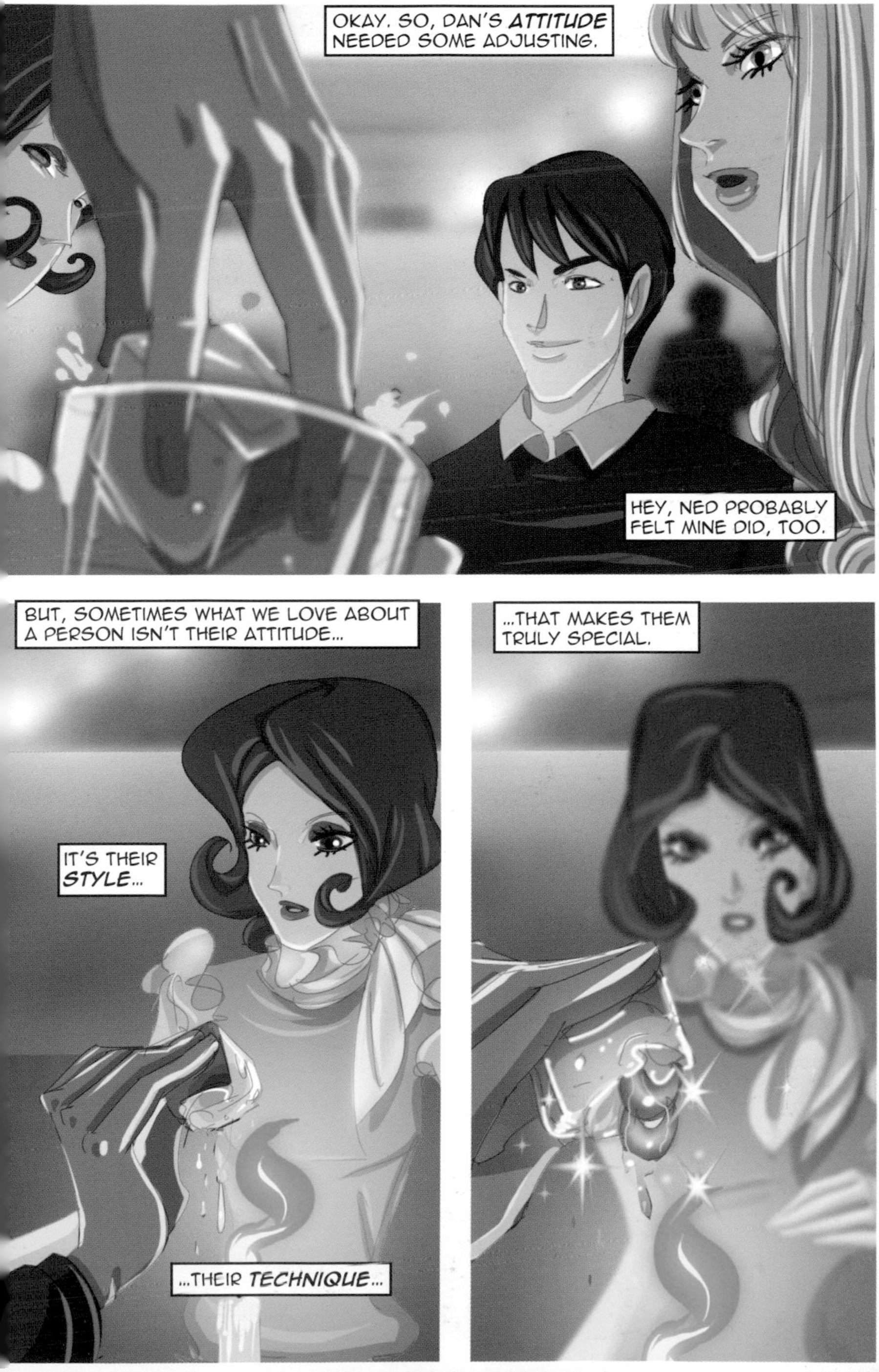
OKAY. SO, DAN'S ATTITUDE NEEDED SOME ADJUSTING.
HEY, NED PROBABLY FELT MINE DID, TOO.
BUT, SOMETIMES WHAT WE LOVE ABOUT A PERSON ISN'T THEIR ATTITUDE...
IT'S THEIR STYLE...
...THEIR TECHNIQUE...
...THAT MAKES THEM TRULY SPECIAL.

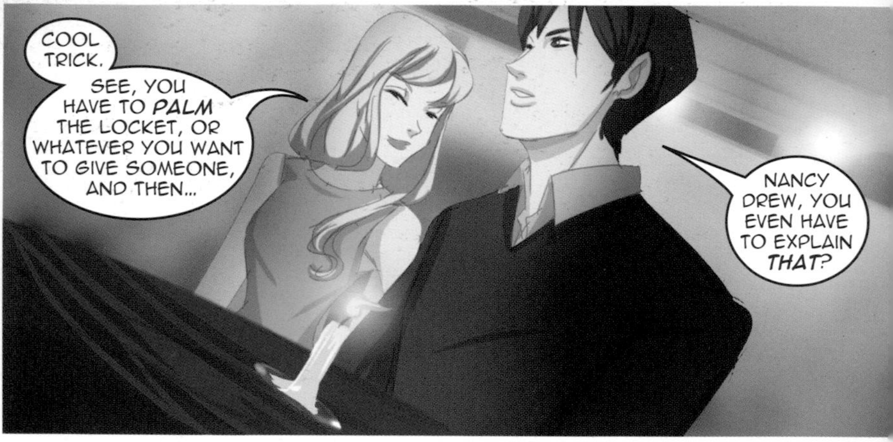
COOL TRICK.
SEE, YOU HAVE TO PALM THE LOCKET, OR WHATEVER YOU WANT TO GIVE SOMEONE, AND THEN...
NANCY DREW, YOU EVEN HAVE TO EXPLAIN THAT?

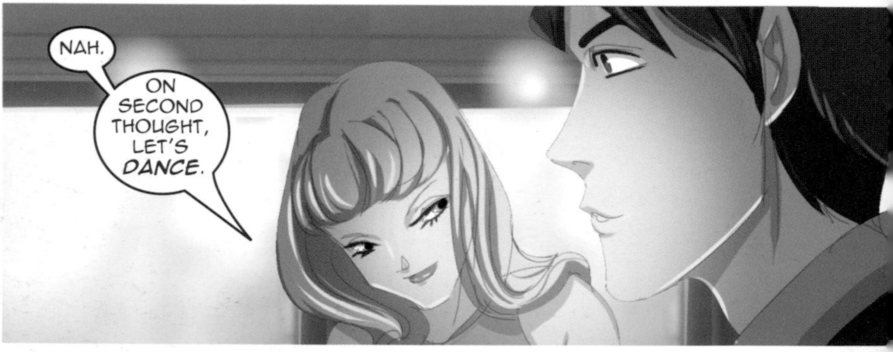
NAH.
ON SECOND THOUGHT, LET'S DANCE.

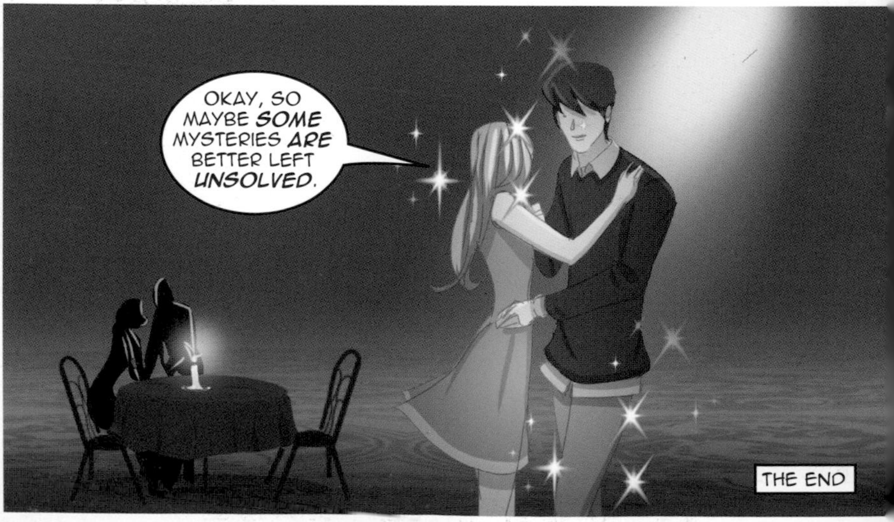
OKAY, SO MAYBE SOME MYSTERIES ARE BETTER LEFT UNSOLVED.
THE END

SPECIAL PREVIEW OF NANCY DREW #15 – "TIGER COUNTER"

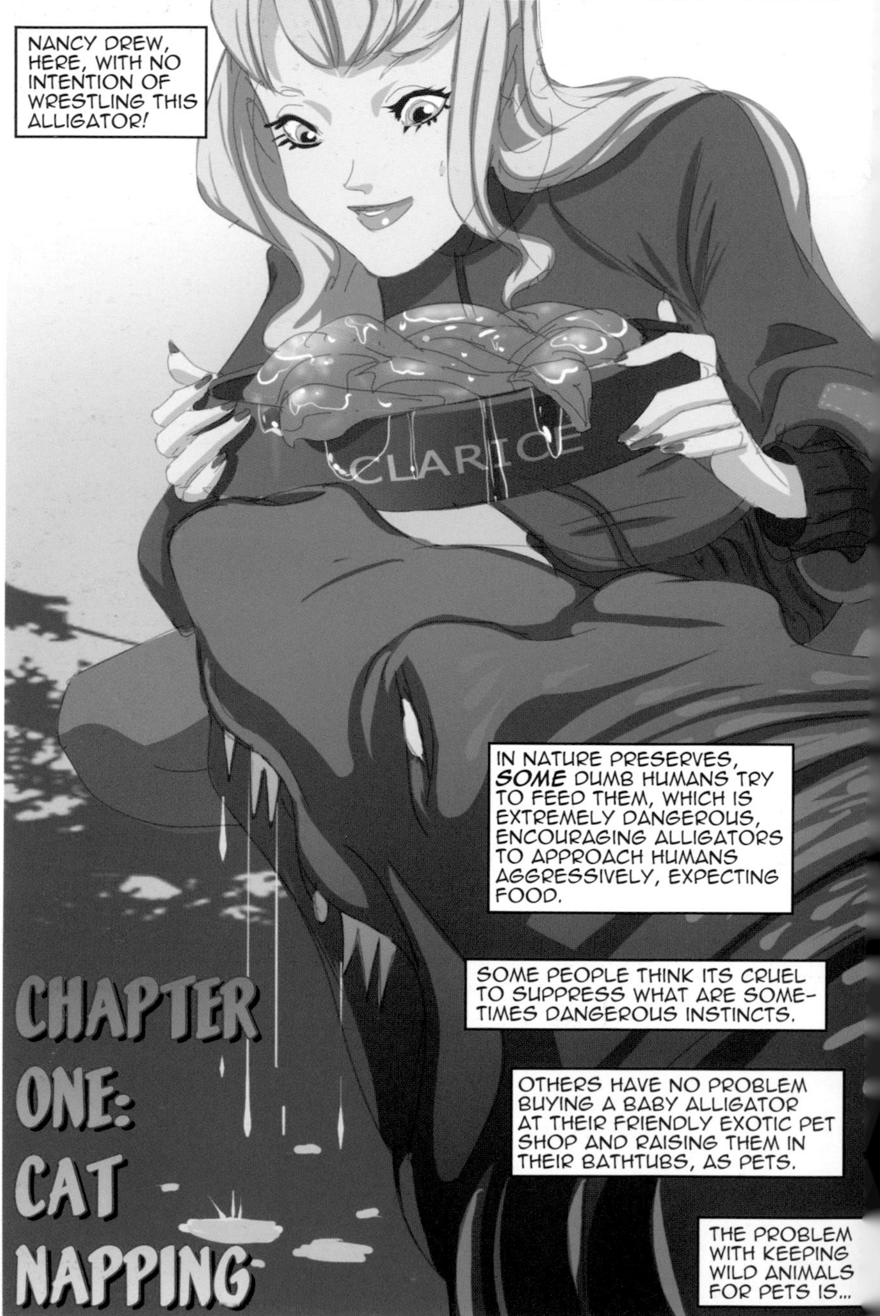
NANCY DREW, HERE, WITH NO INTENTION OF WRESTLING THIS ALLIGATOR!
CLARICE
IN NATURE PRESERVES, SOME DUMB HUMANS TRY TO FEED THEM, WHICH IS EXTREMELY DANGEROUS, ENCOURAGING ALLIGATORS TO APPROACH HUMANS AGGRESSIVELY, EXPECTING FOOD.
SOME PEOPLE THINK ITS CRUEL TO SUPPRESS WHAT ARE SOMETIMES DANGEROUS INSTINCTS.
OTHERS HAVE NO PROBLEM BUYING A BABY ALLIGATOR AT THEIR FRIENDLY EXOTIC PET SHOP AND RAISING THEM IN THEIR BATHTUBS, AS PETS.
THE PROBLEM WITH KEEPING WILD ANIMALS FOR PETS IS...
CHAPTER ONE: CAT NAPPING

...THEY DON'T ALWAYS *BEHAVE* LIKE PETS!

AHHH!

SSSS

IT'S ALL RIGHT, NANCY. EVEN *I* STILL GET A LITTLE JITTERY AROUND THE CRITTERS WITH THAT MANY TEETH.

JACK MARVIN RAN THE RIVER HEIGHTS ANIMAL PROTECTION CENTER. HE'D SAVED JUST ABOUT EVERY IMAGINABLE KIND OF ABANDONED, LOST OR MISTREATED PET.

I'M USUALLY BUSY SOLVING MYSTERIES WITH MY BEST FRIENDS, GEORGE AND BESS.

BUT, MYSTERIES HAD BEEN IN SHORT SUPPLY, LATELY, SO WE ALL DECIDED TO GET IN TOUCH WITH OUR INNER ANIMAL LOVERS BY *VOLUNTEERING*.

RIVER HEIGHTS
ANIMAL PROTECTION
CENTER

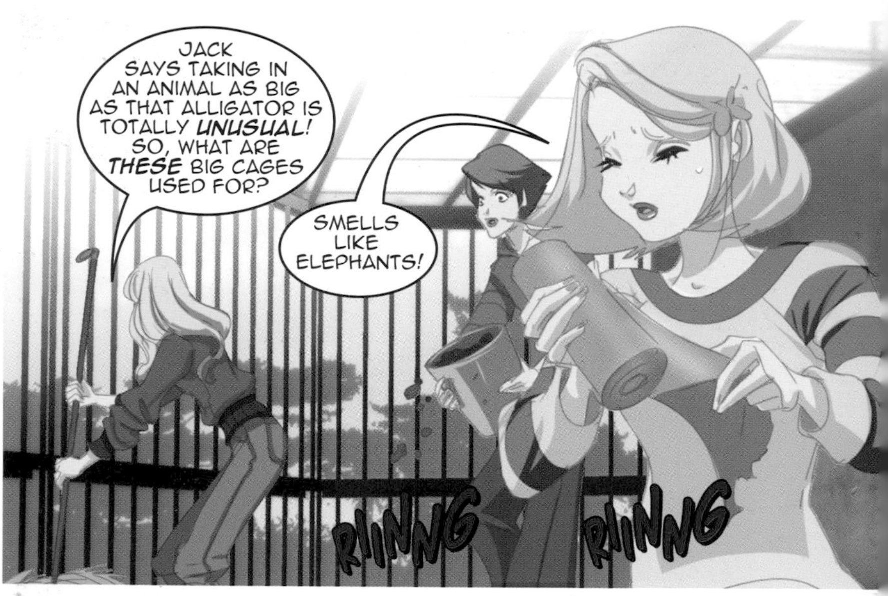
JACK SAYS TAKING IN AN ANIMAL AS BIG AS THAT ALLIGATOR IS TOTALLY UNUSUAL! SO, WHAT ARE THESE BIG CAGES USED FOR?
SMELLS LIKE ELEPHANTS!
RIINNG RIINNG

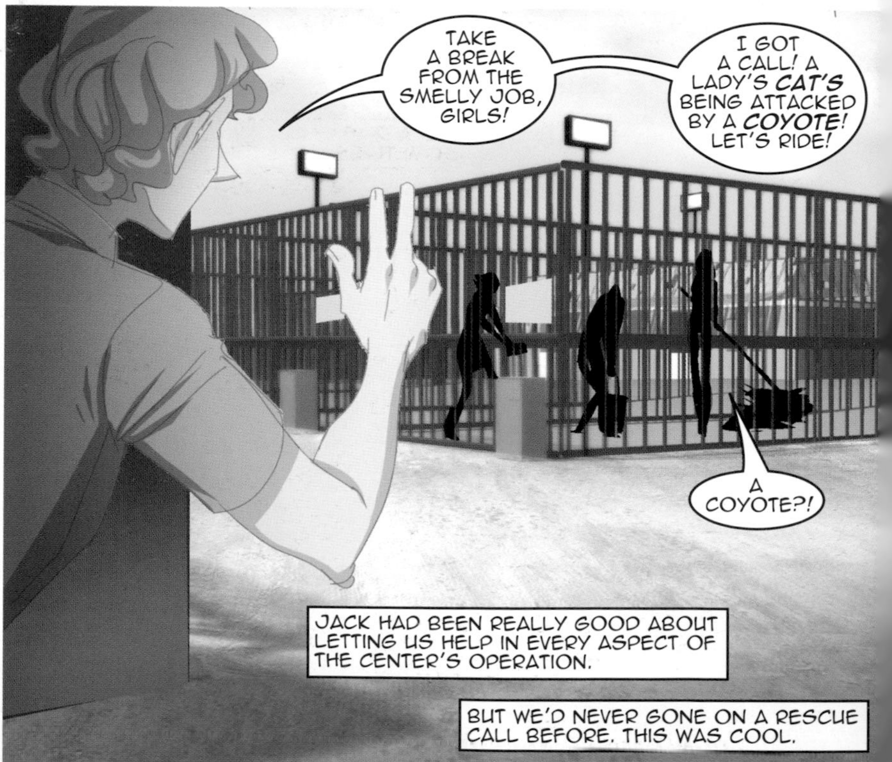
TAKE A BREAK FROM THE SMELLY JOB, GIRLS!
I GOT A CALL! A LADY'S CAT'S BEING ATTACKED BY A COYOTE! LET'S RIDE!
A COYOTE?!
JACK HAD BEEN REALLY GOOD ABOUT LETTING US HELP IN EVERY ASPECT OF THE CENTER'S OPERATION.
BUT WE'D NEVER GONE ON A RESCUE CALL BEFORE. THIS WAS COOL.

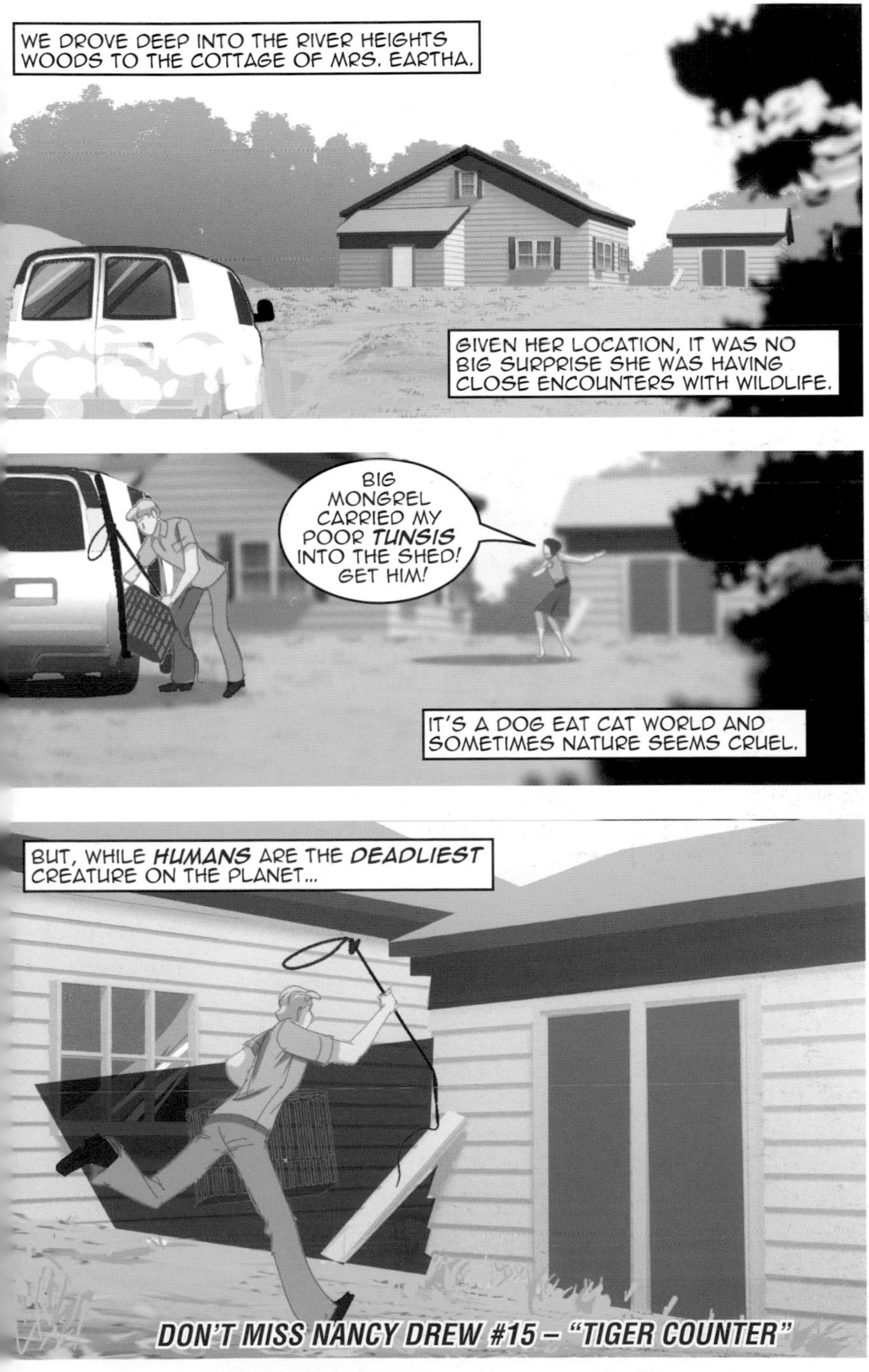
WE DROVE DEEP INTO THE RIVER HEIGHTS WOODS TO THE COTTAGE OF MRS. EARTHA.
GIVEN HER LOCATION, IT WAS NO BIG SURPRISE SHE WAS HAVING CLOSE ENCOUNTERS WITH WILDLIFE.
BIG MONGREL CARRIED MY POOR *TUNSIS* INTO THE SHED! GET HIM!
IT'S A DOG EAT CAT WORLD AND SOMETIMES NATURE SEEMS CRUEL.
BUT, WHILE *HUMANS* ARE THE *DEADLIEST* CREATURE ON THE PLANET...
DON'T MISS NANCY DREW #15 – "TIGER COUNTER"